STEVEN MOORE

OF CURSES AND KINGS

Vinci Books

vinci-books.com

Published by Vinci Books Ltd in 2025

1

Copyright © Steven Moore 2020

The author has asserted their moral right to be identified as the author of this work in accordance with the Copyright, Designs and Patents Act 1988. This work is a work of fiction. Names, characters, places and incidents are the product of the author's imagination or are used fictitiously. Any resemblance to actual persons, living or dead, places and incidents is entirely coincidental.

All rights reserved. No part of this publication may be copied, reproduced, distributed, stored in any retrieval system, or transmitted in any form or by any means, including photocopying, recording, or other electronic or mechanical methods, nor used as a source for any form of machine learning including AI datasets, without the prior written permission of the publisher.

The publisher and the author have made every effort to obtain permissions for any third party material used in this book and to comply with copyright law. Any queries in this respect should be brought to the attention of the publisher and any omissions will be corrected in future editions.

A CIP catalogue record for this book is available from the British Library.

Paperback ISBN: 9781036706838

The EU GPSR authorised representative is Logos Europe, 9 rue Nicolas Poussion, 17000 La Rochelle, France contact@logoseurope.eu

Printed and bound in Great Britain by Clays Ltd, Elcograf S.p.A.

By Steven Moore

The Hiram Kane Archaeological Thriller Series

The Condor Prophecy
The Tiger Temple
The Feathered Serpent
The Samurai Code
Of Curses and Kings
The Shadow of Kailash
The Oak Island Enigma
Killing Koreana

*"To be satisfied with a little, is the greatest wisdom;
and he that increaseth his riches, increaseth his cares;
but a contented mind is a hidden treasure, and trouble findeth it not"*
– Akhenaten, 1351–1334 BC, tenth ruler of the Eighteenth Dynasty

Prologue

London, 2005

Eight men, all dressed in black, moved with stealth into the concrete stairwell of Richmond House, southwest London. The leading man was only recognisable by his eyes, which darted left and right in a well-practiced pattern of survival learned during long shady assignments overseas. With a flick of the wrist, he signalled his men forward.

The men climbed the stairs, their Heckler & Koch MP5-SF Parabellum machine pistols scanning for any movement in the shadows. The stairwell stank of piss and weed. Used vials of crack crunched beneath their tactical duty boots. This occurred often enough to turn an unprepared stomach. These men were wound so tight and were so well-prepared they didn't even notice.

They moved up to the first landing. A bulkhead light bathed the bare concrete in a blue glow, designed to thwart the resident junkies in their attempts to find veins. To anyone else, it might have seemed ethereal.

The men swept the area and headed in silence for the next set of stairs. The last man glanced down over the concrete bannister. Although the city around them seemed quiet, he knew three more tactical units—with enough firepower to bring down a small town—waited half a mile away. They would be watching the whole thing now via the cameras fitted to their Kevlar helmets, and by the drone which hovered two-hundred feet above this hell hole.

The walls surrounding the men bore the names of local gangs. Various words had been scrawled and sprayed on top of each other in a palimpsest of graffiti, as though the battles for space on the once-bare walls were the ultimate expression of their power.

The first man reached the top of the staircase and stopped. He held up his hand and the men behind him paused.

Somewhere nearby, a door slammed. A raised voice echoed through the stark corridors. A baby cried. No footsteps came their way. The men moved on, taking the next staircase with quick steps.

As they reached the third floor, the men turned right towards flat 301. Each of them had memorised the building's layout. To its occupants it was just a high-rise housing estate in southwest London. Yet these men now considered themselves behind enemy lines, and each knew how fast things could change in the theatre of war.

Life and death balanced on a knife edge.

Chapter One

The Kane Estate, England

Present Day

Hiram Kane was in a coma.

At least, to any observer it would've seemed like that. Kane lay on his front, his face wedged into the sun lounger. An unfortunate dribble of saliva dampened his chin. He wasn't aware of it; but if he had been, he wouldn't have cared. It spoke of the tranquility he felt, the safety of his surroundings... the distance he currently enjoyed from things and people that could kill him and wanted to.

He had hardly moved in hours—days? It was exactly what he needed. June this year was especially warm, and he was taking a hard-earned break from... Well, from everything. His body needed it, that was for sure. He still felt the aches and pains from a month ago, still wore the scars, and relished the opportunity for stillness. More than his physical need for rest, his mind needed to recuperate. To recover.

Kane had just returned from a trip to Japan, where a series of traumatising experiences had left him with deep mental scars. In a calculated effort not to end up on any more crazy adventures any time soon, he holed up at his grandparents' house in the English countryside, just on the border between rural Norfolk and Suffolk.

It was the perfect place to find some kind of normality again after the tribulations of the last couple of months, and indeed, of the last several years. With the early summer sun beating down, and a beautiful outdoor pool to laze around, it was the proverbial heaven on Earth. So, a little dribbling right now was just fine with Hiram Kane.

Kane stirred at the sound of a splash in the nearby pool. He rolled over and propped himself on an elbow, just in time to see Alexandria Ridley surface at the far end of the pool. She turned, then powered through the water, one graceful stroke after another. Her strong arms cut through the surface with practised ease.

For a long while Kane had loved Alex Ridley. They had shared many moments together over the last twenty years since they'd met. Such was their affection for one another, most people who met them assumed they were a couple. Yet, for reasons known only to her, Ridley had always held back from making a firm commitment to him, despite his best efforts.

Ridley finally slipped out of the pool after a swift ten lengths, and let the water drip from her lithe body as she walked over towards Kane.

"Hello, handsome. How was the nap? No doubt you were dreaming of me," she teased.

"No doubt," Kane replied. "Who wouldn't? You're a

gorgeous woman, Alexandria Ridley." He grinned. Ridley grinned back.

"You should cut back on the compliments... might just give this girl a complex."

"Get you a drink?"

"Wine. Thanks."

"Be right back." Kane stood from his sun bed, his athletic frame browning nicely after several days slouched in the sun. His body was more or less recovered, and his mind was close to healing too. He glanced at the stump where a finger had once been before it was shot off by a Yakuza gangster. The memories would always remain, bearing testament to a good man that had died in Japan recently. But Kane had made an important decision in the last couple of weeks, probably the most important of his life. Now it was made, there was no point sitting around feeling sorry for himself any more. Life was short; Kane knew that better than most.

It was time to move on.

On bare feet he trotted to the nearby annex where a large fridge chilled a generous stash of beer, wine and champagne. He scooped up his phone from the table. One missed call. He recognised the number. He'd been expecting this call, though not until next week. It didn't matter. When he called back, the conversation would change everything.

That could wait. Taking a drink to Ridley could not.

"M'lady," he said as he approached the love of his life. "One icy glass of sauv blanc."

"Why, thank you," she purred, taking the glass and savouring the crisp first sip. After a second, she sighed with pleasure. "That is so good, thanks."

"And you're so welcome." He had to tell her. "So... I

had a missed call." He gazed at Ridley now, waiting for her reaction.

"From who I think it was?" Kane nodded. "Are you going to call back? It's important, right?"

Kane didn't answer for many seconds as his eyes drifted from Ridley to the huge stand of oak trees bordering the property. He remained silent too, as if waiting for the right words to come. Finally, he turned his gaze back to Ridley. "Yes, it's important, though it can wait until tomorrow. But…"

"But, what?"

"Well… I know we've already made the decision. But…"

"But what, Hiram? It's an amazing opportunity, and just what you need. What *we* need." She reached out and took his hand in hers. "You're the perfect person for the job, I know that."

Kane nodded, the hint of a smile curling his lips. "You're right," he said. "So, we'd better pack our bags. We're going to Egypt."

Chapter Two

Egypt

Present Day

Abbe Abidi placed down his cup of mint tea and leaned back in his chair. He gazed out across the railing of his balcony and squinted against the dazzling orange sun as it dropped closer to the horizon. He scratched at his aquiline nose and glanced at the small glass of tea.

Who the hell am I kidding?

He ducked back inside, poured himself a large scotch and downed it in one gulp. Then he poured another and returned to the balcony.

His fancy apartment in the upmarket area off El-Gaish Road in western Alexandria overlooked popular Abo Haif Sidi Bisher Beach, where the passive waters of the Mediterranean lapped at its shore. The soothing sound of those gentle waves was often the soundtrack Abbe fell asleep to at night. Well, that, and the constant accompaniment of beeping car horns and angry, shouting drivers on what was one of Egypt's busiest roads four storeys below his terrace. Half the reason he went to work so early every morning and left so late most evenings was to avoid the heavy traffic. Besides, it wasn't as if the director of the Alexandria International Museum had anything better to do than be at work anyway.

Except drink. These days he always drank.

Abbe gazed back out at the sinking sun and thought, as usual, of his beloved wife. Fatima had died a couple of years ago. Cancer. Way too young. His children had flown the nest too, both studying abroad and, sadly, not following in the academic footsteps as he'd hoped they would. Abbe's daughter was studying science in Philadelphia and his son, his pride and joy, was following his own passion for media in Berlin. Neither of them had said more than a dozen words to their father in many months. Still, Abbe was proud of them both and was glad they'd taken more after their mother than him. *At least they're seeing the world,* he mused... *more than can be said for me these days.*

After studying antiquities for the best part of four decades, Abbe knew that without Fatima and his kids around, he was turning into an antiquity himself.

Abbe heard an aggressive knock at the apartment door. He finished the scotch in two gulps and stood up. He wasn't expecting company. No one ever came to see him anymore. He made his way to the door and, in the hallway mirror, he glimpsed his bland clothes hanging looser on his already slender frame.

He took a deep breath and opened the door. The bright hallway was empty.

Strange. Abbe scowled and looked around. *Is someone*

playing tricks with me? Then he glanced down at the floor and saw an unmarked envelope on the doormat.

Abbe bent down, his back protesting with sharp pangs of burgeoning age, and retrieved the envelope. He turned, closed the door behind him, then tipped the contents of the envelope into his hand.

He recoiled violently as the contents fluttered to the floor. A wave of dizziness threatened to overwhelm him, and he dropped to his knees. His eyes bulged wide with horror and all colour drained from his cheeks.

Now scattered on the floor around him lay several incognito pictures of his children taken from a distance. In the centre, a piece of paper lay folded in half. With shaking hands, Abbe picked it up. It read:

You will help us!
Conference call tonight.
9 pm.

Chapter Three

London

2005

The leader reached the door of flat 301 and paused. This building was designed so that each flat opened onto an exposed walkway, no doubt to give the occupants some semblance of outside space. The leader glanced around. Operationally, that made things difficult, as the men were visible from the ground or the surrounding towers. He looked over the concrete wall. The yard, fifteen metres below, was empty. He signalled to the men, who arranged themselves in the pre-planned formation: two at each end of the balcony, two behind nearby pillars, and one beside him. They were now invisible.

He examined the door. The light blue paint flaked off in large curls. Someone had attempted to wash off a patch of graffiti. The words were still legible: *Fuck off Pakis.*

He laid his hand against the wood and pushed. The door moved a fraction before the locking mechanism bit. The whole thing was flimsy and would open with nothing more than a shoulder barge.

"Looks weak," he whispered to the man beside him. Normally, they didn't speak before a raid. There was no need to be quiet here. Heavy music blasted from the flat next door. The glass windows rattled in their frames.

They'd planned to blast the door with small explosive charges; looking at it now, it wouldn't be necessary. He glanced left and right down the passageway. Windows of the flat to the right were dark.

The second-in-command nodded and prepared to barge the door with his shoulder. The leader beckoned for two men to join them.

"On my count," he whispered once the men were in formation. "Now!"

Chapter Four

Egypt

Present day

Jabari Nader glanced at the clock on the gym wall. 8:40 pm.
Five more minutes, then I'll go.

He pumped the hefty weights, 2 x twenty-two pound dumbbells, slow and steady for five more minutes. Finally, he placed them down at his feet. He grunted a farewell at a couple of friends struggling beneath gargantuan barbells, then left the gym. Jabari climbed onto his powerful motorbike and screeched away to his flat several blocks along the road. Taking the stairs two at a time for three full flights, his muscle-bound legs powered him upwards. Jabari entered his expansive flat and grabbed a huge carton of orange juice from the fridge; he downed half in one go.

Next, he stepped into the shower and rinsed away the sweat beneath cold water. Once he'd cooled off at last, he draped a large white towel around his powerful body, admiring himself in the full-length mirror as he walked into the lounge, where he took a seat behind his desk. He checked the time on his monitor. 8:57. *Perfect.* Biting into a large apple, Jabari sat back and waited for the conference call to start, a grin creeping across his handsome face.

With a shaved head and hard eyes, Jabari looked like someone who knew how to handle himself. And the man didn't disappoint. After retiring from the Egyptian Special Forces a decade ago, the then thirty-five-year-old had set up his own private security firm. The business catered to all kinds of people, from government officials to actors and singers, and the occasional member of Egyptian royalty. However, someone had approached Jabari recently for a one-off gig. He had turned it down several times, for a variety of reasons, not least the fact that it sounded completely impossible. The final offer had been too good to refuse.

Jabari was told the overall gist of the assignment by a man named Bassam. In a couple of minutes' time he'd be speaking to Bassam's boss, the financier of the project. The mastermind of the gig. That man would also be on the call, as well as two others. The mastermind would inform Jabari and the other men of the plan's finer details. The contact promised Jabari it was to be the job of a lifetime. As he thought of the massive financial rewards assured, his grin spread just that little bit wider.

Chapter Five

London

2005

"Armed police!" they bellowed as the door splintered open. "Armed police. Get down now."

The men swarmed into the flat. As planned, the first three surged forward towards the bedrooms, where the occupants would likely be this late in the evening.

Heavy boots kicked a pair of children's shoes across the hallway.

"Clear!" echoed a shout from the small kitchen. The latent smell of spices hung in the air.

Two officers shoved open the door of the master bedroom and snapped on the light. A man and woman struggled upright, squinting against the light's invasion. The woman screamed. The man cupped a hand above his eyes, his greying hair ruffled by sleep.

"IC4, male and female," the leader barked into his radio.

"Clear!" reverberated another voice from somewhere else in the flat.

"Get up, now!" the chief demanded.

With two firearms pointing at them, the man and woman didn't argue.

The officers led them through to the living room and sat them on the sofa.

"There's a child in here. A little boy," came a call from deeper in the flat.

"Roger that," the leader replied. "Keep him there."

The lead man turned to face the couple. The woman sobbed into her hands. The man shuffled closer to her.

"Don't move!" an officer snarled.

The man held up his hands and froze.

"We're looking for Idris al Halabi," the chief said aggressively.

"He's... he's working," the man stuttered, then glanced at a clock on the wall. "Evening shift at the petrol station. He should be home soon."

"What station?" the chief demanded.

The man gave the name and street of the station. A radio squawked and all officers turned towards the door.

"IC4, male approaching," came the call again.

All eight officers moved suddenly.

Chapter Six

Paris

Present day

Omar Abdel-Rahman glanced up as his butler knocked twice and entered the room.

"It is almost time for your call, sir," said the diminutive servant, Bassam, in his exquisitely manicured English accent. "Are you ready?"

Omar coughed and screwed his eyes shut, then dabbed a handkerchief to his lips. He didn't need to look at it. He knew there'd be flecks of blood there. Bassam looked away.

"Yes, thank you, Bassam. That will be all," Omar replied in his even more refined accent, clipped to within an inch of its life in the dusty halls of Cambridge in the sixties. It was as perfect now as it was then. Back then he'd used his charm to talk his way into the high society of British academia, hobnobbing with such leading archaeological lights as

Jacquetta Hawkes, Thomas Charles Lethbridge and Sir Leonard Woolley.

Bassam silently left his boss's penthouse suite, an opulent space that occupied the entire top floor of the apartment block nestled in one of the most expensive bits of real estate in the world: Avenue Émile-Deschanel, in the 7th Arrondissement, Paris. Not that price mattered to Omar Abdel-Rahman, one of the wealthiest men in all Egypt. Omar had an oversized personality that matched his rotund physique, and a jovial voice that boomed with confidence. His shiny, jet-black coiffured hair added a certain elegance to his appearance, though the out-of-place pencil moustache detracted from what some considered a handsome, though slightly bloated face. His Armani suit cost more than the average Egyptian's annual income, yet despite his wealth and extravagant lifestyle, Omar was considered—by others as well as by himself—a man of the people. He had put millions of his own fortune into a range of charities, and was never one to turn down an invite to celebrity charitable events, where the champagne flowed, and his philanthropic reputation continued to thrive, much like his impressive waistline.

Omar had amassed his personal fortune from the oil industry in the eighties; and, though technically retired, his investments still brought him millions of dollars annually. He spent most of this on his one true passion in life; collecting priceless archaeological artefacts.

Such was the extent of his world-class collection, much of which was secured in his private museum on the floor directly beneath the penthouse suite, that Omar often loaned selections from it to exhibits all around the world. He was unabashedly proud of his collection, and it gave him immense satisfaction. Yet, having the artefacts in his possession was one thing. It was the hunting down and attaining of those supposedly 'unattainable' artefacts that really got Omar's juices flowing.

One such item above all others kept Omar up at nights, more so than any glamorous young suitor could, female or male. Omar had fended off almost as many of both as he'd entertained.

The particular artefact he had firmly in his sights now had been discovered by French soldiers in his Egyptian homeland in 1799. Not long after, it had been sold to the highest bidder. Thus, it has remained in its current home for over two-hundred years; The British Museum.

Though himself worldly and cosmopolitan, Omar Abdel-Rahman knew one thing about ancient archaeological artefacts: they should always come home.

Chapter Seven

London

2005

Idris al Halabi pushed his headphones deeper into his ears and turned the corner towards Richmond House. He couldn't do anything about the other young men shouting insults at him, but at least this way he could pretend not to hear them. He held the other end of the headphones in his fist and wished he'd been able to get a replacement phone already. His mobile had been stolen a week ago, and he wouldn't get paid for another ten days. He'd quickly come to realise that the problem with an honest living was that you only got paid once a month. The other young men from the estate seemed to get paid every day and had all the gadgets and expensive clothes they wanted.

Although that lifestyle had tempted Idris too, he wanted to get out of this shithole by honest means. He wanted to call somewhere else home. Somewhere he didn't have to endure daily racist insults. It seemed to Idris that all the money those other boys earned didn't get them out of the estate. Instead, it got them tied to it for life. The only way those boys ever left the estate was in the back of a police car or an ambulance. Many never came back.

Idris pushed into the stairwell. He tried to breathe through his mouth to prevent the rancid stench from turning his stomach. As usual it didn't work, so he hurried up the stairs.

He reached the third floor and pulled the key from his pocket. With extra shifts at the garage, the A Levels he was studying hard for, and the encouragement of friends at the local mosque, Idris reckoned he could be out of here soon. He would find a nice place to live, and get settled. Then he'd get his younger brother out of here, too.

With plans, hopes and dreams swirling through his mind, Idris hadn't noticed the absence of racist insults thrown his way this evening. The estate was unusually quiet; it hadn't even registered in his mind.

He reached the door of the flat and lifted his key towards the lock. His feet became rooted to the concrete. His stomach turned to iron. His pupils shrunk to pinpricks. The door had been smashed in so violently that it was hanging from one hinge. His brother's shoes were scattered across the floor.

Idris tried to speak, but couldn't find the words.

"Armed police. Freeze!"

Idris heard the shout. A cold understanding followed.

Two men dressed entirely in black strode down the passage towards him. His heart thudded relentlessly. His breath caught in his throat.

Idris looked back the way he had come along the

passage. Another man dressed in the same black stepped out from the gloom.

"Stay right where you are!"

Three guns were levelled at him. There was nowhere to run. *Unless…*

Idris glanced over the balcony. The ground loomed far below. He pictured himself in the videos he'd seen. Locked up. Tortured. Wiped off the face of the Earth. That wasn't going to happen.

Idris pulled a deep breath of the crisp night air and looked up at the sky.

Then he threw himself over the balcony.

Chapter Eight

London

Present day

Salam al Halabi needed to end the call.

"Sure thing, of course. Okay, I've got to run. I'll see you at work tomorrow."

Salam locked his phone and a picture of his mother, father, his brother and Salam himself filled the screen. It was taken fifteen years ago when Salam was only ten. It was the most recent photo he had of them all together.

He slammed the welling emotion away, stashed the phone in his pocket and descended into the London Underground at Holborn. Twenty minutes later he emerged into a warm evening at a bustling Liverpool Street Station; then he made the short walk to his modest one-bedroom flat in Shoreditch. It had been a long, busy, but ultimately good day at work; yet, for the last hour or two Salam's nerves had started to get the better of him. He'd just called his friend, Sophie—where they dating? He wasn't quite sure—because he'd missed her at work and hadn't had time for their usual pint once they'd left The British Museum, where they both worked as assistant curators.

He hadn't had time for that pint, because for Salam, time was seriously ticking.

The twenty-five-year-old hated when he got kept behind at work after hours for one inane meeting or another. Although Salam loved his job as assistant curator, these meetings were almost always a waste of time. This one had been no exception. And this evening, time was something Salam had very little of.

In just half an hour, at 8:00 pm GMT, Salam was to take part in a conference call that would almost certainly change his life.

He kicked off his shoes, fired up his MacBook, then slumped down onto his bony couch. The BBC News reporter on TV was droning some shit or other about the prime minister once more embarrassing himself—Salam believed the blond buffoon did that every time he opened his mouth—so he hit mute on the remote. The flat was cosy and quiet, despite the busy high street just below his first-floor window. He'd made it as homely as possible on his assistant's salary.

Salam felt he'd been overlooked far too long for a promotion at the British Museum, which severely pissed him off. Nevertheless, he worked hard and with diligence. He knew he was up against it. Racial tensions had grown in the last couple of years. Much of Europe seemed to be taking a more conservative, right-wing angle. As a British Muslim of Egyptian descent, Salam knew there were likely to be even tougher times ahead.

Salam ran a hand though his thick black hair, then adjusted his glasses. He glanced at the digital clock on the TV. 7:58 pm. Almost time for the call. Salam's throat suddenly felt dry, and he hustled to refill his water cup in the kitchen, catching a glimpse of the Brick Lane mosque through the window. Feeling a little calmer having seen the mosque, he returned to the sofa and placed his MacBook on his lap.

One more minute…

Chapter Nine

Paris

Present Day

Omar Abdel-Rahman leaned forward and pressed a button on his computer mouse; then he stood up and turned to face a bank of monitors mounted to a wall. Omar was exhilarated that finally, his long-held dream—more a burning desire—was about to commence.

Three other men sat at three separate locations across Europe and Egypt, in two different time zones, each waiting in anticipation of the imminent conference call. Two of the men were nervous, as well as being undeniably excited. The last of them was ambivalent to the actual job—it was just that, a job—yet he couldn't help but wonder about how his life would change if they achieved success.

Despite their very different reasons for becoming involved in the imminent drama, all four men sat by their computers with bated breath. It was to be a conversation that might very well be the defining moment of each of their respective lives.

A huge bay window behind Omar offered a view of the Eiffel Tower just two-hundred and fifty yards to the north west. It was a view he adored. Now he ignored it.

One by one, three smaller screens pinged to life on Omar's Zoom app, each square occupied by a different face. All three of those faces remained passive. Nervous, even.

Omar spread his arms wide, his huge grin almost matching it. "Good evening, gentlemen," he said, "and welcome to the first day of the rest of your lives. Inshallah."

Chapter Ten

Paris

It was time to seal the deal.

Omar Abdel-Rahman looked at each of the faces on the respective screens in turn, holding their gazes before moving to the next set of expectant eyes.

The man in the top left of the four was Abbe Abidi, director of the Alexandria International Museum. Abidi was a man of great standing in the city of Alexandria, his reputation untarnished. However, Omar had done his research.

The director's beloved wife Fatima had died a couple of years ago after a long, gruelling illness. Omar's museum contact had made it clear his boss Abbe had let his standards drop, both personally and professionally. His zest and passion for life were on the wane, and he'd been known to leave work and spend hours in various bars near his apartment before going home.

Omar was a good man, a decent man. He was also an opportunist, and would turn the unfortunate Abbe Abidi's troubles to his advantage.

Next to Abbe Abidi, in the top right, was the youngest member of what Omar hoped would become his inside team, Salam al Halabi. The young Brit was an assistant curator at the British Museum. Omar, through yet another contact in his archaeological network, had learned Salam wasn't exactly satisfied with his career prospects. Not only that, Omar knew Salam was a devout Muslim. Though Omar didn't trouble himself too much with the rise of Islam—didn't trouble himself with it at all in fact, despite being born into that faith—he saw it as another opportunity to turn this knowledge to his advantage. After all, what better reward existed for a young Jihadist than a dozen virgins in Heaven, when all the money in the world wasn't enough?

The third and final piece of the jigsaw was Jabari Hader. His handsome face looked back at Omar from the bottom right of the monitor, and sat atop solid, muscle-bound shoulders. The man had a penetrating stare; Omar was delighted the former Special Forces operative would be working for him, rather than against. He would be a formidable ally.

Known as the owner of the best private security company in Egypt, Jabari had assembled a quality team of former colleagues and trusted associates. Omar had the utmost confidence in Jabari and his men to see this assignment through to its climax. Jabari was a mercenary, plain and simple. He had no known political or religious affiliations, and was simply in it for the money. And money Omar Abdel-Rahman possessed in unlimited quantities.

Thus, Omar was supremely confident of the choice of potential colleagues he'd assembled for what was to be the greatest adventure of his life. It was time to put that confidence to the test.

"Good evening, gentlemen," Omar repeated. "I appreciate you all taking time from your busy schedules to chat with me this evening. I know you've all been contacted by my assistant Bassam. I trust you've all been sufficiently briefed to know why I've called this meeting. I'll assume that the fact you've answered the request is evidence of your commitment? A simple nod will suffice at this stage."

Indeed, all three men nodded, but no one yet spoke. They knew who Omar Abdel-Rahman was. His fame was international. At least, they thought they knew him.

When Omar's assistant Bassam had reached out to each of them after months of diligent research by Omar's team, they had each done some research of their own. They had been invited to get involved in what was obviously a highly-illegal activity. Although they'd been promised enormous financial rewards—as well as other, less tangible rewards in one of their cases—they'd also been promised that no one would be harmed by the daring plot. Naturally, each man wanted to cover his respective bases.

They found out Omar was a very rich man. They learned he was an incredibly generous philanthropist, and that he was famous throughout the world of antiquities for his magnificent collection of priceless artefacts. All he wanted from them was apparently simple; to help him secure one more. Bassam had told them that once it was done, Omar would simply retire from the game and they would all be rich.

None of the three men could think of any good reason

not to get involved, even if it went against some personal principles. The plan sounded well thought out. Success seemed certain. They had all agreed.

Just as Omar had known they would.

Chapter Eleven

The Kane Estate

Monday had soon arrived, and Kane dusted off the remnant cobwebs of a heavy weekend with a brisk run around the estate. Next, he slumped down in a deck chair in the shade of a giant two-hundred-year-old oak, then hit the *call back* button on his mobile. It was answered on the third ring.

"Hiram?"

"Good morning. Yes, it's Hiram, returning your call. How are you, Mr. MacGregor?"

"It's Neil. Thanks so much for calling back."

"Of course. Neil, sorry I didn't call sooner. It's been a busy weekend and… well, I had to be sure of my answer."

"I totally understand. It's a big decision, but we at the British Museum sincerely hope you've made a favourable one for us."

"I appreciate that. I'm honoured you've offered me this incredible opportunity, so with great pride, I formally accept the position. It's a fantastic opportunity, Neil. I'm truly grateful for it."

"That's excellent news. I can't wait to inform the rest of the team. Your grandfather will be delighted. He insisted you were the best man for the job. I couldn't agree more."

Kane ended the call and returned to the house to find his family drinking coffee in the sunlit conservatory. Other than Ridley, and his grandad, who had recommended him for the position, no one else knew about the job offer.

"Erm, I have news," he stated, clearing his throat. "I haven't mentioned it yet because I wasn't sure if it would happen. I received a job offer a few weeks back. I've decided to accept it."

"That's great," Danny said. "Congratulations! Uh, what's the job?"

"For a long time Granddad has been involved with the British Museum in setting up ARC, the Artefact Repatriation Committee. As you all know, the purpose of the committee was to begin the long overdue task of returning some of the world's most important artefacts to their rightful places, usually in the country of their provenance. And… well, I've been offered a position on the committee."

"Not just any position," his granddad chimed in. "Don't do yourself a disservice."

"Right. Well, the ARC has offered me the role of Operations Manager. I'll front a dedicated, highly-skilled team to start returning some of the BM's most famous treasures to where they belong. We begin operations in just two weeks."

"Hiram, that's such wonderful news," said his grandmother, Dee, who placed her frail arms around his chest and squeezed tight.

"Yes, we're very proud of you, Son," added his grandfather. The committee had been his brainchild some thirty years ago. Now it was finally happening. Moreover, after his tireless efforts to get it off the ground all these years, his own grandson was going to be leading it.

Next to step forward and congratulate Kane on the news was his father. "I'm so pleased for you," he said with rare but genuine affection. "I guess I'd rather you'd stay here for a while, but at least it doesn't sound dangerous," he added, and hugged his eldest son.

"Well done, Bro," said Danny, whose grin was almost as wide as Kane's. "I'm proud too."

"Thanks. Hey, maybe I'll need an assistant."

Danny scoffed. "Not a chance. I've been away long enough, and I don't plan on leaving any time soon." They both chuckled, then it was Ridley's turn to offer her congratulations.

"Hiram," she said, spinning him to face her, "you totally deserve the trust the BM is putting in you to bring respect and compassion to this job. There's been a lot of tension about this issue over the years, and we all know this isn't simply a case of loading a box of old relics on a flight and dropping them off elsewhere in the world. It's almost like a diplomatic position, so the fact they want you for it says everything about your character." Ridley paused, glancing around the sitting room at all the members of the family. "In fact, the unquestionable character and dignity of the entire Kane family. I can speak on behalf of the world of archaeology and antiquities when I say those artefacts, and the reputation of the British Museum, could not be in better hands."

Ridley stepped away from Hiram and began a gentle round of applause, to which everyone, including Kane himself, joined in. He was genuinely touched.

"Well, what's the first assignment?" Danny asked.

"You're not lugging a box of dusty old pots to India are you? Or hauling some desiccated Peruvian mummy back to whence it came?"

Kane grinned. "No pots, Danny. Not yet. The first assignment is a big one. Perhaps the biggest. With the cooperation of the UK government, ARC has decided the very first item returned by the BM should make a huge statement, setting an example to other institutions around the world."

"So," Danny said, "what the hell is it?"

Kane took a moment. It really was going to send a powerful message to other museums and galleries across the globe. It was time to do the right thing and return artefacts, many stolen or removed during colonialism, to where they belonged. He could think of no better example than the one he'd be organising.

"My team," he said, "is going to return an object that for two-hundred years has sat front and centre in the British Museum. We've all visited it many times over the years. I remember visiting with Granddad when we were kids, Danny. He taught us who found it, where it was found, and all the other legends attached to the artefact."

Danny looked up. Recognition sparkled in his eyes. He knew what it was. They all did.

"Yes," Kane said, "the Rosetta Stone is going home to Egypt."

Chapter Twelve

Paris

Omar had always known he was touched by genius, and this operation was just the latest in a long history of examples. He had chosen his team well; he knew each carefully selected man needed this almost as much as he did. For example, the youngster Salam al Halabi.

Salam was employed by an institution that, despite his outstanding work, seemed unwilling to elevate him to his rightful place as curator of one of its many departments. He'd worked there longer than most of his colleagues, and he was more passionate and skilled than them all. Yet with growing frustration and anger, Salam remained an assistant as one after another of his peers became curators of his or her own department, striding on in careers that should have been his. It had left Salam bitter.

This all happened to coincide with a growing sense of

nationalism in his country of birth, the United Kingdom. As far as Salam could see, it was becoming less united by the week.

Religious tensions were growing, though Salam knew it was more racial than religious. Of course, Islam wasn't a race at all, but a religious belief. It's just a fact that most Muslims were brown-skinned. Some people were just so ignorant, and it drove Salam mad. He knew as many black so-called Christians as he did white, and as many Arabic Jews as white followers of Judaism. No, the rising angst across his country was definitely racially charged, but labelled by the unscrupulous press as religious tension.

For most of his young life, Salam had been a moderate Muslim. He hadn't followed the Qur'an strictly and had barely been to a mosque. In recent years, however, especially since the *alleged* 7/7 terror attacks in London in 2005 —Salam felt certain those were in fact false flag attacks perpetrated by the British government to stir up the heat— he'd become more and more devout and was now a regular worshipper at the Brick Lane Mosque.

Omar had learned all this. The financial rewards he had promised for Salam's participation would go towards funding the terror cell Salam was flirting with. Failing that, there were always the virgins.

Abbe Abidi was a different case. Omar knew the man was mentally broken. If he kept drinking the way he was, he'd be physically ruined too. He was lost without his wife; it was almost as if he had nothing to live for. The only thing he was still passionate about was history. His lifelong love of archaeology and artefacts was the one thing keeping him sane.

Of Curses and Kings

When Omar's man Bassam first approached him, he scoffed at the idea. The artefact was soon to be coming home to Egypt anyway. Then, it would just be stuck in another museum, remain unappreciated, and soon be forgotten about.

Abbe Abidi toiled with the dilemma. This man, this Omar character, was someone who would appreciate the artefact for what it was. Wouldn't he? *Why shouldn't I help him get his hands on it? Especially considering the fortune it would give me.* It was enough money for Abbe to spend the rest of his life doing whatever the hell he wanted. If he got killed in the process, Abbe knew not a single person alive would miss him. He agreed soon enough.

Omar considered Jabari Hader his masterstroke. The security company owner was already wealthy; and, he counted Sheiks, rock stars and royalty among his regular, highly satisfied clients. He didn't really need the stress of this job, nor the financial rewards. None of those clients were as charismatic as Omar. Not only had Omar sold him the job on the glory of the success—though they could never broadcast it, obviously—Omar promised to cut him into his last will and testament once he, Omar, died. Omar was well aware that any slice of his last will and testament was surely something even the normally unflappable Jabari Hader could ignore.

Omar took a sip of iced water. He'd been coughing more lately, and his throat was always sore. The cool water felt like liquid gold on his tonsils. He placed down the glass, then began the four-way conference call.

"Each of you has been selected with the utmost diligence for the attributes you'll bring to the, um, shall we call it… a repatriation project? Yes, a repatriation project. I'm sorry, *our* project, for it is not mine alone. We each will benefit greatly from its success. It's important for me to know that each of you realises how important *you* are to that success. Quite simply, I cannot achieve what I desire without you. If just one component of our team fails, the project also fails. Failure will bring with it many consequences, though I'm sure you've already considered that." Omar paused, waiting for any objections, though he was certain none would come. "So, gentlemen, despite the risks you're all still here."

"When do we start?" asked the no-nonsense Jabari Hader.

"A good question," Omar replied, "though the answer depends on several factors. For example, how soon can you have your team ready, Mister Hader?"

"They are ready now. I will need a few days to go over the logistics, but that is all."

"Excellent news, and I do not doubt it for a moment. You and your company were selected for exactly that reason. Your reputation goes before you. It also depends on our friend and colleague, Mister Abidi. May I call you Abbe, Mister Abidi?"

"You may, yes," Abbe replied.

"So, Abbe, how are the preparations going at Alexandria International Museum? Is everything there on track?"

"Yes, we are on schedule. We're only awaiting final confirmation from the British Museum, which I believe our colleague Mister al Halabi may have news on?"

Omar watched Salam shift uncomfortably in his seat, evidently far out of his comfort zone. His discomfort would be worth everything he might risk and gain from it. He composed himself before answering.

"That's right, Mister Abidi. Everything's on track at the British Museum, too. I should inform you that there's a new man involved, whose recruitment has given me cause for concern."

"Oh yes? Who is he, and why is it a concern?" Omar asked. "I fail to see how one person might hinder our plans."

"He's a kind of retired explorer, though he's still young, perhaps mid-forties. He's actually quite famous, best known for discovering the lost city of Vilcabamba in Peru, yet he's quiet and unassuming. I met him for the first time when he was introduced as the new head of our team. He's a big man and looks to me as if he'd suffer no fools."

Omar smiled. He wasn't averse to a touch of the dramatics himself. He remembered reading something about Vilcabamba a year or two back, but surely whoever this guy was couldn't affect their plans in any way.

"Tell me, Salam, what is this new fellow's name?"

Salam cleared his throat. "Well, technically he's my new boss. His name is Hiram Kane."

Chapter Thirteen

Somewhere in England

In an abandoned warehouse on a deserted, rural industrial estate, three men sat around a table piled high with takeaway cartons and bottles of scotch. A single naked bulb swung listlessly above them.

Their boss had sent them to the area several days ago. From this dilapidated former self-storage lockup, they'd been out on several reconnaissance missions to a location a few miles away in the countryside. Their plan was simple and confidence of a successful mission was high. They expected their target to offer little resistance. Nor did they expect to receive any outside interference. It would be a simple case of timing and stealth, skills these men possessed in spades. Hence, the relaxed atmosphere and ripe banter between them.

One man sparked up a joint and inhaled deeply. "What are you going to do once we've grabbed the old man, delivered him to the boss, and been paid?" he asked the other two.

"I'm going to convince your wife to leave you and come and live with me," one replied seriously. "She needs a man like me, not a skinny kid like you."

"Oh yeah? I reckon the old timer we're grabbing could kick your arse... I'll probably have to rescue you. Then we'll see who the real man is."

The men chuckled and resumed their game of cards. A few hours from now—late evening, just before it got dark — they would climb into their unmarked transit van and head out into the countryside. They'd been watching their target for a few evenings now and unless something had changed, they knew exactly where he'd be and what he'd be doing.

Easiest snatch they'd ever done.

Chapter Fourteen

Suffolk, England

Kane and Ridley sat facing each other on the train from Suffolk to London. Ridley read, while Kane was content to watch the undulating countryside of his homeland flash past the window. He had spent the majority of his adult life abroad, and had always enjoyed living and working in far off, exotic places. Whenever he was home, however, he realised just how much he missed the simple beauty of the English countryside. Kane was a native of East Anglia, and while it was undoubtedly beautiful geographically—with its vast flattened swathes of patchwork fields, lush pastures and hundreds of miles of idyllic waterways—it was the polar opposite of what he really loved: mountains. Kane wasn't a mountaineer as such. Nevertheless, he loved nothing more than hiking in the hills and trekking across the world's mountainous regions.

Yet, in the same way he wanted to remove danger and

drama from his life, the low-lying landscape of the home counties seemed appropriate; endlessly flat, and very, very safe.

It was just two hours to London, and before they knew it their train was pulling into the cavernous interior of Liverpool Street Station. Kane grabbed his small roller case from the rack, and stepped onto the crowded platform. He found rolling the case awkward, more used to having a backpack slung over his shoulders. Ridley had convinced him it looked more professional to have the case, and he couldn't argue. "More grown up," was what she'd actually said, but Kane doubted it.

They descended into the subterranean world of London's riotous underground where, it seemed to Kane, there dwelled an entirely different species of human. Above ground, people were polite and civilised, holding doors for one another and offering up their seats. Not so in the underground, and Kane hated it. People jostled, argued and glared at one another, as if every day were a Black Friday in Poundland.

Twenty minutes later, Ridley and a relieved Kane exited the underground at Great Russel Square. Kane was a stickler for punctuality, so they were early for his appointment at the British Museum. With an hour to spare, they grabbed takeaway teas and took a slow stroll through quintessentially London-esque Russell Square, revelling at the anonymity of being in the big city. After one full circuit of the green park, they relaxed onto an empty bench. Kane was apprehensive about the imminent meeting.

Ridley seemed to sense it. "Hey." Kane didn't flinch, totally lost in thought. "Hello?" Ridley probed. "Earth to Kane. Bueller?"

He looked around and smiled. "Sorry, I was just… you know, thinking about stuff."

"What stuff? Care to share?"

He shifted to face Ridley. "The BM's putting a lot of faith in me to do this job, right? With everything that's happened lately… I don't know… maybe I'm just not the right guy for the job after all." He looked at his feet, a hint of shame in his eyes. Ridley was having none of it.

"You listen to me," she said. "The things that happened to us, in Peru, and Mexico… there was no way of knowing any of that shit was coming. And then your dramas in Bali and Japan? They were freak events, started by freaks. Nothing like that will ever happen again. You made difficult decisions under horrendous conditions. Because of your bravery and brilliance, you saved many lives. Including mine."

There was such sincerity in those green eyes; deep down Kane knew she was right.

"You've taken a huge decision to leave your beloved Cuzco and the business behind. It was the right thing to do. The only thing."

Kane nodded. "I guess I'm just nervous, that's all. This is a momentous event. Not just for the Rosetta Stone itself, but for diplomatic relations between Britain and Egypt. I might be a good expedition leader. I might even be good at helping people. However, I am *not* a diplomat. I'm just not sure I'm capable of—"

"You are more than capable, Hiram; you are the perfect choice. Yes, you are a diplomat. You're as diplomatic as anyone I've ever known. That's exactly the reason your grandfather recommended you, and exactly the reason you've been chosen. Hiram Senior trusts you. The BM trusts you. I trust you."

Ridley leaned over and kissed Kane on his forehead, then stood and pulled him from the bench. He smiled. He couldn't help it. To him, Alexandria Ridley was simply perfect.

"Come on," she said, "you have an old stone to collect."

Chapter Fifteen

Somewhere in England

In a sprawling garden deep in the English countryside, an old man walked his dog. It was a little after nine in the evening, but it was still light and with the advantage of a high and almost full moon, the passage around the vast expanse of land was well lit.

The dog, an ageing black Labrador named Champ, was weary, but he enjoyed his walks out with his master before bed. If a squirrel happened to stray across their path, Champ was still capable of surprising bursts of speed, though it had been several years since he'd had any success.

Suddenly Champ paused, his saggy ears arcing upright.

"What is it Champ? Seen a squirrel, old boy?"

Champ held perfectly still, as if listening, though the old man knew that his beloved Champ's eyes and ears were nowhere near as sensitive as they once were. The old man held still too, but neither saw nor heard anything in the quiet dusk.

"Come on, boy," he said, "it's just the breeze."

Champ seemed reluctant, resisting his master's gentle encouragement. There was no need for a leash on their own property, and the old man set off without his companion. Reluctantly, Champ followed, and they resumed their walk beneath the rapidly descending darkness.

Bats flitted in and out of the trees chasing bugs. Somewhere an owl let its presence be known.

Just then Champ stopped sharply, and barked, startling the old man. Champ never barked. The owl had fallen silent. Champ barked again, and his master followed where Champ seemed to be looking: into a small copse of ghostly birch trees, their bark glowing silver under the rising moon.

He didn't hear anything. Didn't see it coming.

From the left, opposite to where Champ was looking, two masked men trotted stealthily across the open ground and got to within ten feet before Champ spun towards them. Before he could react, one man had sliced his guts open with a long blade, silencing his barks with three brutal thrusts of the lethal dagger.

Behind him, another man approached from within the birch trees. The old man stood there, mouth and eyes wide, shock rendering him silent. It didn't matter. Two-hundred yards from his large house, and half a mile from the nearest neighbour, no one would hear him if he cried for help.

"What is this? Who are you and what do you want?" he finally said.

The masked intruders shared a glance; then, in a blur of grunts and flying limbs, the old man was wrestled to the ground and restrained. Once they'd gagged and blindfolded him, they pulled him to his feet and marched him across the garden into the forest that ran parallel to the country lane beyond.

Moments later, they'd forced him into their unmarked transit van and were driving calmly through the countryside to a private airfield twenty miles away.

Throughout the entire time, only one of the men had spoken, and only one word. It was in Arabic, and due to the old man's former profession, he understood exactly what it meant.

"Tamin," the attacker had said. *Insurance.*

Chapter Sixteen

The British Museum, London

"Hiram, thanks so much for coming. It's a pleasure to finally see you in person again after all these years."

"Thank you Neil. Yes, it's been too long… May I say, I'm immensely grateful you considered me for this position. I'm determined not to let you down."

"There is no man's judgement I trust more in the world than that of your grandfather. He knows you're the best choice, which means we at the BM know it too. Thus, on behalf of myself, the British Museum and the rest of the ARC team, welcome aboard."

The two men shook hands, and despite his reserved nature, Kane couldn't hide his joy. It was more than just the importance of the job he'd been given and the responsibility he felt. It was the knowledge that he'd be doing something good for the world, something righteous. Finally, it was something safe.

"Right," Ridley said as she led Kane out onto the street

after the meeting, "let me buy you a pint. It's time to celebrate."

"There they are." The man pulled deep on a cigarette, then backed up his comment with a nod in the direction of the museum gates across the street. His eyes were sharp, narrowed in concentration through the tobacco haze.

"I see them... are you sure it's them?" answered his partner.

The first man shot a sideways glance at his colleague and sneered. "I am sure. Let's go... stay casual, and we do not get any closer than this. Okay?"

The second man grunted something unintelligible. The first man grinned, then stubbed out the cigarette beneath the heel of a heavy black boot.

Kane led Ridley back into the main hall of the British Museum; after a couple of celebratory pints, it was to be the first stop on a day spent playing tourists. After the standard security checks at the entrance, they stepped inside the museum, just as a light drizzle began to fall.

"Isn't it something?" Kane said as Ridley watched him marvelling over the very item he had been charged to repatriate to Egypt. The remarkable Rosetta Stone.

Kane felt no sadness that the famous object would soon be leaving the museum. It was to be a milestone event and one of great cultural importance and significance. Nevertheless, in the future it would seem odd to visit the museum with the Rosetta Stone no longer there, after more than two centuries on display. It would definitely leave a void, albeit a happy one.

"Fucking weather," grumbled Nazeer as they hustled across Great Russell Street and through the main gates of the British Museum's sprawling entry plaza. "Just what I fucking needed."

"Always complaining," retorted Atef, "just like a girl."

The two men momentarily lost sight of their quarry, but knew they wouldn't be hard to find once inside as they stood out a mile. Both were tall and striking. Nazeer begrudgingly had to admit that Hiram Kane was handsome for an *ajnabi*, and built like an athlete. As for the woman... Nazeer didn't know too much about her other than her name, that she was half-Egyptian, and that if he got a chance, he'd show her what a real man was like.

Atef and Nazeer stepped into the large atrium-style concourse of the British Museum and paused, searching the crowds for Kane and the Ridley woman, and spotted them heading to the Egyptian Sculpture Gallery on the western side of the massive building. A wry grin caused Nazeer's forehead to wrinkle. *Of course they are*, he thought, and casually led Atef in the same direction.

From the shadows of a megalithic carved statue of Ramses II, Nazeer looked on as Kane grabbed the woman by the hand and moved further into the gallery, pausing at one displayed item after another.

"They're literally stopping at every fucking object," he grunted, "and they all look the same. I don't get what all the fuss is about."

"That's because all you care about is little girls," Atef declared, chuckling. Nazeer didn't respond. Atef knew it's because what he'd said wasn't far from the truth. *To each his own*, he mused, but didn't smile.

After what seemed an interminable amount of time, Nazeer and Atef were finally relieved to be following, at a distance, Kane and the woman out of the cloying, processed air of the museum and out onto the damp London streets again.

"Where the hell are they going next?" Atef pondered as they wandered south, already sick of the assignment and wanting nothing more than to get back to his girlfriend. Twenty minutes later, beneath a grey and threatening sky, they followed their marks up the steps of the National Gallery in Leicester Square, dutifully keeping a safe distance behind so as not to arouse any suspicions.

After the National Gallery, and what had felt like endless hours looking at people who were looking at—what Nazeer and Atef both thought were boring, shitty paintings—they followed Kane and Ridley outside again, relieved to see them heading back in the direction of their hotel.

"Let's hope this is the last fucking stop," Nazeer hissed. He was dismayed when they ducked into a pub near the hotel. He took out his mobile phone.

"Boss, they're in a pub next to the hotel," he said into the phone. "Nothing more to report."

"Good," the boss said. "Send Atef home. You stay there. I want eyes on them until they get back to the hotel."

"Boss, Atef can stay. I need to get home—"

"Are you defying me, Nazeer?"

Nazeer paused, eyes narrowing on Atef, who seemed to sense the gist of the phone call and smirked. "No, boss," Nazeer said quietly. "I understand."

"Put Astef on."

Nazeer handed the phone to Atef, who listened in silence for a few seconds before handing the mobile back to Nazeer.

"Have a lovely evening... with your friends," Atef said, sarcasm dripping from each syllable. "I will be off." With a wink for good measure, Atef turned from Nazeer and trotted off down the road to the nearby Russell Square Underground station.

Nazeer scowled, then turned his attention back on the pub, confident that he would soon teach that jumped-up little prick not to mock him.

After a few quiet pints and dinner at a pub near their hotel, Kane and Ridley made the short walk back to the hotel. Tomorrow was set to be a big day in both their lives. It was the beginning of a new chapter in Kane's life and career, and one he intended to grasp with both hands. If everything went smoothly, in just three days' time they would be embarking on a mission to complete the repatriation of the Rosetta Stone to Egypt.

After it was successfully delivered, Kane's mission was to make the rest of the world follow suit.

Chapter Seventeen

After a quick shower and a generous breakfast at the hotel, Kane said goodbye to Ridley and strolled the thirty minutes it took to get to the British Museum. His appointment was at 8:30. He arrived at 7:53. It wasn't open to the public at that time, but Kane was no longer just a visitor. This was work, and it was with a genuine surge of pride and a palpable sense of responsibility, not to mention a buzz of adrenalin and eagerness to get started, that he approached the imposing building. He swiped his brand-new security card and entered through the *STAFF ONLY* entrance tucked away on Bloomsbury Street.

Kane was greeted in the staff reception and led to the offices of the repatriation team, tucked away at the rear of the Egypt and Sudan gallery. After a couple of fortifying deep breaths, he entered the large, airy office, where a young man was handing out muffins and offering tea and coffee. Kane politely declined both; he was too nervous.

A hum of activity gave an air of excitement to the large room, and the dozen or so people inside seemed as buoyant to be there as Kane was. Several approached him and introduced themselves. Others clustered in small groups as a buzz of euphoria permeated the room. A moment later the director of the British Museum, Neil MacGregor, arrived.

"Morning everyone. It's good to see you all here nice and early today," he stated in his calm yet confident Midlothian brogue. "Before we start, I want to make some quick intros. I'd like to introduce you all to Hiram Kane. By now you all know Hiram will be overseeing the operation to return the Rosetta Stone to Egypt as part of our new ARC team. I'm sure most of you personally know Hiram's esteemed grandfather, Hiram Senior. As a reminder, the Artefacts Repatriation Committee was Hiram Senior's brainchild, and it was his passionate persistence that has finally seen the project get up and running. I'm confident you'll afford our new Hiram the same respect and assistance you would as if it were Hiram Senior here before you now."

Over the next few minutes Neil introduced Kane to every member of the team individually. Their smiles were sincere, their handshakes firm, and Kane immediately felt at home amongst his new colleagues.

MacGregor took centre stage again. "So, team," he said, "you all know why we're here. We've have been tasked with undertaking one of the most important moments in the history of museology… the safe, careful and considerate repatriation to Egypt of our beloved Rosetta Stone. Now, let me be the first to say that I'm very sorry to see the old girl go. She arrived with us here in 1802, and," — Neil lowered his voice to a conspiratorial whisper — "don't say anything, but I believe we still have staff here who remember that day well."

There followed a ripple of good-natured laughter before MacGregor's tone took on a more serious edge. "The reality is, people, that returning the stone to Egypt is one hundred percent the right thing to do. Whether the government of this country agrees with us or not, by returning her to Egypt we're setting a very important precedent for museums all over the world. The Alexandria National Museum has gone to great lengths, not to mention enormous expense, to prove it's ready to receive such an important and valuable artefact. Not only are they ready, however… they are worthy. It has fallen upon us, this great team of dedicated and conscientious experts, to make this happen. I know I can trust you all to see it done, and done well."

Nods of agreement followed as the group fell into serious discussions about logistics, and details of the operation. Separately, MacGregor and the ARC team's general manager, Maria Martorana, brought Kane up to speed on some of the finer points of the process. Once they'd finished chatting, Kane asked the room for a moment of quiet.

"If I may?" he asked, tapping an imaginary glass. "Firstly, I'd like to thank the British Museum, and Neil personally, for the opportunity to lead this fantastic team. My grandfather once told me that one of the greatest cultural crimes of the twentieth century was the continued claim to ownership of some of the great artefacts of the world, and that to keep them was little more than colonialism at arm's length. He said that it was the duty of countries such as Britain and the United States to return what is not theirs, and we have a great opportunity now to show the world how to go about it. My grandfather was right then, and now, more than ever, he is still right. We have to make the world take notice. I see clearly that you're all as dedicated as I am to making this a smooth and successful mission. I should remind you that it's not just the reputation of the fabulous British Museum at stake here. It's also the safety and survival of one of the most important objects ever created by humans. Plus, there's the relationship between the two countries to consider. In light of recent events, both here and in the Middle East, we simply cannot afford for anything to go wrong."

"Well said!" called out a young assistant.

"Here here," said another. "We're with you all the way."

Chapter Eighteen

Though not a massive object, the Rosetta Stone is heavy; weighing a colossal 1,680 pounds, moving it anywhere is a logistical trial. On occasion over the decades, its location in the British Museum changed, as the various display rooms evolved and grew as new artefacts arrived. Every time this happened, it caused a headache for the museum curators because of the sheer weight of the stone itself. There are much bigger, far heavier artefacts in the Egypt section of the museum, including massive sarcophagi, even gargantuan columns from one magnificent temple or another. Yet moving the Rosetta Stone even a few yards around the museum was always a challenge and required a specially built, precision-crafted piece of machinery for the operation.

Now Kane was in charge of moving it. Not only out of the museum, but across two seas and an entire continent.

He had overseen as the artefact had been carefully loaded and secured onto a custom-built pallet the previous evening, and it was ready for the transfer to its new home.

The event had been greeted with mixed emotions by many of the BM's staff, especially those who worked in the Egypt gallery and who regarded the Rosetta Stone as their emblem. Kane understood the dichotomy.

Most first-time visitors to the museum made a beeline to Egyptian Sculpture Room 4 to see the legendary lump of carved rock known as The Rosetta Stone. At first glance it didn't appear to be anything particularly amazing, especially considering it shared Room 4 with stunning temple architecture, elaborate sarcophagi, and not least the wonderfully emotive statues of legendary Pharaohs such as King Ramses II and Amenhotep III.

Kane remembered as if it were yesterday the first time he was ever taken to see the relic by his granddad. He couldn't remember the exact words he had said, but he was absolutely sure it was something along the lines of, *Is that it?* Embarrassingly dismissive, he had to admit now he knew how important it was culturally. At just four feet in height and only a little less in width, and with a depth of a mere ten inches, many new visitors find themselves somewhat underwhelmed by its size, assuming anything famous from ancient Egypt had to be massive.

Physically, the Rosetta Stone is relatively small. Yet its significance to history was anything but. Commissioned approximately 2,200 years ago, the stone was inscribed in two languages, though in three scripts. Egyptian hieroglyphs, Demotic script, (another form of ancient Egyptian), and Greek. It's believed that the remaining section of stone was part of a much larger funerary stelae. The later rediscovery of the Rosetta Stone is how the modern world knows so much about Egypt, its long history and its importance to humanity's cultural understanding of it all cannot be underestimated.

Thus, the artefact's cultural and historical worth was undeniable. Its monetary value, however, was beyond even the most expert of scholarly guesses.

In another part of the world, that did not stop one scholar from speculating. And Omar Abdel-Rahman liked his guess.

Chapter Nineteen

A Week Later

With a charter flight due to leave London City Airport at two o'clock that afternoon, the team got busy. They were in constant communication with their museum counterparts in Alexandria, headed up by the director, a man named Abbe Abidi. There was all the paperwork and documentation involved with the legal side of the repatriation to contend with. There was also the checking and double-checking that the artefact was perfectly secured on its specialised transportation pallet. On several occasions, both Kane and his general operations manager, Maria Martorana, had addressed the gathered press on what was to be an historic occasion. There was so much to be done, and behind the scenes at the British Museum that morning, everything was abuzz with activity. Emotions were running high and a curious mix of pride and sadness set the overall tone of the day.

Once the Rosetta Stone and its ARC transportation crew, headed up by Kane and Martorana, had finally left the British Museum and been ferried east to the airport, along with Ridley and a well-armed private security team, they all boarded the aircraft and Kane finally began to relax.

The first part of his important mission was over.

The flight from London to Alexandria, nestled on the Mediterranean coast in northern Egypt, was just five hours, yet the change in landscape was immeasurable. Kane had always marvelled at just how different the planet could look over relatively short distances. Apart from the obvious geographical contrasts, there was of course the weather, the immense variety of languages and the differences in food. Kane thought his home nation lacked considerably in that department. There were also the cultural differences and religions, not that Kane had any affinity for organised religion of any persuasion.

He gazed out of his window at the Swiss Alps far below, musing that it'd been a while since he'd led an expedition. The reasons for that were obvious, but he missed the wilds.

"What're you thinking about?" Ridley asked as she awoke from a short nap.

"Hey? Oh, nothing really, just mulling."

"Come on, I know you're thinking about something, because you get that funny little wrinkle at the top of your nose." Ridley grinned, and Kane confessed.

"You got me. I was just thinking about people, really. I mean, people are just people, right? Inherently, people should know the difference between what's right and wrong. Shouldn't they?"

"In theory, yes," Ridley agreed. "In theory... hey, you look sad."

Kane inhaled and nodded. "So, it shouldn't matter at all where we come from. All that matters is that we know it's wrong to steal, for example, and we know it's wrong to hurt another living creature."

What he had seen in his recent experiences were multiple examples of the very best and worst of human behaviour. As with most things, it always seemed to be the bad that stayed freshest in the mind, and he had gone up against some bad men. A criminal gang trading in poached tigers as if they were manmade objects. Yakuza gangsters for whom life was worthless. Terrorists that preyed on the weak. Men who kidnaped little girls for revenge.

Ridley was right. Kane was sad. They had both seen and felt too much negativity in recent months. By taking this new job, Kane meant to put most of that behind them.

"I know how you feel," she said, "but you're right, people are inherently good. It's just a crazy, selfish few that spoil it for the rest of us. Well, they try and spoil it. We're okay now, right? We're moving on from all of that danger and negativity. For you, this job will be a doddle... and don't forget, the Egyptian people are lovely." Ridley winked, and Kane offered half a smile at the subtle reminder of her Egyptian heritage.

"You're right," he said, "but all the fighting and the terror stuff now, and so close to home, and the bombings in Syria and the Middle East, and across Africa... it just all seems so bloody senseless." Kane took a few deep breaths, fighting hard to stave off a tear that threatened to spill. Ridley grabbed his hand and squeezed.

"I'm okay. I'm fine," he said, and he thought he almost sounded convincing.

Kane knew his well of empathy ran deep, but he also knew the world was going mad, and deep down he feared that if humans weren't careful, humanity would soon become the next great extinction.

Chapter Twenty

Kane's stomach felt as if it had exited his body.

Despite the clear skies, turbulence buffeted the plane and caused passengers to clutch the seat in front of them or their travelling companion. If they were of a religious persuasion, many prayed to their god for safe passage.

As it was, a couple of hours later and beneath a calm blue sky, their plane touched down at Borg El Arab Airport, just a few miles inland from the Mediterranean coast and thirty miles from the city of Alexandria. If he thought it had been a hot summer in England, then the blast of heat that hit him as she descended the stairs from the plane fairly took his breath away. It was a dry heat, a desert heat, even though they were on the western edge of the fertile Nile Delta. He felt instantly parched, and his throat seemed to constrict more with every passing second. It was so intense that if he hadn't snagged an icy bottle of water from the plane, which he now glugged from, he believed he might have suffocated.

Despite the ferocious temperature and the oppressive, furnace-like conditions, Kane couldn't help but grin.

He was a traveller. It's what he did best. One of the things he enjoyed most about travelling was the massive variety found around the world. Just five hours ago they had boarded a plane in sunny London. It had been 27 degrees centigrade, considered a heatwave in England. Now they were taking their first steps in Egypt, and thermometers were boasting 44 degrees, 39 in the shade. Not that there was any shade. That was okay.

Kane was here for work, and he got to it.

After Ridley was whisked away with some of the team into the modest terminal building by waiting Egyptian officials, Kane was left with Salam, Sophie and Ken, the main coordinators of the repatriation team on the ground. He trusted them implicitly, and they set to work unloading their precious cargo onto the tarmac. Kane was surprised it wasn't actually melting beneath their feet. A forklift truck soon arrived, and its two protruding prongs were expertly positioned between the slats in the pallet. The covered Rosetta Stone was lifted, and the driver, slowly and carefully, steered over to the waiting flatbed truck. When that was done, Kane and his crew were ushered onto a waiting airport vehicle—a glorified golf cart which, mercifully, had a roof—and they followed the truck into a nearby hangar.

Once the dust had settled, literally and figuratively, they disembarked the buggy and approached the now-deposited Rosetta Stone. Kane breathed a deep sigh of relief. They had successfully completed the next stage of the operation. He quietly congratulated his teammates with hearty handshakes.

As was expected, a private on-the-ground security force, led by a man named Jabari Hader, took over. Secure in the knowledge that their cargo was safely stored for the time being, Kane and his teammates followed their Egyptian counterparts out of the hangar and into the main building, where they were reunited with Ridley and the others.

"Well done," Ridley said, hugging Kane. "That's the first and second stages done."

"Thanks. I admit, I'm pretty relieved. I'm off now for a meeting with the Egyptian director of the Alexandria National Museum."

"Yes, at six o'clock," Sophie confirmed, coming to stand beside them. "It's just a forty-minute drive into Alexandria from here, so we'll get checked into the hotel and meet in the lobby later. Say, five thirty?" Kane nodded. "Then it's just a short walk to the museum. Director Abidi will be there to greet you."

"Thanks, Sophie. You too, Salam. So far, so seamless. Great effort everyone. I hope you'll let me buy you all a drink later?"

Kane was glad the first stage was over. It wasn't as if he'd been worried it wouldn't go smoothly. Nevertheless, with such an important artefact, it was still a relief. He also knew it was only half the job done. They next had to deliver the Rosetta Stone to the Alexandria International Museum in the morning, in time for the official handover ceremony. The artefact had first been discovered just a few miles along the coast from the ancient city, and Kane was well aware just how appropriate it was for it to finally be coming home.

At the ceremony, there would be speeches by both the director of the museum in Alexandria, as well as by Neil MacGregor, director of the British Museum, who was flying in later that night, along with Kane's immediate boss, Maria Martorana.

After the handover ceremony was complete, and the

Rosetta Stone was unveiled in its new—and hopefully final—home, Kane's first assignment for the ARC would officially be over.

Chapter Twenty-One

Somewhere in the Mediterranean

"I said keep fucking still," the overseer barked.

The old man would not keep still. Wouldn't keep still at all. When the men holding the him had been tasked with this assignment, they'd all considered it one of the easiest things their boss had ever made them do. It had started out so easily, too. Ghosting him away from his property in England last week had gone off like clockwork. Yet, the moment the old bastard had realised they were taking him out of the country he'd been everything but cooperative. Despite his age, the old man possessed surprising strength, and no little courage. It was clear he was not going to make that easy for them.

"Who on earth are you people anyway?" he asked. "And what do you want with an old man like me?" he added after falling still for a moment. "I mean, how many of you are there? I'm just one old man and there are, what, five of you? Ha... call yourselves men?"

From out of nowhere the old guy lashed out his right foot. He could have no idea who or what was in front of him due to the blindfold he'd been made to wear since the moment of his kidnap. Over the blindfold was a tight hood.

"You motherfucker... uurrgggh!" The guy he'd struck recoiled in agony from the kick that had almost crushed his balls. "I am gonna fucking—"

"No, you will not do anything to our esteemed guest, Nabil. In fact, none of us is going to lay a finger on him. You know our orders. Unharmed." The speaker fell silent.

"Kol khara," spat the man, both his pride and his most precious of areas wounded. "Ibn al kalb!"

All except the enraged victim erupted at their colleague's expense.

"Eat shit you son of a dog?" one of them translated, which only elicited a further episode of laughter as he skulked away into a chair, his humiliation complete.

The overseer's laughter ceased as he stood from his chair and stepped quietly towards his prisoner. Somewhere far above, the container ship's horn sounded, letting them know they were entering busier waters. He crouched down, and leaned in close to the old man. Placing a hand on each of the man's knees to prevent any sudden movements, he spoke.

"I admire your resilience, old timer. But let me offer you a warning. There is still a long way to go until we reach our destination. My orders are to keep you in good shape. Unharmed. Let me tell you this... my orders were to keep only *you* unharmed. Remember, we know where you live. Where all your family lives. I recommend you keep your feet and fists to yourself, is that clear?"

After a few moments, the man in the hood nodded several times to let his adversary know he understood.

"Very good," his captor said. "Now, if you would excuse me, I will leave you in the capable hands of my men." With that, the overseer left the room.

Beneath the hood and blindfold, the prisoner's eyes screwed shut, though the old man almost felt the blazing glare of hatred directed his way from the man whose balls he'd almost destroyed. *Good. Cowardly bastard.*

He had lived a long life. Eventful. Happy and rewarding. He was old, so it didn't matter what they did to him. He had an idea who they were. Not a hundred percent, but an educated guess. He had to play it carefully. He fully expected they were capable of many far worse things, if not to him, then to his beloved family. That was a far greater concern.

Stay calm, he told himself inwardly. *You will get your chance to overcome this. For now, stay calm.*

Chapter Twenty-Two

The Cleopatra Hotel, Alexandria, Egypt

Kane was in deep trouble.

He was attempting to knot a tie for only the second time in at least a decade, and failing miserably. The last time he'd attempted such a challenging feat, prior to his meeting with Neil MacGregor a few weeks ago, he'd convinced Ridley to help. It had only cost him a foot rub. However, this time she seemed to enjoy watching him struggle and he didn't need bailing out just yet. Kane watched her grinning. It was as if he had two left hands, and his strong, chunky fingers simply couldn't get to grips with the basic Windsor knot. Having had one of those fingers shot off by a gangster in Japan a couple of months earlier didn't help. After seeing him almost rip the tie off in frustration, Ridley finally offered her assistance.

"Come here, kiddo, let Mummy get you ready for school," she teased. Kane took it well. He had a solid excuse.

"Anyway, mister," she said, "you look good." She placed her hands on his shoulders and held him at arm's length. "Listen, I'm proud of you. I know what this means to you. I know your family is proud, too, especially your father."

Kane nodded. "Thanks," he said. He knew his dad was proud of him, happy he'd finally taken what his father considered a 'normal' job. By *normal*, Kane believed he actually meant *safe*. He hoped his dad was right about that. In fact, it was the very reason he'd taken this job in the first place. It wasn't dangerous.

"Shall we?" Kane asked as he took Ridley by the elbow.

Ridley looked super-glamorous in a flowing blue dress, equally at home in fancy outfits as she was in her combat trousers, t-shirt and her trademark red bandana. "You look amazing," Kane told her as he led her out of the suite and to the lifts, where they descended two floors to the elegant lobby. They stepped out of the elevator smiling.

Sophie spotted them and hustled over. "You scrub up okay, I guess," she said, bantering easily with Kane, despite only meeting him a couple of weeks before the mission commenced. That's just how Kane made people feel around him. Relaxed, able to be themselves. "Alex, you look lovely."

"You too," Ridley replied, admiring Sophie's outfit. Despite his trousers, shirt and tie, Kane suddenly felt decidedly underdressed.

Sophie appraised her new boss. "Why do you look so nervous?"

"I look nervous? I guess I am a little."

"Everything'll be fine. Look, don't worry, there's no need to be nervous. Remember, the Rosetta Stone's already here in Egypt. That was the most difficult part. The rest'll be a formality, all over in a couple of hours."

"Well, thanks, Soph. Guess we'll know soon enough."

Sophie was right.

An hour later, Kane and Ridley, with new arrivals Neil MacGregor and Maria Martorana, met with the director of Alexandria National Museum, Abbe Abidi. It was a short, somewhat informal meeting before the main events of tomorrow. Kane found Abidi pleasant enough, but also sensed an edginess about him, as if he, too, were feeling the pressure and the momentous occasion looming tomorrow.

They confirmed the timetable of events for the following day, then Kane, along with Ridley and the rest of the team, went for dinner at the hotel's mesmerising oceanside restaurant, complete with palm trees and the intoxicating scent of jasmine drifting on the breeze.

"It's easy to forget we're on the Mediterranean here in Egypt, isn't it?" Ridley said, sipping on a glass of bubbles as they gazed out at the calm sea.

Kane nodded. It was easy to forget that amid such idyllic surroundings, just fifty miles to their west was the northeastern corner of the infamously inhospitable Sahara Desert. To the south was the vast expanse of Africa, a continent that had seen more than its share of suffering. In many areas, its people still suffered. Whether drought, famine, disease, both tribal and civil wars, government coups, outbreaks of lethal tropical diseases like Ebola, and more recently the rise of religious terrorism, the people of Africa were some of the most scarred, disenfranchised on Earth.

It was that last noun, religious terrorism, that weighed heavily on people's minds in recent years. In Egypt, despite what appeared to be the epitome of calm, religious tensions were never far below the surface. The Arab Spring violence of a few years ago had simmered, but the threat of it reigniting at any time was always there. With the exponential growth of ISIS across the region, it had become impossible to predict what might happen. More worryingly than *what*, perhaps, was *where*. Or *when*.

As the evening wore on, the rest of their group moved on to alternative destinations, some to their rooms and others to the hotel casino. Before long it was just Kane and Ridley left. They, too, had moved, and now eased into their chairs on the patio of the *El Faoud Piano Bar* in the *El Salamlek Palace*. The bar was classically detailed with New Kingdom-style columns, and it looked as if it hadn't changed in a hundred years. The view from the upper windows caught their breath, and the fluttering Mediterranean breeze did a good job of taking the heat from the air.

It was only now that Kane truly relaxed. This job was so different from anything he had done previously; it had forced him very far out of his comfort zone. Yet, he had to admit it had all gone well so far, and as he savoured his fifth icy Egyptian beer of the evening, he casually slipped off the damned tie.

Chapter Twenty-Three

The following morning greeted Kane and Ridley with a heady mix of jasmine and frankincense drifting on the air as they enjoyed a leisurely breakfast on their balcony, delighting in the warm breeze that also carried on it the scent of the nearby sea they both loved.

Kane's first job of the day was to corral his team in the lobby at nine o'clock. Then they'd travel back to the airport to oversee the safe delivery of their priceless cargo to the recently restored Alexandria National Museum.

That task was due to be completed by one o'clock that afternoon. Later, in front of an audience of gathered dignitaries, politicians and of course the media, there was to follow the official unveiling event. As part of his detail, Kane was required to make a speech.

He was nervous about it. He had never been entirely comfortable with public speaking, but it only needed to be a few sentences and with Ridley's help he'd written a short speech. He just had to avoid stumbling over his words, which he fully expected to do.

"Morning everyone," he said as he strode with purpose into the hotel lobby. "Not too hungover I hope?" A couple of wry smiles followed, but they all looked sharp and ready to do their jobs. "Okay, let's shuttle back out to the airport, and finally bring the Rosetta Stone home."

The team was soon back out at the hangar. Kane and Maria Martorana watched as the expert movers loaded the Rosetta Stone into a sturdy armoured truck, the kind seen outside banks on collection days. And, Kane mused, in TV dramas and documentaries about heists and robberies…

Despite that, he wasn't sure an armoured truck was necessary. *Surely they don't think anyone's going to try and steal such a famous artefact? Well, better to be safe than sorry,* he supposed, and Kane had to admit it was in his own best interests that the authorities had taken extra care over an object whose monetary value could never be truly measured.

Like a royal funerary procession, the convoy of vehicles crawled west from the airport along the Cairo — Alexandria Agricultural Road, then turned north into the city. It was a short drive, but traffic was heavy and at their careful pace the five-mile drive took over an hour. It didn't matter. That had been expected, and they finally arrived at the rear of the museum in plenty of time. The security vehicle containing team leader Jabari Hader had led the way, closely followed by the armoured truck, then Kane and his team behind that. Bringing up the rear was a second security team.

The heat continued rising as the afternoon wore on, and Kane's shirt was drenched in sweat. He hoped he'd have time to change before the ceremony later.

Once unloaded, the movers carefully wheeled the artefact through the museum's rear loading bay, along a few well-lit corridors and finally into the newly fitted out display room. Here it was to take pride of place. After a couple of hours of painstaking logistics to position the artefact on its custom-built base, the Rosetta Stone was at last *in situ* in Alexandria, just twenty miles from where it was last seen on these shores some two hundred years before. That it was a further two millenia back in the distant past since the rock was first hewn from its black granite quarry was not lost on Kane, who marvelled once again at the impossibility of truly grasping the concept of time.

The curators and museologists at Alexandria National Museum had refurbished the display room beautifully. Crimson drapes hung all around, and dozens of lesser-known yet equally-important artefacts were positioned majestically around the edges of the circular space. The lighting was atmospheric and tasteful, and of course Egypt's national flags hung everywhere. After all, Kane knew it was rightly a moment of immense pride for the nation. In their more-than-justified opinion, it was also long overdue. Today, however, any lingering resentment had been forgotten. The whole country was excited to have one of its most prized cultural objects back on Egyptian soil. Back where it belonged.

As it turned out, Kane did manage to find an hour free before he had to regroup and meet for the ceremony. He and Ridley returned to their suite briefly to freshen up, and so Kane could change his sodden shirt. Ridley still looked as fresh as the proverbial daisy.

"How aren't you sweating buckets?" he asked. "It's roasting out there."

She rolled her eyes. "Two reasons. One, I'm obviously a lot cooler than you," she said, playfully sweeping her hands down her body as if to demonstrate the point. Kane couldn't argue with that assertion. "Two, don't forget I'm half Egyptian. I was born and raised beneath this sun and I suppose I'm just innately used to it. Can't deny it is bloody hot though."

"Bloody hot's an understatement. Anyway, will I do?"

"You look very dapper... you'll definitely do for me. For your bosses, too... one in particular."

"What do you mean? Neil?"

"Ha. Come on, don't tell me you haven't noticed Maria's eyes lingering on you?"

"What? No, don't be daft. She's my boss, and she—"

"She's what?" Ridley said, and winked. "Can't say I blame her..." Ridley draped her arms around Kane, and pulled him in for a hug. "Like I said," she added after she'd let him go, "the woman has taste, boss or otherwise. Come on, let's go."

They headed back to the lobby to meet with Maria, Neil MagGregor, Sophie, Ken and Salam prior to the eagerly anticipated unveiling ceremony. Kane couldn't help himself. He glanced at Maria, his boss, and caught her looking at him, though she quickly averted her eyes.

"Told you," whispered Ridley as she took his arm. "Don't worry, I'll look after you."

Mortified, Kane shook his head and focused on the task at hand. The expansive lobby's style combined both replica and original Egyptian carvings and columns, as well as classical fountains. Exotic Arabic music piped in through hidden speakers. A lot of money adorned this establishment, much of it 'donated' by the many glamorously dressed patrons standing around sipping from flutes of champagne. To the uninitiated—or Kane's cynical eye—it might have looked a little like Vegas. But this was Egypt. This was the real thing.

Once they were gathered around the stunning central fountain, Maria Martorana noticed Salam wasn't yet there.

"Has anyone seen Salam?" she asked. "He's never late." The boss pulled out her smartphone and after a quick scroll clicked on his name in the contacts. The call went straight to answer phone. Whenever they were in working hours, tardiness was strictly a no-no. After a quick survey, it became clear none of the team had seen Salam since the meal last night. Martorana strode to the nearby reception and placed a call to his room.

"No answer," she told the others, who'd followed her over. "This is very strange… very unlike Salam."

As Martorana thought about it a little more, she recalled Salam had seemed a little off-colour over the last few days at work. "Probably wants a promotion," she mused, grinning, "or perhaps he's feeling the strain of this assignment."

She asked a desk manager for a key to his room, saying, "Our colleague might be sick and we need to check on him."

"I am sorry, but I cannot give a room key to anyone who isn't registered to that room."

"It's actually registered to me… and my company credit card. Anyway, it's important we find him," Martorana stated as she fixed here eyes on the man, who seemed to wilt a little. "I'm his boss."

"What I can do," the manager said, "is escort you to the room myself. How is that?"

She shook her head, but said, "Fair enough. Let's go."

Two minutes later Martorana was knocking on Salam's

door. She got no response, and after another minute of waiting with no answer, the manager swiped his master key card and Martorana entered the room. She was surprised to find the room empty. There was no trace of Salam there at all. The bed hadn't even been slept in; it remained perfectly made, as if Salam had never even been there.

"What on Earth?" Martorana's initial annoyance at what she thought had been tardiness was now replaced by concerns regarding his whereabouts. Besides, they had an important job to do, and Salam was a key figure in the logistics of the operation. In short, she needed him. With the clock ticking, they were now on the verge of running late. The show would have to go on without him.

She returned to the others back in the lobby and told them briefly what she'd found. "We can't wait any longer for him to turn up. As you all know, we simply cannot be late. Not even one second. This is our show, and the show must go on. I'll deal with Salam later. Hiram, are you ready?"

"A little nervous, but yes, I'm ready."

"You'll do fine. Okay, team... Let's go."

Chapter Twenty-Four

The Alexandria National Museum

There followed a mix of bemused, concerned expressions among the group as they headed through the lobby. If Kane were to have guessed who among them would be late for this, of all days, last on his list would have been Salam el Halabi. Kane had only been working with the team for a couple of weeks, but he'd found the young curator to be a diligent, attentive and pragmatic member of the group.

It was just a short walk from the hotel to the Alexandria National Museum. Because it was so hot, however, they were all sweating by the time they arrived, making a mockery of Kane's shirt change. It was all to the amusement of Abbe Abidi, the director of the museum, who greeted them just inside the air-conditioned reception area of the museum.

"Welcome, everyone," he said in impeccable English. "How are you finding the heat? It does, erm, get a little warm here in summer." Kane didn't think Director Abidi was being rude, but he obviously found it comical.

"It's certainly warm, that's for sure," Martorana replied, "but we Brits are made of stern stuff. Have you ever seen Lawrence of Arabia?"

The director apparently appreciated the joke. "Too many times," he replied, grinning, "and it gets better every time I watch it." Abidi cleared his throat, snagging the attention of the rest of the team. "Mister MacGregor, Miss Martorana, Mister Kane, and all of your team… Please permit me the opportunity to thank you all personally for your hard work, not only for heartily supporting our repatriation cause, but for actually making it happen." He turned to Kane.

"Mister Kane, I believe your grandfather was integral to this project getting off the ground. Please, do be sure to pass on my personal regards when you return home."

"Thank you, Director Abidi. Yes, my grandfather can be very persuasive when he believes in something passionately. I can attest to just how passionate he was about this. I believe I've brought a similar passion to the repatriation team, and I will endeavour to continue doing so for many years to come. I'll be sure to pass on your kind message."

"Thank you," said the director. "Finally, on behalf of myself, our museum and our country as a whole, I want you to know we are all so very grateful to you and your team. Now, if you'll just follow me, we have a legend to unveil."

Kane had thought Director Abidi seemed a little nervous the first time they'd met, albeit briefly. The man wasn't showing any sign of nerves now. Kane assumed he was simply excited the long-overdue day had finally arrived, something Kane understood well.

They followed Abidi into an office area, where he briefly

ran through the order of proceedings. First on the agenda would be his own speech, he told them, followed by a few words by Kane, who would speak on behalf of the British Museum. The Kane family name is well known in the world of exploration and archaeology, Abidi explained, and to have the Kane name attached to the repatriation project was a definite coup.

"It has ensured plenty of media attention, that's for certain," the director added with a nod towards Kane, then he explained that there would be a short period of time allowed for them to field questions from the congregated said media. "There are news agencies here from all around the world, on what is a truly momentous occasion for us all."

That's what Kane was most nervous about, in truth. He was an outdoor type, not especially comfortable being the centre of anyone's attention. He'd been best man at a couple of his close friend's weddings, and while it was a great honour to be asked, giving best man speeches in front of so many people had probably been the most stressful thing he'd ever done. Still, he felt prepared, and this speech was just another part of his new job. Kane unconsciously reached for his missing finger, the one he'd lost to a bullet in Japan a few months back. He had been very lucky it was only a finger. Compared to that drama and others like it, this would be a doddle.

Once everyone was comfortable with the schedule and that everything was in place, Abidi led them into the central display room. The large, circular room looked magnificent, and Kane thought it a perfect setting for this significant occasion. Dramatic lighting gave him a sense of being inside an ancient Egyptian temple. Photographers were sure to have a field day. The crimson drapes added a sense of regality around the room, and upwards of forty chairs arranged strategically for the press would afford everyone a perfect view.

Most importantly of all, however, positioned at the very centre of the room and draped in a beautiful Egyptian tapestry, sat the legendary artefact they had all travelled from far and wide to see; the Rosetta Stone. For now it remained hidden beneath that elegantly embroidered covering. Yet, and Kane wondered if he was the only one to sense it, it almost seemed to emit some kind of mystical aura around the display room as the time for the unveiling drew ever closer.

Stationed at each entrance to the new gallery were pairs of armed security guards. Beside the object itself stood two more guards, one either side, though these were local police, and not part of Jabari Hader's security team. These men were not armed. It had been decided it would give the wrong impression to the watching media.

The guards on the doors were big men, whose deadpan, expressionless faces appeared as if they hadn't smiled in years. Holstered, automatic pistols served to reinforce the look. Kane felt himself smirk; he was sure it was over the top, but glad they were taking their jobs seriously.

Standing calmly out of sight at the rear of the room was Jabari Hader, owner of the private security firm. He felt his mobile phone vibrate in his pocket. He waited a few seconds, then took it out and read the new message.

Jabari inhaled as the very subtle hint of a smile creased his eyes.

Chapter Twenty-Five

Kane checked his watch. 4:45 pm.

All seats assigned to members of the Associated Press were filled, and behind those media seats another forty reserved exclusively for guests were slowly filling up. Ridley occupied one of those seats, looking beautiful in a flowery yet classy summer dress, her raven-black hair tied in a sophisticated knot. Kane spotted Ridley, and she grinned; she'd caught him checking his watch again, which he seemed to be doing every thirty seconds.

Alongside Ridley sat an assortment of suited officials, their husbands and wives and, Kane had been told, several high-ranking politicians. The atmosphere was building, and a palpable sense of excitement permeated the air.

Finally, after what seemed like an age but was bang on time at exactly 5 pm, museum director Abbe Abidi entered the room. The buzz of anticipation fell to silence.

"Ladies and gentlemen, distinguished guests and members of the press, may I welcome you all with open arms to the Alexandria National Museum. As Director, it is my great honour to be standing here today, and I feel extremely fortunate to be the man tasked with at last revealing to the world what our country has fought for so long to bring home. It is a momentous occasion, and I thank you all for being here to share in it with us. Before that, however, I have a few words of thanks I would like to give.

"I would first like to thank our great friends and colleagues at the esteemed British Museum. I know that we have not always seen eye to eye on the matter of repatriation, but as an institution, you now deserve an enormous amount of credit. It is well known that past governments on both political sides have long resisted our calls for the Rosetta Stone to be returned to Egypt. While their arguments for that might once have been sound, they are no longer such. Nevertheless, you at the British Museum have been under immense pressure to resist that call, and yet you have done what of course is right. The fact that it has come at least one hundred years later than it should have is something we here in Egypt are happy to forgive." Director Abidi smiled, and the humorous quip elicited plenty of laughs from the gathered audience. Kane believed the man was in his element as he continued.

"So, my friends, on behalf of our organisation," he said, "I very much thank you for making our dream of the return of the Rosetta Stone become a reality." Abidi himself led the applause, and was joined by the audience as he thanked the British Museum for what they had done.

"Next, I would personally like to thank the Artefact Repatriation Committee from the British Museum. Under the compassionate and watchful eyes of Mister Neil MacGregor, Miss Maria Martorana, and more recently, Mister Hiram Kane, the committee has worked in close collaboration with our own artefacts commission for several years. Together you have overseen the safe return of our most prized artefact. We know very well what a politically and logistically challenging task it has been, but you have successfully seen it through. Once again, my organisation thanks you."

Director Abidi again led the warm applause, before once more continuing. "Now, ladies and gentlemen, may I introduce to you the man who has overseen the final stages of this whole operation, Mister Hiram Kane. Hiram has followed in the footsteps of his esteemed grandfather, a man who, it could be argued, is also the grandfather of the world's burgeoning repatriation movement. Hiram would like to say a few words on behalf of the British Museum."

More applause as Kane stepped forward on the raised dais and stood in front of the mic.

"Thank you, Director Abidi. I also thank all of you gathered here today. It is with the greatest of pleasure that the British Museum returns The Rosetta Stone to Egypt. As Director Abidi quite rightly says, our two countries have not always agreed upon the rightful ownership of this culturally important artefact, but I hope those tensions are now a thing of the past. The repatriation team we have in place now is determined to, under the right circumstances, begin returning many treasures of the ancient world that currently reside at the British Museum in London.

"Of course, not all of those artefacts are as famous as The Rosetta Stone, yet by returning the stone to Egypt, we hope to set a new precedent that other organisations and governments around the globe can no longer ignore. It is right, and it is just, that such important remnants of the world's great civilisations are returned to their countries of origin, so that the people of those great nations, such as

Egypt, Greece, Iraq and Iran to name just a few, have the chance to visit and experience in person the artefacts that defined each country's cultures and heritages, centuries and, in many cases, thousands of years ago.

"The Rosetta Stone has for decades been critical to our current understanding of Egypt's amazing history, and its people... your people," Kane said, spreading his arms out to the room. "The Egyptian people deserve the chance to experience it in person. My grandfather, Hiram Senior, whom Director Abidi so kindly referred to earlier, said something to me when I was a child that resonates now more than ever. He said, 'There is only one thing worse than stealing artefacts from a country, and that is not giving them back once we've realised it was wrong'. It's a simple-yet-obvious notion, but one which we at the British Museum are determined to see through. I give you my word, here today, that both our dedicated team and I will continue on our path of repatriation. Thank you."

There followed a generous round of applause for Kane's passionate words. Ridley, he noticed, was clapping the loudest.

"So, without any further ado," Kane added, "why don't we finally take a look at the reason we're all here today."

Director Abidi rejoined Kane on the dais. The security guards stepped away to give them room, and Kane and Abidi stood either side of the covered artefact. The shimmering fabric was held in place by two silk ribbons that hung suspended from the ceiling. Each man was handed a pair of scissors, and the director began the countdown.

"Five," he said. "Four."

Kane glanced over at Ridley, who smiled back. His heart raced, but no longer from nerves. He was proud. This was an important moment, and one he was honoured to be a part of.

"Three," continued Abbe. "Two."

This is it, Kane realised. His grandfather had started this process almost three decades earlier, and through his determination and dedication to the project, the moment had finally arrived.

"One!" The director glanced at Kane, who immediately noticed Abidi's smile had disappeared. The director held his gaze for long seconds—uncomfortably long, Kane thought. Finally Abidi smiled back and nodded, and together they raised their scissors and cut the ribbons.

In what seemed to Kane like slow motion, the elaborately embroidered covering first billowed a little, then fell delicately to the tiled floor, revealing…

Kane gasped, as did every single person in the audience. Inside the large glass casing, instead of the magnificent and meticulously carved black granite bulk of The Rosetta Stone, what they saw was…

Nothing!

The Rosetta Stone was gone.

Chapter Twenty-Six

After that initial collective moment of audible shock, utter silence descended upon the display room. To Kane that silence was deafening. Moments passed as a state of disbelief infiltrated the gallery. Kane watched as the media turned to each other, eyes wide in amazement. The two local police officers standing on the dais near Kane seemed confused, unsure how to react, also clearly shocked. The gathered audience muttered in hushed tones, unable to comprehend what they were seeing, or, more to the point, what they were not seeing.

Ridley stood up, eyes on Kane, hands flying to her mouth in utter incredulity.

Martorana stood motionless, blinking rapidly, as if the sheer incomprehension of it had rendered her incapable of a clear thought.

Kane turned to Director Abidi, who stared forward, his eyes fixed somewhere beyond the confines of the display room. He stared for many seconds, unflinching, until finally he closed his eyes. His chest rose as he took a long inhale, held his breath, then slowly exhaled, his chest falling still. His eyes opened now, and Kane witnessed a haunted man standing there beside the empty display cabinet.

Kane was crestfallen. The Rosetta Stone was gone. Three questions loomed large immediately. *Has the Rosetta Stone been… been stolen? If so, how? If yes, when?* It was simply unbelievable.

Not only was it a devastating blow for the world of antiquities, but it had happened on Kane's watch. How could this be happening to him, on his very first repatriation mission? Yet no sooner had those thoughts entered his mind, he dismissed them. It was a selfish way of looking at it. He immediately chided himself and snapped out of it.

The two policemen had yet to react. It was as if they were awaiting instructions from their team leader. Kane looked for Jabari Hader. He was… *Where the hell's he gone?*

The policemen left the dais and moved to check the exits to the room. The higher ranked of the two, Hamdi Felukka, fully expected to see the private security guards stationed outside the doors. They were also missing. This seemed to snap Hamdi and his deputy out of their shell shock, and they sprang into action.

Hamdi snagged his radio and immediately called for reinforcements. Two minutes later, a dozen of his armed team had sealed the room. Everyone in that display room at that moment, while not necessarily a suspect, had to be questioned. Hamdi barked into his radio device.

"Nobody leaves the building… nobody. Seal the exits, have a dozen men block the exits to the car park and have a perimeter set up around the museum. Nobody leaves, you understand?"

With amazing speed and efficiency, Hamdi's men had cordoned off the entire premises of the museum, and within fifteen minutes the entire city was on lockdown. Roads were blocked, and the bus stations were being watched, as were the train station and the huge container port. If the Rosetta Stone was still in Alexandria, Hamdi and his men would find it.

What of the private security team? Hamdi didn't want to believe it. Yet right now, everything pointed towards the likelihood Jabari Hader's private security team were behind the theft. Hamdi had been against the recruitment of external security from the start. He had also let his superiors know his feelings. He took it as a personal insult, as though he and his men weren't up to the task. Hamdi had been promptly waved away, his concerns dismissed.

Hamdi was no fool. He knew that for the right price, anybody could be bought. Whether he was aware of the crime or not, it seemed his boss, the Chief of Alexandria's Police Force, had played a part in this disaster. Hamdi played the scene back in his mind. At the exact moment the director and the man, Kane, had cut the supports to reveal the stone was gone, those hired men should have reacted. Instead of that, they'd simply disappeared.

It had to have been them. It must have been...

Chapter Twenty-Seven

Maria Martorana's face was as pale as a Sahara dawn.

She stood huddled with Kane and the others after they'd congregated on the dais next to the now empty display case. Martorana looked at Kane, their eyes meeting, their shared disbelief clear in each other's pained expressions. In turn she glanced at the rest of the team. She wasn't appraising them for any sign of guilt, but... Well, she had to be sure. As she looked at them one by one, it became apparent to Martorana none of them were involved. She considered herself a good judge of character, and her team looked just as shaken and shocked as she felt. And that was a lot.

Although she didn't want them to, her thoughts turned to the one member of the team missing in action. Salam el Halabi. *Jesus, where the hell is he?*

Hamdi Felukka spoke to Director Abidi, and after asking Martorana and Kane a few questions, Hamdi led them out of the display room and through the police cordon. He then escorted them into the Director's office, closing the door behind them.

"Please, Director Abidi, you must not leave the building until I have given the all clear. The same goes for the rest of you. Okay?"

They all confirmed to the police sergeant that they understood. With a curt nod and a look of determination on his large face, Hamdi left the room, seemingly taking half the room's air with him.

"I... I don't know what to say." Martorana's words came out barely above a whisper. "I just... I just don't know how this could have happened?"

The director sat quietly behind his desk, as if unsure how to respond. His lined forehead creased. His dark eyes showed intense strain. After a long moment, he looked pointedly at Martorana. "Miss Martorana, when people are determined enough to take something they want, then there is very little anyone can do about it."

Kane appraised the man. Director Abidi didn't seem as upset or shocked as he would've expected him to be. In fact, Kane thought he detected the faintest hint of a smile, more in the eyes than in the mouth. He guessed it was probably just his imagination, and let it slide.

"Do you have any idea who this could have been?" Kane asked Abidi. "Do you know of anyone who has the power to pull off something like this? I mean, with all the security around, it could only have been an inside job. Couldn't it?"

Director Abidi looked at Kane, his eyes boring into Kane's for a moment, as if weighing him up. Then his face softened, as if he'd regained his composure.

"Listen, Mister Kane, you know how much I respect you and your family. I can see how it might look as if someone on the inside must be involved... someone within my museum. I refuse to believe, even for a single moment, that any one of my loyal and diligent staff had anything to do with this. It has been my life's dream to see The Rosetta Stone returned to Egypt. Here at the Alexandria National Museum, we employ only skilled, dedicated and honest people, those who share our high morals and a deep love of antiquities." Abidi sighed, and Kane sensed it was a deep sadness that drew his high forehead into a series of even deeper lines.

Kane couldn't take his eyes from the man. To Kane it seemed as if there was something the director wasn't saying.

Abidi apparently noticed Kane's doubts, and again looked directly at him. "Mister Kane, I don't appreciate the way you are looking at me," he said, which snagged Martorana's attention. She now looked at the director too, as if she wasn't sure she'd heard correctly. The man continued. "It is almost as if you're accusing me directly. Is it not so, Hiram? Am I right to think you suspect me of playing a part in this travesty?"

"No... No, sir, I..." Kane said, not expecting the impassioned defence. "It's just, well... we're all in shock, and I'm so confused as to how it could have happened. With all the private security? As well as the police? Quite frankly, it seems impossible."

Kane really wanted to believe the director. He had appeared so passionate about antiquities since they'd met, and he saw in the director many of the qualities he knew his grandfather possessed, as indeed did he himself. Yet despite all that, something wasn't sitting well with Kane.

"Anyway," said Abidi, "sitting around this table isn't going to bring our lost artefact back now, is it? I suggest you and your team return to the hotel and let the security and the police do their work. We have professional people who can deal with this kind of thing, and I am sure the Rosetta Stone will be back here before you know it. I recommend—in fact, I insist—none of you speak to anybody about this. Not until we have more information. Not the press, not your friends. Nobody! The people who already know what's happened… you, me… of course, we can talk amongst ourselves."

"What about the media out there? Surely the whole world will know within the hour." It was Sophie. Kane thought she'd made a good point.

"They won't say anything, I can promise you that," the director declared.

"How can you be so sure?" Martorana asked. Like Kane, she was clearly doubtful anybody could control the press once they had a good story to tell.

The director's eyes locked on Martorana's then, as if daring her to doubt him. "Miss Martorana, I assure you, we have our ways." It was said with such confidence it was difficult not to believe.

The formerly meek director had seemed to grow in stature over the last few minutes. He seemed somehow stronger, more authoritative, as if the drama had brought out a new side to him. It was strange to witness, and Kane still wasn't comfortable with him. There was just something about the man. He didn't seem panicked, not at all desperate, in what must have been one of the lowest points in his career.

It was almost as if he had expected this to happen… as

if he knew it were going to happen. Unable to shake the niggling suspicion that Director Abidi was somehow involved, Kane bit his tongue.

Time would tell, he thought. *It always does.*

Chapter Twenty-Eight

The Cleopatra Hotel

Maria Martorana had just spoken to their boss, British Museum director Neil MacGregor, and she grabbed the group's attention.

"I've just had a brief chat with Neil. As you can probably guess Neil's devastated about what's happened. I filled him in on all the details, the little we know, and he's as confused as we all clearly are. As I walked in, I think I heard Hiram say that we're not personally responsible for the security of the Rosetta Stone," she said, glancing Kane's way. "In that, you're right. That duty fell to the private security guards employed by the museum. However..."

Martorana paused, her gaze scanning the group sitting around the table. What she saw was a mix of emotions, from sadness and confusion, to regret and anger. She also thought she sensed a determination among them, most notably in Kane's eyes. She also saw it in the eyes of Alexandria Ridley. Martorana didn't know Ridley well.

They'd only met a couple of times, and that had only been in the last few weeks. Behind the woman's attractive appearance and warm personality, however, Martorana sensed a tough countenance and fearless nature. She liked that very much, because Ridley reminded Martorana of herself. *Just a decade younger*, she'd mused with a hint of jealousy when they'd first met.

"I don't know about you guys," Martorana continued, "but despite having no official responsibility for the artefact's security, I still feel responsible. Neil's instructed us to sit tight at the hotel and await further instructions. But…"

Martorana was a good-looking woman in her late forties, who counted among her many hobbies a love for extreme sports, adrenalin-fuelled outdoor pursuits and tequila. She was also steadfastly dedicated to her job, and knew she was very good at it. What she was not very good at was sitting around on her arse waiting to be told what to do. Thus, she may have had a direct order from her boss MacGregor, but the director knew her well. Too well. Martorana knew he hardly expected her to follow that remit.

Martorana had more than just a glint in her eye when she continued. "… but some of you know me well, and sitting around twiddling my thumbs is not something I'm prepared to do. For all we know, the stone is still nearby. If it is, it will likely be found within hours. That's only a maybe. At best. My hunch is that whoever stole the Rosetta Stone is a well-funded, highly organised team of criminals; and, the stone is already well beyond the boundaries of this city. I'd stake my reputation, such as it is, on my belief that by now it's already wending its way into the hands of a wealthy collector somewhere. So…"

There was a shifting of atmosphere among the group,

sensing where this was going. Kane broke the silence. "What do you have in mind?"

"I'm going to go out there and find it." Martorana let her eyes wander once more around the table, appraising them, challenging them to say "no." What she saw gave her all the encouragement she needed. "Who's with me?"

Chapter Twenty-Nine

The Outskirts of Alexandria

Fifteen miles beyond Alexandria's city limits, a cluster of men stood around a small white transit van. On the side of the van in large painted letters was written *MUSTAFA'S LAUNDRY SERVICES*. In the back sat a dozen large baskets of soiled table cloths, collected from the city's restaurants. The huge baskets were stacked towards the rear of the van. From a cursory glance inside, nothing would appear unusual. It was just one of dozens and dozens of nearly identical laundry vans that sped around the city after every meal time.

This particular Mustafa's Laundry Services van was not all what it appeared to be. The cargo inside the inconspicuous white vehicle was more valuable than a billion dirty table cloths. A lot more. However, the person who had arranged for this special cargo was not paying for it with money. The currency he was using could not be measured in financial terms. Instead, it was something far more tempting for the people he had employed for the job.

The group of men were hiding out in a modest, indistinct warehouse in the tiny village of El Horaya, just minutes away from Borg el Arab Airport. An aircraft awaited them, though the flight wasn't scheduled until the early hours of the morning. Until then, they were sitting tight and staying out of sight until it was time to leave. The men were relaxed, smoking and drinking, and laughing about how easy it had been to steal the cargo. There were six men in total, though only three of them had been at the museum during the actual robbery. They ranged in age, from nineteen to forty-five, and were a close-knit group. Four of them hailed from the same family.

The only one who wasn't an Egyptian national, though he spoke fluent Arabic, was a young Englishman. Salam el Halabi. Salam had been the secret mastermind of the operation from the UK perspective, and although the others had never met the man before this day, they had heard all about him. Salam el Halabi had been involved in the repatriation process of the Rosetta Stone from the very start. He was one of the chief negotiators between his employers, the British Museum, and Abbe Abidi, director of Alexandria National Museum. In their many talks, talks that had been going on almost a year, Salam and Abidi had learned a lot about each other. Because of the very diplomatic nature of the repatriation, Salam had been required to fly from London to Alexandria on a number of occasions.

During their meetings, in which many more things than artefacts had been spoken of, they'd learned that both were Muslim, and that they both battled internally against Western values. Both men were a contradiction in certain aspects. They'd both been educated in England; they enjoyed many so-called Western luxuries, including cars and drinking, and in Salam's case, women. Abidi had been happily married until his wife died. They had each also discovered a new purpose in life, though for differing reasons. They still had a passion for art and artefacts, and both Salam and Abidi were genuine about their desire for the Rosetta Stone to be repatriated to Egypt.

Beneath that, however, they each had more burning desires. The stone belonged in Egypt, but that fact was becoming a secondary concern. What it had become—what it now represented to both men—was a means of gaining wealth. The artefact was priceless, and in obtaining it, then selling it on, they were both set to make a relative fortune. Each man had a different reason to desire that wealth, though those reasons were something they had not discussed.

Whatever their justifications, stealing the Rosetta Stone had been a masterstroke.

The private jet awaiting the men hunkered down at the warehouse was owned by the man funding the operation. He himself was Muslim, though he didn't care much for the manner the fundamentalists went about their business. What he wanted—the only thing he'd ever really desired—was the Rosetta Stone. If one or more of the people he'd recruited to acquire it for him happened to be Jihadis, so be it. He didn't care. He wanted that stone.

Very soon it would be his.

Chapter Thirty

The Cleopatra Hotel

Was it a threat? Kane wondered, subconsciously clutching at the gold Inca sun disc that had hung around his neck for two decades. It was a sign he was anxious, though he hadn't realised he'd grabbed it.

An hour later Kane, Maria Martorana and the rest of their repatriation team were sitting in the hotel bar in quiet conversation about what had transpired. Director Abidi had advised them—it had seemed more like a threat—not to talk about it in public. Of course, as head honcho of the team, Maria had stepped out to report back to her boss at the British Museum, Neil MacGregor.

"I can't believe it," Sophie muttered. "It didn't occur to me that anything like this could ever happen."

"To think Salam might be involved," Ken said. "Though I can't say I'm surprised."

"What do you mean?" Sophie retorted. "Why would you say that?"

Ken was a valued member of the team. Because he was known for his abrupt attitude and as someone who had little time for niceties, however, Kane had worked out he didn't usually get invited for drinks. "That guy's always been on the edge of the group, sitting alone at dinner, leaving early. It's obvious it was him." Ken wore a look of disgust he didn't try to disguise.

"He's on the edge of the group?" Sophie rolled her eyes. "Just because he's shy and a little quiet doesn't make him a criminal. Whatever happened to 'innocent until proven guilty?'"

"Hey, hey, it's okay," Kane said. "Listen, we're all a little shell-shocked by this. None of us knows what's happened and I'm sure there's a very good reason Salam didn't show up earlier. Let's not jump to any conclusions, okay?"

Ken nodded, seemingly a little embarrassed. "Sorry," he mumbled.

Sophie was fuming. "How dare you accuse Salam of being involved. You hardly know him."

Ken sat up in his chair. "Yeah, well we all know *you* know him, don't we," he said, an insinuating smirk on his face.

Kane knew it was true. Sophie and Salam had been seeing each other for a few months, though apparently they weren't yet a serious couple.

"That's got nothing to do with this. You're nothing but a—"

"Come on, guys," Ridley said. "Arguing isn't going to get us anywhere." Though she wasn't an official member of the team, Ridley had gotten to know the group over the previous days and weeks. Kane was glad. Ridley was a well-liked and popular addition to the travelling party.

"Alex is right," Kane agreed. "We don't know anything

for sure yet. Bickering amongst ourselves and throwing out emotional accusations isn't helping anyone."

Sophie cuffed at a tear forming in the corner of her eye.

Ken nodded. "You're right. Sophie, I'm sorry, okay?"

"I'm sorry too. I just… I can't believe any of this."

"Look, our job was to deliver the artefact to Egypt," Martorana said. "We're not the security, however, and looking after the Rosetta Stone was not our responsibility. So, let's get one thing straight. *We* are *not* to blame here. I admit, the timing of Salam going missing is unfortunate, and doesn't look good. However, maybe we should be worried about him, rather than assuming he's involved."

They all fell quiet for a moment, each appearing lost in thoughts about what might have happened. Finally Kane broke the silence.

"Sophie, listen, did Salam say anything about leaving Alexandria? Did you know he was going to go?"

"I didn't know, honestly. We're not a couple. Not really. We've never even—"

"I'm not interested in your relationship with Salam," Martorana said as she sat down beside Kane. "Yet, we have to consider this; there remains the very real possibility that one of our own team is involved in the most daring archaeological theft of the last hundred years."

Chapter Thirty-One

El Haroya, Alexandria

At the warehouse in El Haroya, the waiting men were growing increasingly impatient to leave. The laundry van was no longer a laundry van. Two of the gang had given the vehicle a spray-paint and a new logo. The once-white van was now black, and labelled *FAROUK'S FREIGHT FOODS.*

Whenever the moment to leave did arrive, their plan was simple. The men were to load into the van, where the Rosetta Stone was already secured, then leave the warehouse under the cover of darkness. They were to drive to the nearby airport, and head to the private hangar where they would transfer their infamous cargo onto a waiting private jet destined for Cairo. Darkness was imminent, the late-summer sun dipping rapidly towards the scorched sands of the northern desert. They didn't have much longer long to wait, but tensions were rising.

The actual theft had gone off without a hitch. The man

who had funded the theft, the mysterious tycoon, had also supplied the security team led by Jabari Hader. With him pulling strings, it had been plain sailing. Jabari was also in charge of this part of the operation, and the men were merely waiting for his confirmation that it was time to leave.

They respected Jabari Hader, a quiet yet confident man who didn't say much. Yet, because of the innate authority he exuded, when he did speak, everyone listened. Besides which, he scared them. His hard eyes screamed danger, and not one of them employed under his lead would dare cross him.

The men didn't have the same respect for the Brit, Salam el Halabi. He was younger. They knew he was better educated than them. Despite being Muslim, he wasn't Egyptian. However, they knew that it was largely because of his organisational skills in London that things had gone so well to this point. The men at least owed him their attention when he addressed them now.

"Listen," Salam said, his voice lacking the confidence of Jabari's, "I know we have successfully stolen the artefact. Do not think for a moment that the job is finished." Salam knew the men spoke decent English, but it was their second language so he spoke to them in Arabic. "In fact, it is far from over. Stealing it was the easy part. I do not think you should underestimate the British team. Believe me, Maria Martorana is a tough woman, and—"

Several of the men snorted their derision. Some Egyptian men of their generation thought very little of women, especially an infidel woman from England. If they had lacked respect for Salam el Halabi before, now they looked at him with utter contempt. Salam had expected this reaction and tried hard to ignore them.

"Mark my words, Martorana and her team are not

going to let this go," he said. "They will do whatever they can to get the artefact back. It is not just Martorana. The man, Hiram Kane, is dangerous to this mission, I believe more so even than Martorana."

Some of the men had started muttering amongst themselves, no longer interested in what the kid from England had to say. Salam continued anyway, almost as if for himself.

"When my boss recruited Kane I knew this would become much more difficult. He's only an explorer, an expedition leader, but he is a tough man." It were as if Salam himself was starting to doubt their chances of success, even though he believed the hardest stage was already completed. The thought of Martorana and Kane coming after them filled him with nagging doubts. Yet, he was committed now. There was no turning back. In any case, his career, such as it was, was clearly over. There was no chance he could get away with his role in the theft. It was obvious now that he was involved, so there was little point in not seeing it through to its conclusion. Besides, Salam el Halabi wanted his payment.

He pondered the men before him. It was clear they didn't believe the British team was any threat, and that it was just his Western softness getting the better of him. Maybe they were right. Perhaps he wasn't as devout a Muslim as they were. Yet, the sole reason he was involved in this in the first place was so he could prove just how devout he was. He was set to make a massive amount of money from his part in the plan, and he was fully committed to using that money to help fund the growing Jihadi movement back in Shoreditch at the Brick Lane Mosque.

He was serious about the threat he believed Kane posed.

He'd heard all the stories about the man's exploits around the world, and knew without doubt Kane should not be taken lightly. He'd felt it was a bitter blow to the mission the day he'd been recruited by the British Museum. As for Martorana, Salam had known she was a tough woman since the first day he'd started working at the BM. Like all staff at the institution, Salam had heard about the time an armed man attempted to hold a group of school children hostage in one of the BM's galleries. The moment Martorana had learned about the threat, she'd rushed straight down there and addressed the man; she convinced him to approach her, thus leaving the half dozen children behind a large display case. Once she realised the children were no longer in any physical danger, she tackled him, slammed him into the tiled floor and restrained him until the security staff arrived.

It turned out the man's gun was fake, and that he was mentally unstable. Martorana hadn't known that, and had risked her life to protect the kids. She was brave and fearless, Salam knew, but that bravery was more than matched by her intelligence and fierce determination, not to mention her formidable athleticism. Salam couldn't shake the feeling that, sooner or later, Martorana and Kane would ultimately have the final say in this drama.

For now, however, Salam knew there was no possible way they had any idea where he, Jabari Hader and their crew were waiting out. For the time being, they were safe. It was just another hour or so until their departure after sunset. As six-thirty came around, and a nearby Muezzin hailed the faithful over the loudspeaker at the nearest mosque, Salam was glad it was time for evening prayer. He joined the other men on their makeshift prayer carpets, and as they fell to their knees and faced southeast to Mecca, the haunting voice of the muezzin drifted to them across fields and tiny rural villages.

Salam was devout, but as he muttered his prayers to Allah, he couldn't help his mind drifting to Sophie. He had asked—no, he had even begged her—not to come to Egypt on this mission. He cared for her, and had suggested it might be dangerous. She had laughed off his concerns, but thanked him for caring. She had insisted she remain on the team. In the end, there was nothing more he could say. He didn't want to betray her this way; fundamentally, Sophie was not his priority.

Salam's priority was Jihad, and if it ever came to be that Sophie stood between him and his ultimate objective, he would not hesitate to take any necessary steps to prevent it. *Inshallah*, it wouldn't come to that.

Salam el Halabi prayed just a little harder.

Chapter Thirty-Two

The Cleopatra Hotel

Kane saw a grim determination had settled onto Maria Martorana's face.

Nobody had said anything for several moments, and silence hung around the table as Kane and the others absorbed Martorana's declaration and subsequent question. She'd told them calmly that she felt responsible for the theft, and that she was going out there to find the artefact. It was her duty, she'd said. In many ways, Kane agreed with her.

And, it wasn't just a simple case of agreeing to go with her because he respected her and because she was technically his boss. Good people didn't steal priceless artefacts, which meant it had probably been orchestrated by dangerous criminals. That was way above the others' pay grade. Yet, Kane felt what she felt and it was not above his. He glanced about the table, and sensed they all felt the same. They shouldn't have, but they'd all taken the theft personally.

Martorana took a deep breath and sat down. She realised she'd gotten a little carried away just now, and softened her stance.

"Look, I understand this might be a little unorthodox, maybe dangerous. Okay, certainly dangerous. Definitely off the record. Therefore, I totally understand if any of you would prefer to stay out of this. In fact, those of you with families, I insist you stay out of it." As soon as she'd said that last sentence, she smiled. None of the group were married, including her. Aside from Kane and Ridley, who were in a relationship, that left recently-divorced Ken, and Sophie, who was apparently dating one of the alleged criminals. Martorana almost laughed. Almost. But she didn't. They were entering menacing territory. What she was asking of them was tantamount to professional negligence.

Martorana herself wasn't married. She'd been in a long relationship with one man, James, for almost two decades, but they'd decided the world was already over-populated and had never had children. Nor had they ever seen the need to get married. James had died a few years previous in a caving accident in north Wales. Maria wasn't the moping type, nor would James have wanted her to be. After a couple of years, she had emotionally moved on. Rather than feeling sorry for herself, something James would've hated, she threw herself into her passions, including her work at the BM. Every chance she got she could be found skydiving, trekking, SCUBA diving and kitesurfing. She had yet to go caving again, and knew she never would.

Yet if there was a more active and adventurous forty-nine-year-old woman out there, Maria hadn't met her.

Chapter Thirty-Three

Kane glanced at Ridley, who met his eyes.

He had learned over a long period it was futile to suggest Ridley take the safe option and go home. She was braver and tougher than anyone he had ever met—braver and tougher than even he was. It would be a waste of time even asking. In fact, she would be insulted. He bit his tongue.

It was Sophie who finally broke the silence. "I feel this is mostly my fault. I should've noticed something. Salam never actually said anything, but… Well, he has been a little distant lately, especially the last few weeks. I should've noticed. I'm… I'm sorry."

"Maybe he's not involved at all," Martorana said, though she didn't look convinced. "It might all just be a misunderstanding." Kane guessed she didn't believe it. By now, neither did the others.

Sophie looked at Maria. "I appreciate that, but I think we can all agree he's somehow involved. Shit, I feel so stupid."

"Listen, there'll be time later to worry about what we all might've missed back in London," Kane told her. "That time isn't now."

"Hiram's right," Maria agreed. "Without Salam, we are five people. We're not going to get any protection from our government. We don't even know who it is that's taken our artefact. It's my firm belief that as the leader of this project, I have a moral responsibility to do whatever I can to find that artefact and return it to its rightful place here at the Alexandria National Museum." Martorana paused, seemingly gauging their reactions. Finally, she nodded, apparently satisfied she was doing the right thing. "So, I ask you again… who's with me?"

"I'm with you," Kane declared. "This is my project too, and I feel the same way you do. I didn't join ARC to sit back idly and watch someone ruin our mission. I'm in."

Martorana nodded. Kane didn't think she'd surprised by his willingness to stay on the mission.

"Me too," Ridley said. "Hundred percent."

Martorana looked at Ridley. Kane did too, and saw in her eyes the same fierce determination he saw in Martorana's. *Good*, Kane thought, *very good*.

"Of course, I'm staying too," declared Sophie. "I want to help. Please don't send me home." Martorana nodded. "Besides," Sophie continued, a new layer of fight in her voice, "if I get my hands on Salam and it turns out he is part of this, the bastard's going to wish he'd never met me!"

There followed a ripple of stifled laughter at Sophie's declaration, a welcome moment of lightheartedness. It didn't last long. What they were getting into was very likely fraught with danger.

Ken didn't speak for long moments. His deep, broad accent was reminiscent of rumbling thunder and he rarely had anything good to say. Kane suspected that had something to do with his recent divorce, but kept that thought to himself. Right now his gruff colleague looked torn, perhaps even vulnerable.

"Ken?" Maritorana probed.

He looked up, a hint of shame in his eyes. "I want to stay, Maria, I really do. But—"

"It's okay, Ken," she cut in. "Whatever it is, it's okay."

"You know I had the custody battle with my ex-wife over our girls?" Martorana nodded. "The court ruled in my favour. I've been granted joint access and… next weekend it's my turn. I can't stay, just in case anything—"

"That's totally understandable Ken. You should go home and be with your daughters. Don't feel bad. You've been an important member of the team and you've completed your role perfectly. I formally release you of your duties."

Ken seemed to cuff a tear from his eye, then inhaled a deep breath. "Thanks, boss. If anything were to happen to me…"

"Once the police confirm we've had nothing to do with this, we'll get you on the first flight home to your girls."

Ken said goodbye to his colleagues, apologised once more and told them he was going to his hotel room to let his family know.

That left just Kane, Martorana, Ridley and Sophie on the team. Kane had to admit he had no idea where to start. They were a team of four, and as Martorana had explained, it was all totally off the record. They'd get no official help from the government, nor the British Museum, though he secretly suspected that Neil MacGregor would do everything he could to support them with whatever they needed.

Their 'team', such as it was, did happen to include his

badass partner Ridley. Kane side-eyed Martorana too and thought she looked as if she could handle just about anything. With those two alongside him, Kane believed they were in good shape, whatever might happen. His only concern was Sophie Clarke. Sophie was a diligent worker who, he learned, had progressed quickly in her fledgling career at the British Museum. That was in the calm, safe and sterile confines of a museum, and spoke nothing of her abilities in the field. She was young, twenty-five, Kane knew, and passionate. Most importantly, she wanted to be there, wanted to help, and that was the kind of person Kane needed around on what could well turn out to be a very dangerous new assignment.

If it were only him, Kane would go full tilt after the artefact. But in truth, this was Martorana's mission. Losing the Rosetta Stone was easily the lowest point in her long and distinguished career in antiquities. Other than people dying, it was the lowest point in his career too. He knew Martorana would do everything in her power to get it back, as would he.

He glanced at his boss now, and caught her grinning. She shared what had tickled her with the others.

"It's ironic, isn't it…" she said.

"What's ironic?" Kane asked.

"That we've worked so hard for so long to give the Rosetta Stone away, and now all we want is to get it back."

Chapter Thirty-Four

El Haroya

Jabari Hader was ready.

After what had seemed like an eternity, Jabari quietly entered the remote warehouse and gathered his men together. It was time to go. He had just received confirmation from their man at the airport that the private jet provided by Omar Abdel-Rahman had touched down and was ready and waiting at his private hangar.

Salam el Halabi approached Jabari. "Is everything ready?"

"Yes, Salam. Mister Abdel-Rahman's contact has called to confirm everything is arranged. We must go now."

"Is all in order at the destination?" Salam asked.

Jabari stared at the young Brit. This was the first time they had met in person, although they had spoken on several conference calls, along with Abbe Abidi and, of course, Omar Abdel-Rahman. Jabari hadn't really formed much of an opinion about the Brit from their calls, but he was starting to understand why some of the others had taken a dislike to him, not to mention a distrust.

"I already told you, everything is ready." He let his eyes linger a little longer, and watched Salam flinch as he narrowed them into hard-edged slits. "Do you think I can not do my job, Salam?"

Salam shuffled back a little, unable to withstand the power of Jabari's glare. "No. I mean, yes. Of course I think you can do your job. I am… I'm just nervous, that's—"

"Do not be nervous. And get in the fucking van. Now!"

Salam had never been in any kind of situation like this before, and he realised he was so far out of his comfort zone that he suddenly felt nauseous. Any doubts he'd had leading up to the event he had managed to quash, by focusing on the main purpose of what he was doing. Now, here in a remote warehouse and surrounded by hard-core Jihadis, not to mention the dangerous-looking Jabari Hader before him… all those doubts came flooding back. It was all Salam could do to stop himself from running out of that warehouse, and getting as far away from there as possible and forgetting any of it had ever happened…

He didn't run. He stood there, frozen to the spot, almost certain now that if he did try and get away, he wouldn't make it more than twenty yards before he was shot in the back, then buried somewhere in the fucking desert where his skin would be ripped to shreds by wild foxes and vultures would pick clean his bones.

Ten minutes later the *FAROUK'S FREIGHT FOODS* van eased to a stop at the private airport entrance, reserved only for VIP guests and those with special licenses. The man at the booth, an automatic weapon hanging loose at his side, stepped up to the van's tinted window. He looked inside, acknowledged Jabari Hader with a curt nod and clicked a button in his security booth. The barrier rose slowly, and the black van accelerated through the entrance. A moment later, it pulled to a stop in the private hangar. The electronic doors slid shut behind it.

The men clambered out of the van as a forklift truck angled over. After a painstakingly careful transfer of the Rosetta Stone onto the British Aerospace-built Hawker Beechcraft 800XP, the men, including Jabari and Salam, climbed aboard.

The pilot, apparently a personal friend of Omar Abdel-Rahman, ordered the six passengers to strap themselves in. After waiting while the hangar doors once more slid open, he steered the Hawker out onto the private runway.

Salam looked through his window. He wasn't an experienced traveller anyway, but being locked into this tiny yet powerful jet with a bunch of men who didn't give one shit about him... he was reminded again just how far he'd stepped out of his comfort zone. The bubble of his simple life back in London. His visits to the Brick Lane mosque. His job at the British Museum. Sophie... That comfortable life had never seemed as far away as it did now.

Salam closed his eyes and muttered *"Allāhu akbar"* as the Hawker sped down the runway and lifted off into the darkness, the repeated mantra of *Allāhu akbar, Allāhu akbar, Allāhu akbar* echoing in his ears.

Chapter Thirty-Five

The Cleopatra Hotel

It was game on.

The team had confirmed their commitment, both to their mission and to each other. Kane suggested they leave the hotel and find somewhere more private to talk, so they left the bar and filed out through the reception. At a nearby coffee shop they ordered drinks then found an outside table. They chose to sit outside rather than in the air-conditioned interior, because only foreigners were daft enough to brave the late afternoon heat. Thus, there would be no one to listen to their conversation. Mercifully, a large umbrella shaded them from the worst of the relentless sun.

They sat in silence for a moment, unsure where to begin. It had all happened so fast. Martorana had acted quickly to pull this team together, but they hadn't yet had a moment to digest what had happened. It was Ridley who finally broke the quiet.

"I just don't understand how this could've actually been

done. Weren't the security teams guarding the stone over night? Doesn't the museum have CCTV everywhere?"

"Yes, the museum has CCTV," Martorana confirmed, "and yes, guards have been posted throughout the building ever since the stone arrived. So it had to be an inside job. Who else has the ability to organise this from within?"

"Other than Director Abidi?" Sophie asked.

Martorana had been calm for too long. Now she seethed with rage and scarcely tried to conceal it. "It *had* to be him. The slimy bastard has probably been planning it for a long time."

"Yes, and he somehow convinced Salam to get involved during his visits to Alexandria—" Sophie stopped herself and glanced at her boss. "Sorry," she added.

"It's fine. I think you're probably right, by the way."

"You know, the more I think about it, the more convinced I am he was involved." Sophie was clearly angry, probably as much with herself for not noticing Salam's involvement. Martorana retained a shred of hope they were wrong, but it didn't look that way.

"Let's think about it. With the help of our own Salam in London," she continued, "and his expertise of the actual artefact itself, if they found the right security team, corrupt, obviously, then it might not have actually been that difficult. I wouldn't be surprised if the police had been paid off, too, though it didn't appear like it, the way they hustled afterwards."

"I agree," Kane said, nodding. "What about this? Since the Arab Spring revolution, tourism in the entire region has dwindled, especially in Egypt, a country that relies almost exclusively on tourist money. I've seen it myself. I was on a diving trip at Nuweiba on the Red Sea right during the Arab Spring, and while the locals were still friendly, they were desperate for business. Desperate to the point of almost being aggressive. The people here are really suffering. If someone's willing to invest good money to bribe the guards, even get them involved in their criminal scheme, those with families to feed might find it very difficult to say "no." The security guards must've been involved. For what it's worth, my money's on Director Abidi being behind it."

Kane's fists clenched unconsciously. It was his first assignment for the Artefact Repatriation Committee. It had turned into a disaster. He knew he hadn't done anything wrong, knew he shouldn't take it personally. But that was Kane's nature. He was a proud man from a proud family. They'd earned an outstanding reputation in the world of exploration and antiquities. It stung to think of their name, especially his grandfather's name, ever being associated with the theft of the Rosetta Stone. Kane was angry; he would not rest until justice was served.

Ridley apparently recognised how he was feeling. She didn't say anything, but she rested her hand on his shoulder. It was just enough for him to take a deep breath and a moment to calm down. He glanced at her and inhaled. Next he looked at Martorana, recognising in her eyes that same determination he saw in Sophie's. Innately, he knew Ridley felt the same.

"Look," he said, "I don't want to throw any wild accusations about, but the moment I saw Abidi I sensed something off about him. I wasn't sure what… his mannerisms, the look in his eye, maybe his edginess. When I held his gaze he seemed uncomfortable, almost squirming away from me. It doesn't mean it was definitely him, obviously, but if I were a betting man that's where my two quid would be."

Chapter Thirty-Six

"What do we know of Salam?" Ridley asked. "I don't know him well. I've only met him twice I think. He seemed nice enough… it's hard to believe he's a criminal."

All eyes settled on Sophie.

The assistant curator thought about if for a few seconds. She remained quiet, as if unsure of what to say. She clearly felt betrayed by Salam. Until they were sure, had some concrete evidence of his involvement, Sophie figured it was unfair to talk about him. "I… I don't know, really, I mean…"

"Listen, Sophie," Martorana said, "I know it's difficult. For now, let's assume Salam's innocence. Tell us what you know."

Sophie breathed deeply. She felt conflicted. Her gut told her Salam was involved. Her mind told her she had a duty to her job. As a lover of art and antiquities, she had a vested interest in seeing the Rosetta Stone returned. "Salam and I have been seeing each other casually for a few months, since early spring I guess. He's a lovely man; kind, always polite.

He can be secretive. I've never met his family... he said they wouldn't approve. You know he's Muslim, though I don't think he's super devout. His family is very devout, and he told me right from the beginning it was best his family didn't know about us."

She paused, as if working through things in her mind. Martorana didn't rush her. Ridley took the moment to go back inside and order another round of drinks. Sophie continued.

"I thought that was okay. I guess. I didn't want to push anything. To be honest we were both too focused on work to worry about it. I guessed that if we continued seeing each other, I'd eventually be introduced to the family. Salam seemed to get more distant. I know he was spending more and more time at that mosque near his flat, though I didn't think much about it. He often told me how he hated violence, especially the terrorist stuff by what he called 'Islamists'. He seemed ashamed of them. 'Not in my name', he said. I'm sure he meant it." Sophie paused again. Sadness seemed to creep into her eyes. It was difficult for her to think of Salam lying to her, about being someone he wasn't. She had cared for him, and it stung.

Martorana was starting to think there was more to Salam than she'd believed. She hoped beyond hope she wrong. Yet, the words *Islamists* and *terrorists* kept popping into her mind.

"I didn't think much about any of this really. Once we were both assigned to the repatriation project, he tried to talk me out of it. Said he thought I should opt out, without really giving any good reasons. It was a little weird. Like I said, I didn't really think about it. It's a great opportunity for me, one I've been working towards for years... I'm glad

I'm here." She forced a smile. The strain showed in her eyes.

"We're happy you're here too," Kane said, wanting her to continue but unwilling to pressure her.

Sophie took a few deep breaths and seemed to compose herself, just as Ridley returned with the drinks. She handed Sophie her iced espresso. She accepted it, inhaled deeply and took a couple of sips.

"Thanks. Listen, I've been excited about this ever since I applied for the committee. This assignment is without doubt the biggest moment of my career so far. I wasn't going to miss it for anything." She swiped a solitary tear from her cheek. Fresh resolve slid slowly onto her face. "None of that matters. Whether Salam is involved or not, it won't cloud my judgment, nor my determination to do whatever I can to help get the Rosetta Stone back. You have my word." Her stoicism left the others in little doubt she meant it.

Now they just had to work out what the hell to do. They were an unofficial team, though it was understood Director MacGregor would "unofficially" help as much as possible. The number one priority was to learn the whereabouts of the Rosetta Stone.

"So, what do we do?" Ridley asked.

"We need to work out who took it, or at least who funded the theft," Kane said. "Once we know that, we can probably trace where the stone has gone. We have to move fast. For all we know it could already be out of the country."

"Right," Martorana said. "All of you listen to me now, and listen carefully. Under no circumstance are we to do anything that might put our lives at risk. At the end of the day, no matter how much we care for our jobs, our so-called duty... our egos... If things get out of hand, we back off and let the authorities do their work. Is that clear?"

They each nodded his or her agreement, taking a moment to ponder exactly what might happen. As of now, Kane knew, they had very little information to work with. They had their suspicions about who might be involved. Very likely Director Abidi. Probably Salam el Halabi. The private security team. There had to be another player, someone to bankroll the operation. *Find that person,* Kane thought, *we find the Rosetta Stone.*

"Abidi is director of the museum. Fact," Kane declared. "Corruption is rife in Egypt. Fact. Salam knows more about the actual artefact than anyone else. Fact. Are the police involved? Probably. Are those security guys with the big guns a part of it all? Very likely. Will we get any help from anyone on the ground here in Egypt? I can't answer that because I don't know anyone."

No one could offer any leads in that department. Kane cracked what had become a trademark wry smile.

"Then, my friends, it seems as if we're on our own."

Chapter Thirty-Seven

Paris

"Inshallah." Omar Abdel-Rahman stood up from his desk. "Inshallah," he stated again, before he ended the call with Jabari Hader.

Omar was a big man who enjoyed life and all its indulgences. Even standing up from his chair required a decent amount of effort. This had become especially apparent in recent months, given what he'd learned from his private doctor a year ago. Yet Omar didn't have time to worry about such trivialities as his health. With a chubby hand he picked up his flute of 1820 Juglar Cuvee, one the world's most expensive champagnes. He took a few steps to the wide window, inhaling a deep breath before sipping at the bubbles. *There's only one thing better than the best champagne,* he mused, *and that's the best champagne accompanied with even better news.*

The view before him would never get old, and Omar admired his unrivalled vista of the Eiffel Tower, twinkling against the night sky just a few hundred steps away. Yet, in just thirty minutes he would be leaving his Paris apartment. It was time to go home. He wondered ruefully if it would be for the last time.

Usually, when Omar acquired a new artefact, he had it delivered to Paris. Exactly below where he now stood was one of the greatest private collections of artefacts anywhere in the world. His collection was something of which he was immensely proud. He had become a very famous and respected collector of antiquities over the years. There was, however, one difference between the magnificent array of relic downstairs and the new piece he'd just been informed had been successfully acquired in the last few hours. Those items in his private collection below were all legally his. He had paid a lot of money—no, a veritable fortune—for each and every piece he owned. All had been registered in his name.

The new piece was coming to him via very different, far less honourable methods. There had been other artefacts that had come to him that way too. He was okay with that. He was a true aficionado. Omar knew it was better for him to have those items than other, less genuine collectors, even if it meant having to acquire them in somewhat underhanded ways. Those illegally attained pieces were at his top secret gallery at his home in Luxor, and he adored every single one of them.

There was his cherished Rembrandt, stolen from the Isabella Stewart Gardener Museum, and for which he'd paid $20,000,000 back in 2006. He would always have a special place in his heart for the *Kamakura-period Honjō Masamune*, one of the most famous swords ever made. He'd brought that piece from a shady thief out of Brussels in 2013. Most scholars agree that the sword had been lost to history, yet it now sat in Omar's collection. They were just two examples of many. He'd spent upwards of half a billion dollars on his collection of antiquities, some legal, others less so.

The piece he was to receive tomorrow, the piece he had desired his whole life, was on another level altogether. It was the one artefact indispensable to the world's knowledge of his country's long, rich and varied history. The one artefact that, without which, humankind would never have learned about the Boy King, Tutankhamun, or Queen Hatshepsut, or the heroic pharaoh Ramses the Great and the heretic king, Akhenaten. It was probably one of the most sought-after objects in the world of black-market antiquities of all time. Nobody thought it could ever be stolen.

Nobody, that was, except Omar Abdel-Rahman. And he had done it. He had put together a team of highly skilled, strategically positioned players who had done his bidding for him. They had achieved the impossible. The Rosetta Stone was his.

Omar finished the last drops of the champagne and waddled back to his desk. He pressed a button on the phone. Three seconds later his servant, Bassam, hurried through the door.

"Yes, sir?" Bassam said, his English accent shinier than a freshly minted penny.

"Have the jet prepared. We're going home."

Chapter Thirty-Eight

Alexandria National Museum

What the hell are we missing now? Kane mused.

He glanced down at the stump of his destroyed finger, the top half missing. It didn't hurt, though sometimes he still felt it; it was a common phenomenon among amputees. He was glad it was only a finger, and grinned inwardly; his missing finger served to keep him on his toes.

With so little information to work with, Kane and the others had only one real option: they had to question everybody they could at the museum. They believed there must be someone there who hadn't been corrupted. Even if they found out who was innocent, getting the opportunity to speak to them wasn't going to be easy. If, as Kane suspected, criminals controlled most of—if not all the staff—it would be almost impossible.

They had to try. Kane suggested they split into two pairs. Ridley paired with Martorana, Kane with Sophie, meaning at least one official member of the ARC team occupied each pair. Albeit, they were no longer official.

Kane found it hard to believe every single member of staff at the museum was working with the criminals. If it were true, then his innate hope for humanity would further diminish. There was only one way to find out. So, they headed back to the museum, Kane more hopeful than confident.

The area surrounding Alexandria National Museum was on near total lockdown. Members of the press had at last been allowed to leave. They were filtering out as Kane and Sophie approached. They paused, seeing if there was anyone from the press they recognised. There wasn't.

A moment later, however, two reporters spotted Kane and made a beeline to the world-famous expedition leader. One approached while the other, a woman, held back.

"Mister Kane, may I ask you a few questions? I'm Julian Wright, with the *Daily News* here in Egypt."

Kane thought quickly. It might be a good chance to learn a little about who the criminals might be. The best case scenario was that it was simply an art theft for art's sake. It didn't justify anything, but at least he could understand it. Much worse than that was that the Rosetta Stone had been stolen to raise funds for far more nefarious means… like funding a terror group. Sadly, that's how it was shaping up. Kane wasn't a praying man… he'd never prayed in his life. If he were, he'd have prayed he was completely wrong about that.

He held out his hand to the reporter, who shook it. "Of course," Kane said, "though I should tell you I'm no longer working officially. Our repatriation team from the British Museum has been ordered to step down. But we can chat."

Julian Wright led Kane and Sophie to the same coffee shop they'd just left, far from the drone of activity at the museum. Wright ordered the drinks; this time Kane was glad they'd opted for the air-conditioning inside. Wright looked to be in his late forties, though his handsome face showed evidence of years working in Egypt's harsh, dry climate. He appeared confident and exuded a calm disposition. Sitting opposite Kane and Sophie, Wright snagged a notepad and a pen from an equally worn-out satchel and looked at them from across the table.

A wry smile broke across his stubbled face. "What a mess, huh?" There wasn't a trace of derision, though, and he appeared sorry for what had happened.

"What a mess is right," Kane answered. "We're still in shock to be honest, as will the whole world be once the story gets out. Aren't you guys supposed to keep quiet for a while?"

"Yep. We've been ordered by the police and other officials to say nothing about the theft until the morning. If the Rosetta Stone hasn't been recovered by eight o'clock tomorrow morning, we're allowed to go public. It's quite the story."

"Yes. Quite the story," Kane agreed. *Quite the understatement too*, he mused, but kept that to himself. "I'm sure it's difficult not being able to write about it yet, right?"

"The archaeological story of the decade? No shit... whoever breaks this story will be dining out on it forever."

Kane glanced around the cafe, then out onto the patio and the street beyond. Leaning in a little to Wright, he said, "Listen, as I said, we're officially off duty now, but—"

"But what, Mister Kane?"

"It's Hiram. Off duty, but that doesn't mean we aren't going to—"

Sophie placed her hand on Kane's forearm. "Maybe we shouldn't—"

"But what, Hiram?" Wright repeated.

Kane looked at Sophie. "This might be of great help to us," he said. "It's fine."

Kane looked back at Wright, attempting to appraise his integrity. You could never be sure, yet he felt as if Julian were one of the good guys. So, he just came out with it. "We're going to try to recover the Rosetta Stone ourselves." He sat back in his chair, waiting for a reaction. Julian leaned back too, eyes slightly wider but evidently trying hard to hide his surprise. Kane continued. "We feel responsible, of course, and we're going to try our best to put things right."

Julian nodded. "That's admirable, truly, though I advise caution. There're some dangerous people around here, very dangerous. I strongly recommend you don't go snooping around too much. Very dangerous."

Sophie sat up and said, "Are you saying you know who might be involved? Who stole the Rosetta Stone?"

"No. I'm absolutely not saying that. It's just, well…" Now it was Julian's turn to look around, careful to ensure no one was listening to their conversation. "Look, there's been a growing number of militant groups in Egypt the last few years. A lot of young Egyptians are still disillusioned with the way their country's being run. They're seeking, shall we say… an outlet? Something to belong to. Those outlets need funds."

"You mean Islamic groups? Terrorists?"

Julian didn't answer verbally. He didn't need to. His subtle nod answered the question, clearly and concisely. It was not what Kane wanted to hear. Not what he wanted to hear at all.

Terrorists. It seemed as if Julian was indirectly suggesting a terrorist group was involved with the theft. He had to ask. "Listen... Julian... are you suggesting terrorists stole the Rosetta Stone?"

Julian squirmed a little in his seat at the direct question. They were sitting in the rear of the coffee shop, and currently the only customers. The one girl working the counter was outside disposing of some rubbish and couldn't possibly hear what they were saying. Julian looked beyond the girl into the street. There was no one around. He looked at Kane, a pensive look etched into his worn features. Finally, he nodded.

"Yes. That's my best guess. In fact," Julian added quietly, "I'm almost certain of it."

Chapter Thirty-Nine

Something had to give. It wasn't this guy.

"No, you can not come through," barked the security guard for the second time.

"We're working with the museum," Martorana protested, flashing him her official lanyard.

The man grinned, then his features hardened as he turned away.

While Kane and Sophie had chanced upon their meeting with Julian Wright, Martorana and Ridley hadn't been so fortunate. The moment they'd approached the museum, they were stopped at the heavily guarded street outside. A police cordon had been set up, and working alongside the police were many armed security guards. Who had actually employed them wasn't clear. There was simply no way in. Despite Martorana's protests they were denied access.

They hustled around towards another entrance reserved for official staff and tried again, Martorana declaring her position as head of the Artefact Repatriation Committee at the British Museum to gain access, waving her lanyard around as if she were an air traffic controller.

Despite her annoyance, Martorana couldn't help but grin, and she had to stifle a flat-out chuckle when one particularly snooty policeman said, his face deadpan: "British Museum? Ma'am, it would not matter if you were Queen Elizabeth herself, nobody is getting in."

Realising they were wasting their time, they backed away from the police cordon just in time to spot Kane and Sophie appear from around the corner. They were walking alongside another man they didn't know.

"Hey," Martorana said as they met, but soon noticed Kane's usually upbeat personality was gone. In its place a look of serious concern.

"We need to talk," was all he said, and he led them in a hurry back to the hotel.

Chapter Forty

The Cleopatra Hotel

In Sophie's room, Kane introduced his colledgues to Julian Wright while Sophie ordered a pot of tea via room service. Julian gave a quick rundown of who he was and what he might be able to do to help them. On the hustle over to the hotel, he informed Kane he'd decided to tell them everything he thought he knew.

"Just to be sure you're all clear on this," he said, "what I'm telling you is definitely not concrete evidence. Consider it an informed opinion."

Martorana nodded. Julian cleared his throat.

"For a number of months now, there have been unconfirmed rumours on the ground here in Egypt. They purport that an Islamic group closely linked with ISIS—and that had been defeated in the north Sinai region by UN troops—has now set up a series of camps somewhere along the Nile. No one knows for sure where. It's been suggested it might even be in the Luxor area."

"Luxor?" Ridley said. "Isn't that where Karnak Temple is?"

"As well as the Valleys of the Kings and Queens," Kane confirmed.

"When you think about it," Martorana said, "it makes perfect sense. The Valley of the Kings has hundreds of undiscovered tombs and underground complexes. Same for the Valley of the Queens. Since the war on terror started up in the Sinai region, hardly any teams are digging in Egypt anymore. Archaeological funding's being spent elsewhere. Understandably I suppose. Put simply, many research teams are afraid to stay and work in Egypt. The country's been on edge for many years now, and things like this will only make it worse. Tourists no longer visit those areas in such great numbers, so it makes sense to situate terror camps somewhere like the Valley of the Kings."

"Hidden in plain sight, so to speak," Sophie suggested.

"Like I said," Julian added, "it's just speculation, though I've heard it from more than one source."

Like the others, Kane was growing increasingly certain that terrorists were now the most likely culprits of the theft. He looked at Ridley, both glad and worried she was there. "What do they hope to do with the stone, assuming it was them?" she asked. "I mean, a world-famous artefact like that's not exactly easy to sell. I'm assuming that's what they want, right? Sell it to fund terror campaigns?"

Kane nodded. "Much as I hate to believe that's the case, it looks that way. Selling the stone? Not a problem. You know as well as I there are dozens of people around the world who would die to get their hands on it." He winced at the unfortunate turn of his own phrase. "Sorry."

"You're right though," Julian said. "There are a lot of rich collectors, even here in Egypt. Wealthy tycoons, oil barons, even some museums aren't beyond…" The reporter stopped himself suddenly, as if considering a thought. A long moment later he slowly nodded, as if confirming what he had just recalled. "A few years ago," he continued, "there were a series of thefts, most of them from lesser-known galleries around Egypt. It was the usual stuff. Artefacts from the various Kingdoms, weapons, stones from temples, even the odd mummy. It transpired one tycoon by the name of Omar Abdel-Rahman was accused of masterminding the thefts to grow his personal collection. He vehemently denied it all, claiming someone as rich as him didn't need to steal artefacts when he could quite happily buy them. He's a bit of a celebrity in Egypt, and in Paris, where he has a magnificent private collection. Eventually, someone else was arrested, and mysteriously all the stolen items were returned. That guy, more or less an unknown, went to prison. The world forgot about Omar for a while, but lately he's been showing his face out and about in public, mostly in Paris. This was about three years ago. The thefts all around Egypt stopped. But…" He paused, allowing the others to catch his drift.

"But?" Martorana said. "You still think this Omar has something to do with the theft of the Rosetta Stone? The greatest artefact of all?"

Julian nodded. "I was never convinced Omar was innocent. He's almost a hero in some parts and has been known to donate millions of dollars to various charitable causes. He's a character, that's for sure, a kind of slightly shady Robin Hood. He's never hidden his love and, some would say, his obsession, for antiquities."

"You think he's guilty now?" Kane asked, almost sure where this was leading.

"Yes. In fact, now I think about it I'm almost certain.

Omar's Muslim, though he's openly against terrorism and is not considered to be involved in any terror groups. He is, however, a very passionate advocate for the preservation of Egyptian history, suggesting he's in support of the repatriation of these wonderful artefacts. What if he doesn't trust the corrupt Egyptian authorities to take the best care of them? He wouldn't be unjustified in thinking that, based on his country's previous record."

"You're saying that, in essence, he's stealing the artefact for its own good, before someone else does? That sounds a little far-fetched," Ridley said, clearly doubting Julian's theory.

"What about the terror angle?" Sophie asked, having remained quiet until now. "What about Salam?"

"I don't know Omar personally, but I've learned from my time here in-country that he's pretty unscrupulous, despite his public philanthropy. If by stealing the Rosetta Stone somehow inadvertently funded terrorism... well, I don't think he'd lose much sleep over it, as long as he got his hands on the prize."

They all fell quiet for a few moments, as if trying to put together the pieces of an increasingly complicated puzzle. Kane was bewildered. After a couple of minutes he broke the heavy silence.

"In a nutshell, what you're saying is that we've returned the Rosetta Stone to Egypt, only for a group of terrorists to steal it for a rich tycoon, because he doesn't want it to be stolen. A corollary of which is that the Egyptian terrorists use the theft to make a fortune to support their campaign of terror in... in Egypt? Is that the size of it?"

Julain's half smile, half grimace was answer enough.

"Fucking hell. You couldn't make this stuff up." Kane exhaled through his teeth, head shaking in anger. Yet, at the same time he was overwhelmed with sadness. He had taken a position with the British Museum's Artefact Repatriation Committee precisely to avoid bastards like this. Yet, once more, here he was, unwittingly putting himself and his beloved Ridley in danger. He felt sick to his stomach. He glanced over at Ridley, someone he could rely on to make the best of any situation. She looked helpless. Not afraid, because Alex Ridley wasn't afraid of anything. Her helplessness was more worrying for Kane. If she felt helpless, the toughest person he'd ever known, then what the hell could he himself do? In that exact moment he made a decision. He was turning his back on it. He would fly home to England with Ridley, go directly to the Kane estate, then take early retirement into a peaceful life and disappear into the English countryside.

He stood up, all strength for the challenge seemingly gone. "I'm... I'm sorry, Maria... I just can't do this anymore. I thought these dramas were behind me. When I accepted the job with the repatriation committee, I..." Kane looked at Ridley, and then looked away. Quietly, he added, "I have too much to lose. I'm leaving."

Chapter Forty-One

A sense of déjà vu washed over Nazeer as he made sure he remained out of sight. It was like London all over again, though without the rain. He cuffed a bead of sweat from his forehead. *Rather sweat than cold rain*, he mused as he glanced at his partner Atef. Atef smirked. *One of these days,* thought Nazeer, *I'll wipe that fucking smirk right off his—*

Nazeer's attention quickly refocused as Atef nodded over his shoulder towards the coffee shop. Nazeer turned to see the doors opening and Hiram Kane and his colleagues step out onto the dusty street. Nazeer and Atef tucked themselves a little tighter against the adobe wall they stood behind and watched on as Kane led the others, including the journalist, back towards the nearby hotel.

After it was safe, they followed, keeping out of sight behind thick-trunked palm trees that lined the wide road. Once Kane and the others reached the hotel Nazeer held them back, waiting until the group had disappeared inside. Ten minutes later, they too stepped inside.

Nazeer and Atef paused just inside the grand entrance,

loitering casually until the man they knew who worked on the concierge desk appeared. They needed a moment to speak to their associate and convince him to part with certain information. It would only cost them a few Egyptian pounds. With so much at stake, their boss would have happily paid thousands for the same simple info. Two minutes later, after sliding a blank envelope discreetly across the polished wood counter, their associate consulted some paperwork. He then scribbled something on a scrap of paper and slid it towards Nazeer. He glanced down at the message, nodded, then turned. A moment later, they were gone. For the equivalent of ten US dollars, they had Hiram Kane's room number.

"This is the room," Nazeer growled in rapid-fire Arabic. "Number twenty-three."

They looked up and down the long corridor. There was no one about. They glanced at each other.

"Ready?"

Atef nodded. Both men drew their guns.

Nazeer swiped his master key card, and in half a second they burst into the room, guns held out in front of them.

No one there.

Nazeer kicked open the bathroom door and, like in a classic—or cheesy—horror movie, he slashed back the shower curtain.

Nothing.

Both men cursed. They were too late.

Hiram Kane was gone.

Chapter Forty-Two

Ridley looked up at Kane for a long moment, holding his gaze in hers.

She understood what he was saying, and she appreciated how difficult it must have been for him to say it. Ridley knew how passionate he was about the repatriation program. He had been for years, ever since his grandfather had started the ball rolling decades earlier, educating him how important he believed the process was.

Ridley also knew how much Kane hated violence and injustice. Did he really want to leave? She doubted it. He wouldn't ever knowingly put her in danger, she knew that. Which meant he was doing it only for her. That didn't sit well with Alexandria Ridley. Didn't sit well with her at all.

She felt sure that if she hadn't been there, Kane would be doing everything he could to track down the Rosetta Stone and return it to the right people. Perhaps even more importantly than that, he'd somehow find a way to *relieve* the terrorists of their windfall. So, how could they not continue on with their mission? It didn't matter what he said... they had a responsibility to try.

She stood and walked over to Kane and took him by the hand. Turning to the others, she said, "Could you give us a moment, please?" Martorana and Sophie both nodded, and Ridley led Kane out into the corridor.

Then she changed tact. "I cannot fucking believe you want to leave. What the fuck are you playing at?"

Kane spun on his heels in obvious shock and turned to face Ridley. He tried to say something but his words failed.

"You listen to me, Hiram. Don't you dare for one minute think of leaving here because of some outdated notion of chivalry. Don't you dare. You know I won't leave, so I will not let you trick me into it by saying *you* are going."

Kane stared at Ridley, looking deep into her eyes. *Too clever...*

He screwed his eyes tightly shut, trying to hide what he was thinking. Then he opened them again, and the slightest hint of his trademark wry smile curled one corner of his mouth.

"You bastard," Ridley said, seething and grinning at the same time. "You're not leaving."

"Of course not, but you can't blame me for trying to get you to. I love you, Alexandria Ridley, and I want you to be safe, that's all. So please, why don't you get a flight with—"

"Mister Kane, Miss Ridley... Are you okay?" A member of the hotel staff came racing breathlessly along the corridor. "Are you hurt?" The man wore a serious, concerned look on his face.

"No... no, we're fine. Why? What's happened?" Kane asked.

"Oh, praise Allah. I was so worried."

"What on Earth's going on?" Ridley asked.

Kane stepped closer. "Yes, tell us, man, what's going on?"

The man caught his breath and looked Kane directly in the eye. "Someone just tried to kill you."

Chapter Forty-Three

Kane slammed his palms against the wall, causing a painting hanging nearby to crash to the floor.

After learning of the break-in to his room, Kane's mentality shifted entirely. Memories of his recent near-death experiences due to the actions of one bastard after another came flooding back on a surge of rage. He had wanted to stay away from trouble, stay away from the kinds of people that would break into a hotel room and try to kill him.

In truth, it wasn't himself he was concerned about. He was with Ridley, someone he would do anything for. He would gladly give up his own life to protect her, or anyone else for that matter. As those bad memories roared into his mind, so that rage thundered through his veins. *Nobody threatens Alex's life. Nobody!*

With heightened resolve, forged from both anger and crystal-clear intentions of doing what was right, Kane was now determined to act decisively. He took Ridley by the hand and joined the others back in Sophie's room. The hotel worker had posted two security guards outside the door.

Inside, they started to formulate a plan.

Julian asked if he could join them, both in his role as reporter for the *Egypt Daily News*, and also as someone who wanted to see the right thing done. He told them he'd gotten into reporting in the first place for adventure and to raise awareness of the world's problems. Ever since he'd been stationed in Egypt these last few years, he'd felt and seen first-hand the growing tensions in the area.

Besides, he explained, he figured he knew as much as anyone about what was really happening in Egypt these days and would be a valuable source of contacts. Thus, he was welcomed on board. Kane agreed with Martorana when she told Julian she was glad of the field experience of the reporter. She looked around at the group.

"I know you're all still here because you want to be. I just need you to be one hundred percent sure of something; this is *not* officially our problem. We are *not* an official team. The British Museum has requested we stand down from our official duty; we are to return home as soon as we're cleared by the authorities to do so. In a nutshell, we are *not* to go after the Rosetta Stone ourselves. That is the official stance... Is that clear?"

She paused and looked each of the group in the eye.

"We understand," Sophie confirmed. Kane saw fire in her eyes. "What is your *unofficial* stance?"

"As you know, I've already spoken with Director MacGregor. He knows I'm staying on. He insisted, at least formally and through official channels, everyone else must return to London." She nodded. "We've all seen it. Too many people turn their back on such things, which is the very reason the world has descended to its current state. Just look at our own country and the BREXIT fuc... that farce. Too many people believe what they read in shitty newspapers... no offence, Julian," she added, as she continued her impassioned tirade. "The UK. The US. France... everywhere. The populace make ill-informed decisions. The lack of people stepping forward to rally against unhinged leadership worldwide. The bombing runs against so-called targets in Syria, where thousands of innocent people died every day because people turned a blind eye and pretended things weren't as bad as they really were. Myanmar. Tibet. Venezuela. It's a long list. Too many people, too many times, did nothing. *Do*, nothing! Well not me! From the looks in all your eyes, not you either!"

Kane stood up, utterly impressed by his boss's passion for justice. It was something he'd always shared. He knew Ridley did too. "We have a chance to do something," he said, "stand up for what's right, stand up against what's wrong, and take our own personal stand against terrorism. We might just be able to complete our job, too."

"What a nice bonus that would be!" Martorana declared, though her expression remained stoic.

They all looked at Julian Wright now for some kind of starting point, some spark of inspiration from which they could formulate a plan. He sat still and quiet for a moment, looking at nothing in particular. Then, after almost a minute his eyes widened and he smiled. He stood and said, "Let's go for a ride."

Chapter Forty-Four

They left Sophie's room, stepping out past the security, and made their way to their own rooms to collect the rest of their things before regrouping down in the lobby. The man who'd informed them of the attack in Kane's room waved them over.

"Please be careful, Mister Kane," he said. "Those men are dangerous. Here is a photo taken from the hotel's closed-circuit cameras." He handed the printed image to Kane.

Julian leaned in to look. "Oh, shit!"

"What is it?" Ridley asked. "Who are they?"

"I'm pretty sure they're members of a local gang affiliated with some of the underground criminal factions in the city and beyond. That can only mean one thing. I hate to tell you this, but I believe a journalist colleague of mine was killed by that gang a year ago for getting too close to uncovering some of their activity. It's thought she was abducted, taken out to the desert, and... Well, she hasn't been seen since. I think they were going to kill you. I'm sure of it. We have to leave. Now!"

"They're probably still out there somewhere. It was only half an hour ago," Martorana confirmed. "What do we do?"

The man behind the counter stepped around to the front. "I know you do not know me and right now it might be difficult to trust me, but I want to help you."

Kane looked into his eyes and saw only honesty there. He turned to Julian. "What do you think? Do you know this guy?"

"I don't. Generally this hotel has an impeccable reputation."

"Excuse me, but the man who revealed your room number has gone, Mister Kane. He only started working here a few days ago... now I think we know why. You can trust me, and, *Inshallah*, I hope you will."

Kane looked at Ridley, who nodded. "Okay," Kane said. "What shall we do?"

The desk clerk hustled them wordlessly behind his otherwise-unmanned desk, through some kind of administrative room and out through another door. Then he led them quietly down the stairwell to a back entrance. Once there, he turned to them. "I really wish you all luck. Please, be safe. I'm ashamed of some of my countrymen. Now, you should go."

Julian had parked his car a block away. After scanning the area and seeing nobody around, they strode quickly out of the staff car park. Several minutes later they were loaded into Julian's beaten-up old Fiat, and were soon speeding through the city.

Chapter Forty-Five

Desouk

They hurtled towards the outskirts of the city in the dusty, dented Fiat.

The now-dark streets were devoid of human activity, though there were plenty of stray dogs and cats on the prowl scavenging for dinner. It wasn't only slim pickings for Egypt's struggling humans.

Now a little after sunset, the locals were either at prayer in their mosque or, in the case of most women, cooking the evening's dinner.

It wasn't far to where Julian was headed, maybe ninety minutes he told them, depending on A, his car, and B, the state of the deteriorating roads. He just hoped they'd managed to leave the area of the hotel without being spotted. Julian had lived in Alexandria for close to half a decade now. He knew the city inside out. He had plenty of friends, both expats and locals. Right now he needed a friend. There was one former colleague who lived in Desouk, a small town on the Nile about fifty miles east of Alexandria. It was a quiet town and was little more than an overgrown fishing village. The friend was a Scotsman he had worked with at the newspaper when he first arrived. Jim Burns had taken the young reporter under his wing, and they had grown close over too many evenings spent drinking illicit booze in more than a few of Alexandria's seedy neighbourhoods.

Jim had retired two years ago, though he and Julian remained friends and in contact. Julian knew the old-timer lived peacefully with his Egyptian wife on an old canal boat on The Nile. Although he hadn't actually visited Jim in over a year, he knew it was the perfect place to seek refuge for a few hours, maybe a day or two. There they'd put together a plan. Jim Burns knew just about every criminal in the city. Not that he himself was corrupt, but he knew how to deal with the shady elements, knew how to roll with those on the wrong side of the law, and was respected for never giving up their names. They would be safe, and they would probably get the sources or inspiration they needed.

A few minutes shy of two hours later, Julian eased his car along the dark riverside lane, eventually pulling up alongside the river boat owned by Jim Burns and his wife, Adara.

"You guys wait here. Jim doesn't believe in phones now he's retired. He boycotts them with a passion, so I couldn't call ahead. He definitely won't be expecting visitors. He might have a gun."

Julian slid out of the car and walked in the darkness towards the boat. A single exposed bulb hung from a TV aerial on top of the cabin and provided just enough light to guide him safely along the bank. Once he was close enough he called out to his old friend. "Jim? Hey Jimmy, you in there?"

There came no reply, and after waiting a couple of minutes, Julian called again, this time a little louder. "Jimmy? I have Scotch."

A light flicked on inside the boat. Several seconds later the door opened. "If it's not single malt you can fuck—"

"Single malt!"

"Then you're most welcome." Jim Burns was a big man to whom years of heavy drinking had provided a rotund and ruddy appearance. He'd claim often it was hard-earned. Even in the dim light, Julian saw his friend hadn't lost his usual swagger. He guessed Jim was at least half way through his daily bottle of Scotch.

"Well, what're you waiting for, laddie? Come on down ya young whipper snapper."

Jim greeted his friend on the deck with a powerful hug and an even heartier slap on the back, which almost caused Julian to topple over the side into the dark—possibly croc-infested—waters of the Nile. They stepped inside the simple yet cosy home. Julian didn't waste any time.

He quickly explained what had occurred at the museum and whom he had met. He wasn't surprised to learn that Jim—who seemed to know about most things that happened almost before they had—already knew about the theft. Julian didn't ask how he knew about it so quickly, all the way out here on the edge of civilisation. Instead, he asked the big man if he and his new companions could lay low for a while.

Just a few minutes later, Kane, Martorana and the others were sitting around the table in the boat's main living area, all with a generous glass of Scotch in front of them.

"It's good of you to help us out like this," Martorana said. "We appreciate it."

"A pleasure, my girl. As you might imagine I don't get many visitors out this way. It's nice to see young folks... actually, it's nice to see anyone who isn't a grizzled old fisherman, if I'm honest, which is what I'm fast becoming."

Julian had noticed Jim's wife, Adara, wasn't there, which was unusual. He wanted to ask about her. Something told him he already knew the truth. He didn't have to wait long until for confirmation.

"My wife, Adara, died last year. I guess I don't get out much anymore. To be fair, that suits me just fine. I'm tired, Julian," he said, just a trace of sadness in his wisened eyes, "but I'm happy enough living out the rest of my days a lonely old man. Cheers," he added, raising his glass. They all raised their glasses too.

"I'm really sorry, Jim," Julian said. "I didn't know. How did Adara die?"

"Her heart," Jim told them. "Been having issues nigh on a year. When the heart attack came it was sudden, all over in seconds, thank God. She's in a better place now, that's for sure. But here I am. Despite being lonely sometimes, I'm pretty content watching the world go by on the Nile every day, sometimes on the deck fishing, others from right there on that armchair. I won't deny the view sometimes gets a bit blurry." Jim raised his glass once more, his wicked grin leaving no doubt as to how he spent his days.

"Anyway," he said, "seems you kids have a lot more on your plate than I do. The question is..." Jim paused, glancing at his new, unexpected guests. "The question is," he repeated, "what are we going to do about it?"

Chapter Forty-Six

Cairo International Airport

It flew like a missile.

Out of the blackness of the night, the super-sleek, super-fast Hawker Jet ghosted down onto the private runway at Cairo International Airport. The pilot taxied the bird slowly to the private hangar. After making the final instrument checks, he shut down the engines.

Jabari Hader had arranged with Omar Abdel-Rahman to get the stone out of Alexandria as quickly as possible. After a day or so, Omar was then to fly on to Cairo, make the transaction, then discreetly return with the Rosetta Stone to Alexandria where it would be installed in his private collection. The idea of getting the stone out of the city was to create a decoy and lead any would-be searchers on a wild goose chase. That's what Omar had in mind.

Jabari had other ideas.

Salam el Halabi wished it were over already. His nerves had been growing increasingly frayed since he'd snuck away from the Artefact Repatriation Committee team at the hotel and later joined Jabari Hader. The security leader scared him. The whole fucking thing scared him. If he wasn't in such deep shit he would've already bailed out.

He knew he couldn't. Salam knew there was no way he wasn't already guilty by association of playing a part in the greatest archaeological heist of all time. If he ran now, Jabari's men would take him out, of that he was certain. He really only saw one way of surviving this now; complete the transaction, then hope that his financial rewards would enable him to hide somewhere safe forever. If he were to even get it.

The transaction was to take place directly in this hangar. That was, if everything went to plan. It was a simple trade, yet the people involved were obviously not the greatest example of fine, upstanding members of society. Salam had been that once. Now he knew he was no better than these others. They probably trusted him only as much as he trusted them. Somewhere a fraction above zero.

In essence, the transaction was simple. One archaeological artefact in exchange for a shitload of money. The handover had been scheduled for lunch time the following day, when the buyer, the same man who funded the entire operation, was arriving by another private jet from his home somewhere overseas. Until that moment Jabari, Salam and the others were instructed to sit tight and await Omar's arrival. The hangar was equipped with a comfy sleeping area, high above on a custom-built mezzanine floor. There was also a lounge and a kitchen area where they could prepare food and relax.

Salam was far from relaxed. He was so anxious to get

the business done and get the hell out of there that he feared he might suffer a panic attack. As soon as the doors of the jet opened, he climbed out of the plane, leapt down the short stairway and trotted outside the hangar for some air. Every minute they were in possession of the artefact was another minute the police—the genuine police, not the ones on Jabari's payroll—Interpol, the FBI, MI6 and other organisations had to find them.

On top of that, Salam could not shift the burgeoning fear that his boss Martorana and her new assistant Kane still had some part to play in all this. He somehow knew they wouldn't just let it go. That worried him more than anything. He'd seen the way Martorana worked, and knew how her mind operated. She was a fucking devil disguised as a museum curator. As for Kane… the man screamed justice. Salam didn't know what was worse… facing the malignant, psychotic glare of Jabari Hader, or the wrath of Martorana and Kane. Going to an Egyptian prison might be the best of all options. Maybe even dying in the desert and being eaten by rats.

Salam wanted to get the transaction done right now. So be it. *Inshallah*, things would go well, and Salam had no real reason to believe they wouldn't. With a couple of long, deep breaths, he went back inside and found a spot on one of the sofas upstairs.

All there was left to do now was wait. He lay back and closed his eyes, his usual mantra of *Allāhu akbar, Allāhu akbar, Allāhu akbar* strangely absent from his thoughts.

Chapter Forty-Seven

Desouk

Julian stared at Jim. "Did you say, 'What are *we* going to do about it?'"

Jim nodded, eyes glinting.

"We didn't come here to get you involved, Jim, only to ask a few questions."

"Now you listen here, sunshine, I might be a doddery old fart, but that's not gonna stop me coming with you on this... whatever this is. A treasure hunt?" Jim's eyes sparkled and the others couldn't tell if he were serious or joking.

In truth, Jim Burns was more than ready to help. In fact, he was desperate for it.

He had been a reporter for decades. Yet if he were being honest—now that his wife wasn't about to keep him in order—it was the adventure he craved, which was what had led him into journalism in the first place. He'd lived and worked all over the world since first cutting his teeth reporting on Glasgow's gritty streets in the eighties. He had seen his fair share of action. For the last decade and a half, however, since he'd met Adara and largely left his wild days behind—at least when she'd been watching—he had called Egypt home.

He was drawn to the honesty and integrity of the people. With no shortage of history, both ancient, modern and constantly-in-the-making, it made the perfect country in which to phase out his career and ease into a well-earned retirement. Doing it alone hadn't been part of the plan. In the months since his wife had died he had been drinking heavily to dilute his sadness. Not that he hadn't always drunk a lot. In the journalism world Jim Burns' binges in expat bars were almost legendary. His reputation for partying was almost as strong as his reputation for getting the big scoop. The fact he looked a lot like classic hell raiser Oliver Reed wasn't lost on Kane and the others; he looked just as tough as the legendary British actor.

Jim had always had his finger on the pulse of everything that was happening in Egypt. In fact, he and Julian had formed quite a team when they were colleagues. The younger man just hoped his intuition about his old friend was right. That, if there was something going on in the darkest shadows of Alexandria—and indeed beyond—Jim Burns would know about it.

"Listen," Jim said, "you're very safe here, at least for now. Hardly anyone knows I live here; those who do can be trusted. It's safe for you to stay here for now." He paused, his eyes narrowing a little. "For now," he repeated for emphasis. "I have to warn you, historically Egypt has a way of giving up her secrets, however well kept. If people are looking for you, and you're probably correct in thinking they are, then it's only a matter of time until they find you. I think it's safe for you to spend a night here. Come first light tomorrow, I suggest *we* should all be long gone. Which means *we* need to make a plan."

"*We?*" Julian repeated. "Jim, honestly I don't think—"

"Of course, *we*. I'm coming along. Whether it looks like it or not, there's plenty of life in this old pooch yet. Besides, you're going to need me."

Defeated, Julian glanced first at Kane, then Martorana, hoping for backup. It wasn't forthcoming.

Kane took up the reins. "Look, Jim, we really appreciate your help. What we need now is some inspiration, a hint about who might be behind this. Do you have anything?"

The big man smiled. Despite his darkened, bloodshot eyes Kane saw the excitement that sparkled there. "I have more than just a hint. I once interviewed one of the richest men in Egypt, in fact, one of the richest men in the whole region… Omar Abdel-Rahman. He's a former oil tycoon who's well known throughout the world of artefacts for his unrivalled collections in Paris and Luxor."

"Jim, we know this already," Julian said, "but that's—"

"Go on, Jim," cut in Martorana, eager to lean on the man's vast experience and obvious contacts.

Jim flashed Julian a look, but continued. "Right. Omar told me in that interview that it was his dream to see the Rosetta Stone returned to Egypt. However, off the record he joked that one day he would own it himself. I did not think he was joking. Back then I believed he was serious. I always have. Now it seems there's some criminal element, maybe even terrorists, involved in the theft. Think about it. To successfully pull off such an undertaking must mean there was a lot of money behind it. Now, I'm not saying Omar's a terrorist. In fact, I very much doubt it. He's always declared himself a liberal Muslim, moderate at the most. The man is not a terrorist."

Jim leaned over and snagged up his Scotch, took a long, slow gulp, then placed it down again. He glanced at those gathered around his modest living room. A conspiratorial glint returned to his eye.

"However, a criminal? Omar would call himself a Saviour of artefacts. A God of historical preservation. The Messiah of antiquities, if you will. Yes, I believe he is technically a criminal, at least when it comes to getting his hands on a certain strata of priceless artefacts. I think that to find the Rosetta Stone, you first need to find the tycoon. And I know just where to start looking."

Jim Burns explained that through his network of underground contacts he'd learned that, since the overthrow of Muslim Brotherhood President Mohamed Morsi, and the defeat of terrorist group Sinai Province, Sinai Province had actually moved its operations out of the Sinai area. They'd relocated into the valleys around Luxor, an area synonymous with legendary places such as The Valleys of The Kings and Queens. It was home of many famous temples, too, such as the magnificent structure at Karnak and the Temple of Luxor itself, not to mention the tomb of the most famous of all pharaohs, Tutankhamun himself.

In the vast matrix of known and unknown tunnels and caves in the endless valleys, it became the perfect place to set up a secret terrorist camp. With half of Egypt's security forces and military intrinsically intertwined with the Muslim Brotherhood, it wouldn't be a difficult secret to keep.

"But how does that link to the Rosetta Stone?" Kane asked. "I mean, we don't really know for sure who stole it." The question was reasonable. Burns answered honestly.

"I know we have no concrete evidence. There is no

other known criminal group either smart or organised enough to have pulled off what is one of the greatest art thefts in history. I'm certain that whoever did this, they must be an established and efficient group, not to mention well-funded, and willing to risk everything for the greatest prize. There is only one man wealthy or passionate enough to buy such infamous and stolen goods."

"Omar Abdel-Rahman," Ridley said.

"Exactly," Jim Burns told them. "Big Omar, perhaps the greatest art thief in history. Now, Julian, be a good lad and pour us all another round of Scotch."

Chapter Forty-Eight

Cairo International Airport

Salam bolted upright, heart thudding beneath his ribs.

He'd nodded off on the couch, and dreamt he was being executed by Jabari Hader. He shook his head clear of the fearful dream. Salam was sweating in the oppressive heat of the hangar, and wiped his forehead on the sleeve of his shirt. He stood and stretched, waiting while his heart rate returned to normal. He glanced over at another sofa and caught Jabari staring at him. He needed some air.

An hour later, after stepping out of the hangar to try to calm his shredded nerves, he returned upstairs onto the mezzanine section and made himself a drink. Salam started to think about his former colleagues. They were good people, largely. Although they were infidels, he had enjoyed his time working with them. Maria Martorana was a good boss, who had always encouraged him, ever since he'd first been employed by the British Museum. It was an institution he once admired, yet it remained the antithesis of everything the rest of his family believed in.

True, they were British nationals, yet they'd never really adopted Western values and still held strongly to their Islamic beliefs. That, in itself, was fine. For decades Britain had prided itself on being a multicultural society, perhaps especially in London, where families from all over the world and of all creeds and colours had lived side by side for decades. Yet in recent years, a new tension had started to spread like a cancer.

Increasingly, different ethnic groups had tended to stick together. This was no more highlighted than after the London bombings in 2005. There are many who still believe the entire tragic incident on the 7th of July—in which more than fifty people were murdered, and in which Salam's older brother lost his life after the police tried to arrest him—was a conspiracy, an inside job, a false flag operation orchestrated by the British government to instil fear among the citizens of London. The theory that the bombings were orchestrated in order to help garner support for the Iraq war and for Blair's New Labour party has never gone away. Since then, racial divisions have grown ever wider.

So, when Salam, the family's youngest son, graduated from university and immediately secured a prestigious position at the British Museum, it had angered his parents. The British Museum was an ancient institution. It thrived on displaying artefacts from other countries, many of which were collected during the often reprehensible colonial period. It was understandable why many people disliked the establishment. Salam thought differently. He was later employed as part of the developing Artefact Repatriation

Committee. He saw it as a great chance to do something good, something that might help ease relations between countries that were primarily of different religious faiths and customs. It was his way of bringing those different faiths and cultures together.

Then things changed. Though he hated to use the word radical, he was beginning to fit that tabloid-driven moniker. He had always attended the mosque, ever since he was old enough. For a young kid in London, going to the mosque was more about the social scene, and hanging out with his mates. As he got older, however, and especially as the city he lived in and called home began to change, Salam had become more and more interested in the word of Allah. That interest had only been enhanced by more recent events, not only in the Middle East, but all over the world. Idiots in the West, who continuously spouted off their hateful and bigoted rhetoric, had done more for the Islamic cause than any act by groups like ISIS and Al-Qaeda. More and more, formerly moderate Muslims like Salam were becoming radicalised.

So it had been for Salam. He had met and got to know a few influential imams at the Brick Lane mosque; they had encouraged him to join their fight against the infidels. He'd resisted for years. Ultimately, the senseless bombings in Syria and elsewhere, and the constant persecution of the Palestinians, had turned his head so much that he had become a committed Jihadist. Since his position within the Repatriation Committee had afforded him access to delicate information about the details of the Rosetta Stone, and its imminent repatriation to Egypt, he had devised his plan to steal it.

So far so good. They just needed to make the transaction tomorrow, and his radical group, a small London cell with close links to ISIS, would receive the single biggest financial input in its history.

Then, they were set to unleash hell on the corrupted and godless infidels of London.

Chapter Forty-Nine

Desouk

Inside, Ridley fought to hold it together.

She'd been quiet since they'd arrived at Jim's houseboat, though her mind was far from passive. Egypt was the country in which she'd been born. Although she hadn't grown up or lived here since she was just a few months old, it was still somewhere she had fond feelings about and a lifelong connection to. It was literally in her DNA. The fact that her man Hiram Kane was the one responsible for the safe return of the Rosetta Stone, only to have it stolen on his watch, linked her even more closely to the events.

That, and the fact that once more they had been drawn into the world of dangerous criminals and terrorists… It hit her hard.

Rather than all this making her afraid for the safety of Kane and herself and making her want to get as far away from Egypt as possible, it somehow had the opposite effect.

It galvanised her, made her angry, made her more determined than ever to do the right thing.

"We have to go after them," she yelled, standing up abruptly and knocking a bottle off the table. She ignored it and continued. "Getting back the stone? That's a given. More important than that now is that we have a link to the terrorist bastards. We've been given a chance to reveal their base, help put a stop to their activities."

"I know how you feel, Alex, I really do. I agree with you about the stone," Kane said. "Getting involved with terrorists? If we do that, we'd have to be so careful... make a plan, get help. We've had enough experience of that lately, and we—"

"—and we were lucky to survive," Ridley finished. "I know that, yet we can't just sit around here doing nothing!" Ridley's eyes went wide as she slammed her palms down on the table.

"Hiram's right," Martorana chimed in. "Besides, we aren't vigilantes, nor are we soldiers. We're nothing more than passionate archaeologists and historians. Shit, my job title is Repatriations Coordinator. We just aren't skilled or equipped enough to get involved with terrorists without getting the right help."

"For what it's worth," added Julian, "as was shown in Sinai, when you shut down one organisation, it just emerges bigger and stronger somewhere else. I agree, we're in no position to get involved directly with the Muslim Brotherhood, however big the story might be."

"No. You're wrong. We have to," Ridley protested. "It's a moral obligation to start now, before it's too late. You all know what's happening to innocent people around the world, hundreds, thousands of people being murdered by terrorists. We can't just sit here drinking and doing nothing. We just can't."

The room fell silent. They agreed with Ridley in principle. The weight of the situation was overwhelming. They were a group of people who didn't know the first thing about terrorism other than what they read in papers and saw on the news. Unfortunately, Kane and Ridley had seen firsthand what men and women with religious agendas were capable of. Yet their experience involved small and isolated groups, nothing like the vast network of Jihadists that might be involved in this.

In addition to Kane and Ridley were two journalists, an assistant museum curator and a repatriations coordinator. That was it. They weren't exactly the SAS. Still, there was something in Ridley's impassioned plea that struck a chord in all of them. They had an opportunity to do some good. Maybe not undermine the entire terrorist cell, but at least cause them serious problems. It was the unlikely voice of Sophie that broke the thoughtful silence.

"Guys. Look, I know I'm the least qualified of us to speak up on this situation… I'm not even a fully fledged museum curator yet." She smiled wryly, though her eyes were sincere and focused. "I have been personally betrayed by these people. He… I am one hundred percent determined to at least try to recover the Rosetta Stone. If we have a chance to stop these religious nut cases? I believe we have to try."

All were taken aback by the grit behind Sophie's sudden outburst. It only served to make them question what they should do.

They looked at each other, one to another, and saw in

each other's eyes a determination to finish the job they had started. There was something more. All of them in the lounge of Jim Burns' houseboat had in one way or another been affected by terrorism. Kane and Ridley recently in Peru and Mexico. Sophie's probable betrayal by Salam. Maria Martorana had lost a cousin in the concert shooting in Paris. Julian Wright, the reporter, had known many colleagues who had died in the course of their work, most recently, the girl who had been kidnapped and almost certainly assassinated in Egypt. Not least, Jim Burns himself, who, although his wife had officially died of a heart attack, in his own heart he believed it stemmed from the pain of seeing what had become of her beloved Egypt.

As their collective resolve grew, they all knew without doubt what they'd be getting into. They just needed someone to take control of the situation. As team leader for the Rosetta Stone's repatriation, Kane was responsible for its recovery, along with Martorana. However, he didn't know if he was the right man to lead this new group of people. He glanced at Jim Burns, who had long ago put down his bottle of Scotch. There was a fire in those deep blue eyes, which had intensified over the last few minutes. When he rose from his chair, it was as if a different man stood before them.

"My friends, new and old," he said. "It seems we are a team of sorts. A team with two objectives. The first? Recover the lost artefact. Second? Kick some terrorist arse."

Chapter Fifty

Abbe Abidi's Apartment, Alexandria

Now that the storm of chaos had finally calmed down back at the Alexandria National Museum, Director Abbe Abidi was allowed to leave the premises and return to his apartment a few blocks away. It had been a crazy twenty-four hours. Now it was over.

Abbe had gotten away with it.

When he had first been approached about participating in the theft, anonymously to begin with, he had been absolutely against it. He was a serious professional and an educated man, who had spent his life and career rising to his current position as director of his beloved museum. Something soon became clear to Abbe after that initial contact. In no uncertain terms, he was informed that if he didn't collaborate, then he was of no use to them. Thus, his life was forfeit. Worse still, it was suggested that his adult children would probably have some kind of unfortunate *accident* in the near future.

Of Curses and Kings

To begin with Abbe resisted. He had reluctantly joined the initial conference call in order to learn who it was hassling him and his family. He wasn't impressed, and dismissed it all out of hand as some amateur crooks seriously over-reaching. What the lead man had suggested went against all his long-held principles, and for several days he didn't take the threat on his and his children's lives at all seriously.

However, one morning a few days after that initial contact, as he retrieved the mail from his box in the lobby of his apartment building, everything changed. He pulled the sickeningly familiar envelope from the box and with shaky hands he slid out the contents. Instant dizziness wobbled him where he stood. His face blanched to a deathly grey.

"Sir? Mister Abidi, are you okay?" called over the on-duty concierge.

Abbe glanced up.

"Sir? May I assist you?"

The director ignored the man and scraped up the two items that had fallen to the floor. He held them in his open hands, disbelief threatening to ruin him. The first, one of his daughter's t-shirts. Bloodstained. The second, his son's favourite NY Yankees baseball cap. Abbe knew they were the real thing because despite their ages, his wife Fatima insisted on sewing their names inside all their clothes. There was another note. All this one said, was:

DO NOT DOUBT WHAT WE WILL DO.
YOU WILL HELP US!

In that moment Abbe knew he no longer had any choice. Anyone could take photos from a distance. To get these items would have required direct contact with his beloved children.

Since the heist had now gone off smoothly, largely down to his internal help, he should have been able to relax. He had spoken recently to his kids and they were fine. They knew nothing of any threats and had not been contacted by any strangers, dangerous or otherwise. His son did admit to having misplaced his baseball cap. Abbe decided not to mention anything about that.

Yet, he could not relax. The leader of the plot, Omar Abdel-Rahman, had told him that he was going keep the Rosetta Stone in his possession... for its own good. Abbe knew of Omar. Anyone who worked with antiquities, especially in Egypt, knew of him, if not in person then at least by reputation. Abbe had to admit that at least the artefact would be in good hands, albeit dirty ones.

The fact that his kids were safe, added to the fact Omar was also paying him a fortune for his cooperation, helped Abbe keep his thoughts to himself.

Even though he'd had very little choice other than do what the group demanded of him, something new was niggling at his soul. Omar had insisted they were in essence a marginally criminal group doing something good for humanity, despite the threats of violence. Omar had even labelled himself the Egyptian Robin Hood. Abbe hadn't laughed.

Now Abbe had started to speculate there was in fact an Islamic fundamentalist group behind Omar's criminal façade. To think that he might be complicit in some organised terror group was abhorrent to him and causing him severe stress. Yes, he was Muslim. He even considered himself reasonably devout. Yet there was no way he could condone the atrocities done in the name of Allah being committed all over the modern world. Then again, by helping the criminals steal the Rosetta Stone, he was coming to understand that possibly, that is just what he had done.

He had to know. If it were true, Abbe couldn't live with himself. He was beginning to feel the enormity of what he'd done tighten its grip on his soul and on his sanity.

Chapter Fifty-One

Desouk

The sun rose quickly, emerging as a fireball over the eastern Sinai desert and radiating warmth on Kane's face as he stretched away the night and the previous evening's drinks. Between them they'd consumed a fair amount of scotch; as more of a beer man, Kane smiled wryly as he assessed his headache. Luckily, not that bad. He awoke early and crept out of the houseboat, hoping to get some fresh air on deck. He was soon joined by Ridley, who sidled up next to him, both now enjoying the sun's warmth.

"How do you feel?" she asked. "That was quite a night."

"It was. Jim is some character. That story about the croc that slipped aboard his deck while he slept… lucky bugger." Kane shook his head as he remembered the story. He instantly regretted it.

"He's a great storyteller. What I meant was, how do you feel about the plan?"

"Ah. Well, we have no other leads. With what we've

learned from Julian and Jim about this man Omar, and his ability to buy what he wants, it seems as if he's surely the prime suspect. I think we need to go and find out for ourselves."

Kane sighed. He was torn between doing the right thing regarding his job, and doing the right thing for Ridley. He knew she'd never forgive him if they didn't at least make an effort to retrieve the Rosetta Stone. More importantly, he would never forgive himself. They would, of course, have to be very careful; they had all promised each other not to make any decisions alone. They were a team, albeit a random group of people with differing skills. What they did possess was a togetherness, a collection of like-minded and passionate people who had reached a point of sadness with the world and were sick of people doing what they wanted. All men and woman had their limits. This group had reached theirs.

They were going after the Rosetta Stone, and they were going to do what they could to bring down the terrorists.

Before that, however, they had to go into hiding, or at least head somewhere less exposed. As Jim suggested, they were literally sitting ducks here on the houseboat. Though their location was remote, Kane knew better than to take any chances.

Chapter Fifty-Two

The Next Day

After making a couple of quick calls using Martorana's mobile phone, Jim had checked them into the airport hotel at Borg El Arab International, where they hunkered down, made more plans and waited to find out what the next step was to be.

Jim Burns explained he'd enjoyed a friendly relationship with Omar Abdel-Rahman. The mega-rich tycoon had always been a jovial and willing entertainer to his friend in the press. They had often called upon each other for information. Jim connected with Omar for his newspaper articles. In turn, Omar used Jim for information about his rivals.

So, it was of little surprise when the previous day Jim had contacted Omar's office to ask if he was available for an interview. Just an hour later, a meeting was confirmed. They'd set it for lunch time today at Omar's mansion in

Alexandria. Jim had also asked if Maria Martorana, Kane and Alex Ridley could join them. That was also approved.

Thankfully, the evening had passed uneventfully. Before they knew it, the time had come to go and visit Omar. So Jim, Martorana, Kane and Ridley took the long cab ride west from their hotel to Omar's near-palatial mansion.

A mix of excitement and trepidation fluttered in Kane's stomach. This could be a major breakthrough in locating the lost artefact. It could also spell danger. Jim had assured them Omar wasn't a dangerous man. Kane knew better than to trust anyone these days. Yet, he trusted Jim, despite knowing him for less than twenty-four hours.

They arrived at the massive gated compound, known as *Alyawtubia*—Utopia, in Arabic—where they waited at the guard house. After a few moments, in which the guard dutifully called the house to confirm that the guests had been invited, the gates swung open and the cab eased forward between large, enigmatic fountains and statues, and some of the most remarkable examples of topiary Kane had ever seen. When witnessing bushes shaped like pyramids and the Great Sphinx, then it's obvious you're amid serious wealth. Kane thought it looked more like a fancy hotel than someone's house.

They exited the cab, and were swiftly ushered into an ante-chamber by a tuxedoed butler named Bassam, who politely asked them to wait a moment. They had barely taken a seat, when not a minute later the door opened and the smiling Omar Abdel-Rahman greeted them warmly, shaking their hands and beckoning them inside what to Kane was one of the most spectacularly appointed rooms he had ever seen. It was more a gallery of artefacts, in truth. Combined with a collection of paintings from world-renowned artists, such as Cezanne and Renoir—Omar was obviously partial to the Impressionists—this room stunned the senses in its juxtaposition of world-class art from all around the globe.

Next, Kane's eyes were drawn to a shelf in the back corner of the room. On that shelf were a series of gold discs which he instantly recognised as Incan. Kane was famous throughout the world for being the man to have rediscovered Vilcabamba, the lost Inca city, and with it, the legendary lost hoard of Atahualpa's gold. That amazing discovery was widely considered one of the greatest archaeological finds of the last century, and one of Kane's proudest moments. Of course, that expedition deep into the Andes had not all gone to plan… two separate terrorist groups had seen to that. Kane blinked away the sad memories and turned to his host, Omar, who eyed him with a knowing smile.

"Mr. Kane, it's a great honour to meet such a distinguished man in the field of discovery. I have read all about your successes. I was sorry to hear about your recent tribulations in Mexico. For those poor children who lost their lives, I say it was a tragedy of the highest order."

Kane nodded. *This man knows his stuff.* "Thank you, sir, I appreciate that. Please, call me Hiram."

Omar smiled, nodded, then added, "Yet it was an amazing discovery you made in Peru, both the lost city and the gold, was it not?"

Kane couldn't deny that it was in fact the discovery of a lifetime. He returned what seemed to be Omar's genuine smile.

Omar ushered them into a row of plush leather seats opposite his desk, which he sat behind with no short amount of effort. Omar was a big man, who looked to be mere hours from a cardiac arrest.

"So, Jim, am I to assume this has something to do with the Rosetta Stone?"

Jim's eyes widened. "Um, well, yes, you can assume that." Jim smiled, but then the smile faded and his expression turned serious. "Look, before I go on I want to assure you I am not accusing you of being involved with the theft of the stone."

"Are you sure? I know you're fully aware of my long-held passion for it to be returned to my beloved Alexandria."

"Well, were you involved? I mean, did you have something to do with the theft?"

For a moment Omar's eyes narrowed, and it appeared as if he were angry. Then his face softened. "You always were direct with your questions, Jim, which I appreciate. No, since you ask, I had nothing to do with the theft of the Rosetta Stone. I won't say I haven't acquired other important artefacts by, shall we say, somewhat less than scrupulous means. As you know, the objects in my collection are safer with me than in many of our less-than-secure galleries and museums. I seek to make no profit from the things I collect. I only hope to ensure their survival and safekeeping."

It was an impassioned case-making exercise. Jim knew Omar well, and he didn't seem at all convinced to Kane. Jim tried a new tack.

"Look, Omar, we believe the Rosetta Stone has been stolen by a gang connected to terrorists. They're probably going to try to sell the artefact to a wealthy collector, then use the vast amounts of money involved to arm themselves and become more powerful. You understand why I've come to you. You're the only collector I know wealthy enough, and with enough influence, to broker such a deal. So I ask you again, knowing as I do that you yourself are not directly involved with terror... would you still buy the Rosetta Stone if you knew what it would be funding?"

Omar stared at Jim for a long moment, a vague expression on his face. Finally, he seemed to snap out of his trance. He stood up and walked slowly to a large painting that hung on the wall behind his desk. The painting was a depiction of an archaeological site at the exact moment Napoleon's soldiers found the buried artefact that came to be known as the Rosetta Stone.

Kane had no idea where this drama was leading, but he was on full alert.

Chapter Fifty-Three

Alyawtubia

Omar stood stock-still, arms clasped behind his back and staring at the art work for a full minute. Finally, he spoke.

"Of course, at the time of its discovery no one even knew what it was, nor how it would shape the world's understanding of our magnificent Egyptian history. It would be hard to argue against the idea that the Rosetta Stone is the single most important archaeological discovery of all time." He turned to face the four guests sitting opposite his desk. Kane thought an announcement of regret was coming. An admission of guilt.

"There we are. I'm sorry to inform you, and naturally, I wish it were different, that I know nothing of the whereabouts of the Rosetta Stone. I truly wish I did."

Kane was deflated. He felt sure the larger-than-life figure addressing the group was the missing part of the puzzle. He glanced at the others and saw they felt the same as he did.

"Damn it. I... I'm sorry to have wasted your time," Jim told them, glancing at the others. Then to Omar, he said, "I shouldn't have doubted you, old friend. I guess I was just desperate to help recover the artefact."

Omar stepped over to Jim and placed his meaty hands on his friend's shoulders. "It is fine, Jim. You are right to have asked me. I am indeed the only one capable of such an arrangement. Alas, you were wrong. So, there it is," he said again, backing away from his friend and shuffling over to a drinks cabinet. "Can I offer anyone a drink?"

"No, thanks," Martorana said. "Come on, we need to get going," she added, addressing the others.

Kane, Jim and Martorana made their way to the door. Only Ridley remained seated, her face impassive and thoughtful. As Kane glanced down at her, confused at why she wasn't getting ready to leave, she stood up.

"Just give me a minute, okay?"

Kane angled his head to one side, appraising his love. He knew better than to question her scheme. Instead he asked, "You okay?"

"Yep, I'm fine. I just have a couple of questions for our friend here. Wait in the car. I'll be down in a few. Maria, do you mind?"

Martorana glanced back at Ridley. Like Kane, she seemed to think Ridley was onto something, so she nodded. "See you in the car."

Omar took a seat behind his desk as the others filed out, a bemused look on his face. Then, when it was just Omar and Ridley left alone in his expansive office and the door had closed, his smile faded. In its place was another expression. Though he tried to hide it, Ridley was onto him.

"Why, Omar?"

Omar's eyes shifted away from Alex, unable to meet her penetrating gaze. "Why what?" he said after a long moment of uncomfortable silence.

"I think you know. Jim was right, wasn't he? About you being a part of the theft somehow."

Omar now met Ridley's eyes and held them, clearly trying hard to remain calm. Inside, the usually unflappable oil tycoon and legendary artefacts collector was obviously shaken to his core. His eyes followed Ridley as she stepped over to a large window that afforded an amazing view over Omar's beautiful gardens and beyond that, the eastern most edge of the Libyan Desert. For a moment Ridley was stunned into silence by the immense beauty before her. This was her homeland. Somewhere within a few miles of here was the location of her birth. She was half-Egyptian, and it was the Egyptian in her that believed Omar was lying. She saw it in his small brown eyes and sensed that as a fellow Egyptian he was suffering a great deal of inner conflict by lying to her.

Ridley sensed rather than saw Omar as he quietly took a spot next to her at the window. *Come on, Omar,* she thought, *just tell me the truth.*

Omar cleared his throat and dabbed at his lips with a handkerchief. To Ridley he sounded sick, but she didn't look, nor did she say anything. Instead, she remained silent and waited, almost sensing Omar's internal struggle. She was certain he wasn't telling the truth. Three whole minutes passed before he finally spoke.

"I'm so sorry, Miss Ridley. I... I thought I was doing the right thing."

Chapter Fifty-Four

Alexandria

As in most cities, there exists in Alexandria an underbelly of nefarious people, those who seek to make a living by any means possible. Networks of contacts spread around like tendrils, prodding and probing, gathering information which can be used for and against people. Always for profit. Never for good.

Today was no different.

Julian's journalist colleague, the woman with whom he had approached Hiram Kane outside the hotel soon after the theft, had slipped quietly away. Amid the mayhem, Julian hadn't noticed. The two weren't exactly friends, though in the world of journalism they had many of the same contacts. It was often a case of *you scratch my back, I'll share my source.*

Laura Hogan hadn't slipped away very far. In fact, she'd stayed close enough to have followed Julian's journey with Kane and his team, tracing them all the way to Jim Burns' houseboat. She knew not to tread on Julian's footsteps on this one. Yet, she wanted the scoop too. Thus, she made a few calls. Unfortunately, Laura wasn't as experienced on the ground in Alexandria as she'd have liked. She hadn't quite worked out which of her contacts she could trust. So, when she contacted one of her sources, a local thug named Ibrahim, it was a call made in good faith. Ibrahim had told Laura he would look into the information she wanted. That was twenty-four hours ago. She'd not heard back from Ibrahim since.

No sooner had Kane and his team's taxi disappeared inside the gates that led up the drive to Omar's massive property, than a young local man pulled out his mobile phone and placed a call.

"It is me, Ibrahim."

"Did you follow them? Where are they?"

"Yes, I followed them. They have just gone into the tycoon's property."

There followed a long silence.

"Boss? Are you there?"

"I am here. Listen, Ibrahim, wait there. Let me know when they leave the property."

"Okay, boss."

"Speak soon, Ibrahim."

"*Inshallah*, Jabari."

Chapter Fifty-Five

Alyawtubia

"Listen, Omar," Ridley began gently. If she had to turn aggressive, she would. "You know this better than anyone. If wonderful artefacts such as the Rosetta Stone continue to go missing, it is the Egyptian people who get the blame. Egyptians like you and I." She placed a hand on his shoulder, hoping to encourage truth from the big man. "We will always be thought of as liars and thieves. Sure, in the distant past ancient tombs and palaces were robbed, probably by the very people that helped build them. In more recent times, it was Western explorers, pilfering the tombs under the banner of archaeology and exploration but often it was merely a case of greedy, insensitive colonial powers, grabbing what they could for financial gain and the glory of having those monuments on display in their own countries, and to hell with Egypt. That was the past, Omar, a dark and murky past. It's why Hiram's grandfather, now Hiram and Maria, have worked so hard to have the Rosetta Stone brought back to Egypt, only for it to have been stolen by some—"

"... some bastard like me?"

Omar and Ridley turned to face each other. Omar smiled, but it was a smile etched with sadness. He nodded, then said, "Why don't you take a seat, dear Alex. I'll have Bassam bring your friends back up. I think they'll want to hear what I have to say."

After hearing the seismic admission that Omar was, indeed, the man who had masterminded the theft, Kane, Martorana and the others listened on in shock as he told them more. After he'd finished, he looked at them all, one by one. Kane saw the anguish in his eyes.

"Jim, you were right, of course. In summary, it was I who organised the theft of the Rosetta Stone. You are also correct that I'm probably the only person alive who could have done so. Yet, I implore all of you, and Alex, I especially wish you to believe me, when I tell you that by acquiring the Rosetta Stone via that criminal enterprise you speak of, I was only hoping to secure the safety of the artefact for eternity. However, your visit has made me realise the error of my ways. I turned a blind eye to what I suspected of some of those people. It was a... I've made a terrible, terrible mistake."

Omar closed his eyes for a moment, then opened them again and faced Maria Martorana. "I am very sorry to have put you through this, Miss Martorana. To you, Mr. Kane," he said, turning to face him, "I am also very sorry. Now you know the truth. The problem is, I am not yet in possession of the artefact. If I have learned anything about this city and its slimy, slippery inhabitants, I am probably being betrayed at this very moment. I am due to collect the stone at a private hangar in Cairo later this afternoon."

"Why Cairo?" Jim asked.

"A decoy," Omar said, the hint of a smile in his eyes. "To throw scavengers like you off the scent." The smile faded. "I should call my lead contact, let them know I'm on my way, and tell them that everything is going to plan."

"Good idea," agreed Martorana. "May we listen in?"

Omar nodded, then picked up the phone from the vast desk and dialled a number, setting it to loud speaker. It rang only once before being answered.

"Jabari."

"Jabari, this is Omar. I'm calling to let you know I am on my way to Cairo. I will be there on time, as arranged. Is everything in order?"

There followed a long pause.

"Jabari? Are you there?"

"Yes, I am here."

"Is everything okay in Cairo?"

A brief pause, then, "Yes, Omar. All is well."

"Very good then. I will see you this evening." Omar ended the call.

"That didn't sound good," Jim said.

"He seemed hesitant, for sure," Kane agreed.

Omar closed his eyes. "I admit, I fear he senses something isn't right."

"What will he do?" Kane asked.

"I suspect Jabari Hader is only in it for the money. He will not get any more for it from anyone else than he would from me. However, if he were smart, and I believe he is, he'll have a plan B, some other buyer lined up. If he suspects something is amiss, I'm sure he won't waste any time in making contact with those other buyers, while destroying any trail of evidence that might connect him to me."

"Shit! So guys, what do we do?" It was Jim who'd asked. For once he was out of ideas.

"Salam el Halabi," Martorana said. "We need to find Salam. Perhaps there's still a chance he can help us. We have to try. We must."

Ibrahim ducked his head lower.

He was sitting in a car parked a hundred yards along the road from Omar Abdel-Rahman's disgustingly large mansion. He watched as the gates swung open and a shiny black Range Rover sped out onto the road. He ducked lower still as the vehicle approached, but not low enough that he failed to see Omar in the back seat, in conversation with the journalist Jim Burns and the other man, Hiram Kane. There were also two woman, Martorana something, and another.

"Ibn il-'aHba," he muttered. *Son of a whore.* He pulled out his phone and called Jabari.

"Ibrahim. Report."

"Omar just left with Kane and two women. And that mother fucker, Burns."

There was a long pause, then, "I think we can assume the bastard has betrayed us. Ibn il-'aHba!" he said, though he remained calm. "No problem. Follow them, Ibrahim. Report back as soon as you know where they are going."

"Okay, Jabari," Ibrahim replied. Jabari Hader had already hung up.

Chapter Fifty-Six

Cairo International Airport

Jabari paced about the makeshift office in the hangar. He had expected this might happen. It didn't matter. He was ready. He had always doubted the bravery of the fat fucker tycoon, Omar Abdel-Rahman. The man had grown accustomed to always getting what he wanted. He was so rich that he had conjured up the risky plan to steal the Rosetta Stone. Now it seemed he had lost his nerve. It was a blow. There was no one else who could pay the huge sum of money Omar was offering for the Rosetta Stone. The other problem now was that Omar knew the plan. Praise Allah, Omar had created their fucking plan. That meant that if he had betrayed them, which Jabari now felt certain was true, then it wouldn't be long before armed police arrived at the hangar.

They had to leave. And soon.

Salam finally nodded off again, but it was far from a peaceful sleep. He dreamt. In his dreams, everything was going wrong. The plot of his dream was sporadic. It made little sense, one scene merging with another. He saw the faces of his former colleagues, those he'd betrayed. He saw Sophie's eyes, large, open and tearful. She knew about what he'd done. He saw the Rosetta Stone, but it was destroyed after being riddled by bullets from a gun he himself was holding. Scorpions crawled over his face. Somewhere, a snake hissed. Omar was standing over him in his sleep, waiting for him to wake so he could kill him for his failures.

"Salam." No response.

The large, shadowy figure loomed like a giant, blocking out the light. It called down to him like a pharaoh as he lay there shaking from fear and shame at what he had done. Sophie was there too. She held her hand out and offered to help; though as he reached out for her, Jabari sliced down on his wrist with an ancient Egyptian sword and...

Just like before he awoke with a start, and clutched at his wrist, half expecting to feel his hand gone.

"Salam!" Jabari hissed. This time the man grabbed at his wrist to wake him. "Salam, wake up. Change of plan. We have to move. Now."

Salam opened his eyes, immediately angling his gaze to where he was certain his hand used to be. He blinked hard and shook his head. His hand was still there. Shielding his eyes against the harsh glare of the hangar's industrial lights, he looked at his watch. 3:15 pm.

"You've been asleep a long time. We need to go. We roll out in fifteen minutes," Jabari told him, his voice hard. The security man fixed his eyes on Salam for a few extra seconds, then turned and left him there.

Salam swung his legs off the edge of the couch. He was glad the man had turned away. It meant he couldn't see the first tears running down his cheeks.

Chapter Fifty-Seven

Hany Malek, Omar's chief pilot, sat drinking coffee and reading a newspaper in the cabin of the Hawker Jet. With no word from Omar, he didn't expect them to get going for a while yet. Hany smiled as Jabari Hader approached. Hany knew Jabari was Omar's operations man.

Jabari pulled a gun from his waistband in one swift movement and levelled it at Hany. The smile dropped from Hany's face.

"We go now," Jabari said. "Move."

Hany Malek remained seated. He scowled up at Jabari. "What the fuck is going on?"

"You will stand up and get into the cockpit . Then you will take off. Then you will fly me exactly where I tell you to fly me. Understand?"

"You will never get away—"

Hany was too slow. With devastating speed Jabari slammed the pistol into his temple, rendering him almost unconscious. His head lolled to the side. Jabari picked up the cup of coffee and threw the hot liquid into the pilot's face. Luckily it wasn't boiling. Hany spluttered and swore as coffee ran down his crisp white shirt.

"Let me try again," Jabari said, his voice barely above a whisper. "You will get in that fucking plane, and you will fly me to Luxor. Now! Let's move."

Jabari hauled Hany Malek to his feet and ushered him towards the plane, just as the other members of his team appeared from up on the mezzanine.

Had he heard right? Salam wasn't certain. He thought he'd heard Jabari say Luxor. Whether he'd heard correctly or not, he couldn't miss the blood streaming from the right temple of the pilot, staining his white shirt a dark crimson. *What the hell's going on? This isn't part of the plan.* They were supposed to be waiting in Cairo for Omar Abdel-Rahman to show up later that evening. Salam was due to fly back to Alexandria with Omar, the mastermind of the plan. Once there, Salam's final duty was to help the tycoon install the Rosetta Stone into a custom-built display area in his private collection. Then, using his unrivalled expertise, he was to give the man a personal viewing, complete with a history lesson of the priceless—and now infamous—artefact.

Only then would Salam be paid his fee. Then he'd be free to leave, eminently wealthier than he had been before. As he took a seat in the Hawker Jet now, however, he was certain they were well off-script.

Chapter Fifty-Eight

Alexandria

"I'm going to make a call," Kane told Ridley.

A pair of Omar's chauffeur-driven Range Rovers powered through the streets and back towards their hotel. Omar, Martorana and Julian rode in one. Ridley and Kane sat in the back of the other.

Kane dug the phone from his pocket and looked down at it. Whenever he was in trouble, whenever something seemed insurmountable or impossible, there was just one person Kane wanted to talk to. One man who inspired him to keep going, whatever the circumstances. A smile crept onto his face as he selected the landline number of the Kane estate. He tapped 'Call.'

A moment of silence fizzed down the line.

The Range Rover slowed for two labouring trucks to pass each other and then accelerated past. Its thick wheels made quick progress across the dusty highway, dodging over-laden mules, men hauling mud bricks on carts and broken down rust buckets. There was a stark contrast with the other entities on the roads and the two top-of-the-range SUVs whizzing by.

A distant ringing tone started to buzz down the line. Kane clamped it closer to his ear. He imagined the bell on the old handset ringing through the wood-panelled halls of the Kane residence. That rickety old house was his second favourite place on the planet, second only to the Peruvian mountains, which meant so much to both Kane and his grandfather.

The ringing tone sounded ten times and then cut to silence. Kane pulled the phone away from his ear and looked at the screen. 'Call ended' flashed, before being replaced by the picture Kane had taken of them all at the party only days ago. It seemed so long ago now. The smile dropped from Kane's face and something gripped his stomach.

"What's wrong?" Ridley asked, threading her arm beneath Kane's and gripping his hand.

"No answer."

"You know what that man's like… he only comes inside to sleep."

Kane forced a smile and looked through the window. "Yes, you're right," he said as the built-up area gave way for a short time to a stretch of featureless desert. "That's probably it."

Ridley squeezed Kane's hand harder as his sense of disquiet grew.

Chapter Fifty-Nine

Cairo International Airport

Hany heard Jabari and glanced over his shoulder. "Keep an eye on the kid," Jabari demanded of one of his team, making sure Salam saw his gun.

Jabari had hustled them all onto the Hawker Jet, ensuring Salam was seated at the rear of the cabin.

"If he moves, shoot him." Jabari's colleague nodded, then Jabari moved through the cabin and took a seat next to the pilot. Hany didn't want to die today; he decided to be compliant.

"We fly to Luxor," Jabari told him. "Do not test me."

Hany Malek looked to his right, and was met by Jabari's icy stare. Without any doubt, Hany knew the man was a killer. Hany would fly him to Luxor. *Fuck, I'll fly him to the moon if that's what he wants.* Hany had three beloved kids and a wife at home in Alexandria. He at least wanted to see his kids again.

Salam sat frozen in his seat. Things were unravelling. Deep down, he always suspected they would. *Who the hell do I think I am, getting involved in an international criminal group and stealing artefacts, in order to fund an amateur two-bit terrorist group back in Shoreditch?*

Yet, he still believed in the principles of Jihad, at least those he'd been convinced of at the Brick Lane Mosque. His stomach rolled and his head swam with confusion.

He gazed across at the prisoner strapped into the chair opposite him. The old man was stoic. He appeared fearless as he kept his eyes dead ahead, displaying zero emotion. *Why isn't he scared?* Salam wondered. *He bloody well should be.* Salam's chin fell to his chest, his mind swirling with doubts and anguish and fear and regret and a hundred other emotions.

As the Hawker roared down the runway and arced up into the air like an arrow, Salam closed his eyes, now certain he had made the biggest mistake of his life.

Salam jolted awake.

Despite all the turmoil, he'd somehow dropped off to sleep. He glanced wearily at his watch. They'd been in the air just half an hour. It had been long enough for the man who was tasked with watching him to have also fallen asleep too. Salam looked over at the prisoner seated opposite him. He was taken aback when he realised the man was staring right back at him.

Of course, they knew each other. The man's attitude seemed to have shifted. Rather than the stoic, emotionless expression he'd kept affixed on his face since his arrival the day before, now there was something else there, some new emotion. He didn't say anything. Salam sensed in his eyes the man was trying to impart a message to him, some kind of communication. He couldn't speak; he knew people were listening.

Yet, Salam thought he knew what the old man was trying to tell him across the cabin of the Hawker. Salam took a deep breath. He leaned out a little way into the aisle of the jet. No one moved. Most of their small team were either asleep or probably watching porn on their phones. The door to the cockpit was closed. He took his chances.

Salam reached into his pocket and pulled out his own phone. The man across the aisle nodded. The display showed a dozen missed calls. Five from Sophie. The same amount from his boss, Martorana. Two unknown numbers. He checked his inbox. Several messages from Sophie. Three more from his boss. Guilt made his mouth dry.

He clicked on the most recent message from Sophie. It was simple.

: Salam, it isn't too late. Please, tell me where you are! You can tell me, it's okay. Whatever you've done, it's alright.

He leaned back in the seat and closed his eyes again. Then he looked over at the old man, who nodded, almost as if he were reading Salam's mind, telling him, *Go on, kid, send the damn message.*

Salam checked the network signal. He was surprised to see he still had one bar. He began to type…

Chapter Sixty

The Cleopatra Hotel

The twin Range Rovers screeched to a stop outside the hotel. Jim and Martorana leapt from the rear of the leading vehicle, as Omar eased his bulk out as fast as he could. Kane and Ridley emerged from the one behind.

They hustled into the air-conditioned bliss of the foyer and saw Sophie and Julian waiting for them. They all felt on edge. After rounding them all up into his room, Kane sat them down. Martorana explained what was happening and introduced the others to Omar, who took a moment to offer his apologies and confirm his dedication to help them in any way he could.

After a brief coughing fit, Omar added, "It is my belief that the group will no longer come back to Alexandria. If my hunch is right, they'll either stay in Cairo and try to make a deal on the black market there, which I think would be more or less impossible, or…"

"Or what, Omar?" asked Jim. "Come on, old friend…

this is not the time for holding anything back. Tell us your thoughts."

Omar nodded. "Luxor. I can't be sure, but—"

"Shit," Sophie suddenly burst out, surprising them all. "It's Salam." Sophie's eyebrows rose in an arch, suggesting surprise, though her narrow eyes betrayed a hint of disappointment. The smile below really confused them.

Chapter Sixty-One

Abbe Abidi's Apartment, Alexandria

Director Abidi took a last glance at the sun as it finally dipped beyond the horizon. He then stepped through the French doors, closed them to shut off the incessant noise from below, and returned to his study.

Abbe almost always felt a sense of comfort in his study, surrounded by a collection of academic books three decades in the making, several of which he'd authored himself. It was his quiet zone, somewhere to think clearly and forget about what he'd lost since Fatima had passed away. It was his sanctuary. Now all he could think about was what he had done and the irreparable damage he had caused.

Abbe caught a glimpse of himself in a mirror as he stood beside his desk. His dark hair was fading to grey at the sides... *I'm sure I'm greyer than I was this morning*, he thought. It was also thinning rapidly, though that was a trait he'd inherited from his father. His father had been the director of the museum before him, a man famous across Egypt in their particular corner of the academic world.

Abbe's father, Adil Abidi, was a man—*the* man—who'd campaigned vehemently for the Egyptian antiquities department to push for museums around the world to begin repatriating Egypt's lost artefacts. He wouldn't say *lost*. He'd say *stolen*. When he had died a decade ago, he'd left not only a large void in the Abidi family, but large boots to fill at Alexandria International Museum, boots Abbe had been trying his utmost to fill ever since he'd stepped into the role of director. Whether he'd succeeded or not was no longer a question. He had not. Not only that, he had betrayed his father, as well as betraying his country, and his profession. Abbe knew his much-desired legacy was in complete tatters, never to be recovered.

Tonight, Abbe's office didn't feel like a relaxing sanctuary. He slumped heavily into his creaking, ancient leather chair at an equally-antiquated desk and slid open a drawer. He grabbed out a small plastic bottle and snapped off the lid. He threw back two of the painkillers to stave off the pounding headache that had come on suddenly, then threw back two more just to be sure. He washed them down with a deep gulp of freshly poured scotch.

After a long inhale, Abbe closed his eyes and prayed his headache would go away. He also prayed that tonight he wouldn't have another of those God-awful dreams that had been plaguing his nights lately.

Chapter Sixty-Two

Somewhere Over Egypt

Salam's attention was snatched by movement at the front of the cabin. He glanced up in time to see Jabari ease out through the narrow door of the cockpit and move towards him at the rear of the aisle. Salam looked on as Jabari immediately noticed the man who he'd tasked with watching him had fallen asleep. In a lightning-fast movement, Jabari slammed the back of his hand viciously against the sleeping man's cheek, rocking his head against the seat.

"I am... I am sorry, boss. I—"

Jabari pulled a knife from his waistband and in one slick movement raked it across the man's throat, cutting off his words. Jabari stepped back as the man's lifeblood flowed from the gaping gash. He didn't blink as he addressed the others in the cabin.

"This is what happens when people do not do their duty. It does not matter if you work for me or if you are my enemy. I am in control here and you do as I say." He wiped the blood from the knife on the dying man's shirt. He didn't blink once.

The old man strapped into the seat across from Salam had turned his head just enough to see what his captor had done; murder a man in cold blood. It sickened him. He didn't flinch. At least now he knew what these bastards were capable of.

Fuck! Salam knew he had just a matter of seconds to get the text away. Jabari's eyes locked on Salam's. Then the security chief rushed towards him, sensing something was going on. As Salam pressed SEND, he prayed the text message would go through.

Suddenly, the restrained old captive stuck his leg out across the aisle. Jabari slammed into it, stumbling forward just as Salam's screen displayed the word SENT.

Jabari kicked the old man's legs away and scrambled to Salam's seat and snatched the phone from him. Then, in a flash of bulging biceps and snarling teeth, he crashed a fist into Salam's jaw, sending the young Brit to oblivion.

Jabari turned to the old man. In a calm voice, in English, he said, "I could say you will live to regret that. But you will not live. You will surely die. Before you die, I will take something very precious from you. I will make you watch."

Chapter Sixty-Three

Alexandria

"Salam?" Martorana asked. "What the hell did he say?"

They climbed into the vehicles and sped back towards El Borg Arab, where Omar's other jet awaited in the private, exclusive part of the airport.

It was always primed and ready to go anywhere in the world at thirty minutes' notice. So, no sooner had Salam's text message pinged into Sophie's inbox, than Omar had called his pilot and demanded he set an immediate course for Luxor.

"How long's the flight?" Ridley asked.

"On a commercial liner, about six hours I think. On my jet? Two, maybe three?" Omar smiled, but Ridley sensed no joy there. In her opinion, the man displayed genuine remorse. She only hoped she was right.

Of Curses and Kings

The drive from the airport hotel took less than ten minutes, and just half hour after receiving the text from Salam, they were airborne and arrowing directly south towards one of the most archaeologically rich places on the planet.

Kane glanced out of the window. He had been to Luxor before and had always wanted to return. Now that old familiar feeling came to him as he looked down at the green-fringed Nile below, snaking south and providing a lifeline to the millions of people that relied on its life-giving properties to survive.

Why? Why is this happening again? Why are people such bastards?

Chapter Sixty-Four

The Hawker Jet

Jabari descended on Salam like a plague of Egypt.

Salam felt certain he would die. The bridge of his nose cracked. It sounded like snapping a carrot in half. He felt concrete fists pummelling his flesh. His ears screamed as adrenalin pumped through them. Yet, as quickly as it began, it stopped.

For Jabari it was too easy. He found no pleasure in beating the weaker man. He preferred an opponent who fought back, not a cowering mongrel like this British wannabe Jihadist.

Barely conscious, Salam hauled himself against the side of the jet between the seats where he'd crouched beneath Jabari's devastating blows. One eye was swollen shut. His nose was destroyed, and streamed with blood. His ears rang from the adrenalin. Nausea roiled in his guts. Yet, to his great surprise, he was breathing and for now, alive, though he feared he was soon to become the latest object buried beneath Egypt's ancient sands and never, ever to be seen again.

Finally mustering sufficient energy, Salam was able to pull himself back into his seat. Once there, he let his eyes close to await whatever fate Jabari had in store for him when they touched down in Luxor. It was almost over. Salam knew it. He closed his eyes and waited to die.

It was just a couple of hours later when they arrived at Luxor's modest international airport. In a blur of action and swirling dust and barked orders, the group of men—and the Rosetta Stone—were transferred from the Hawker Jet into a series of unmarked cars and vans. Within minutes, the convoy was streaming out of the airport's industrial sector onto the highway. Soon after that they were making their way southwest towards Luxor Bridge. Once across, they then veered northwest towards the world-famous Valleys of the Kings and Queens to, if all went well, make the transaction of a lifetime.

In the rear of the same 4-wheel-drive vehicle as Jabari, Salam sat quietly. Nausea still bubbled away in his stomach and his head pounded from the beating Jabari had inflicted. He was blindfolded, and thankful for it; though the rough cloth pressed callously against his injuries, the blinding Egyptian sun would do nothing for his world-class headache. He was still alive. That was something. He was glad he couldn't see anything. At this point Salam believed that the less he knew about what was happening, the better. He'd once believed that knowledge was power. Not in this case. Not even close. Ignorance was bliss.

If my brother hadn't been so dead set on trying to change things, then he wouldn't be so dead.

Now Salam had made the same mistake.

Up front, Jabari was in hushed conversation with the driver about their destination. "You know the way?" he asked.

The driver turned to him, lips curved in a rueful grin. "I am Egyptian. Of course I know the way. You think I am a stupid dog? Do you?"

Jabari didn't answer. Instead, he quietly turned in his seat and let his gaze settle on Salam in the back. Salam twitched a little. Jabari nodded. "Yes, I know the way. If one does not know the way to Egypt's greatest female pharaoh then one is not Egyptian." He kept his eyes fixed on Salam.

Salam's ears still rang, but not enough that he couldn't hear the conversation in the front. *Greatest female pharaoh?* He fidgeted a bit in his seat.

"As I said, I am Egyptian. A good Egyptian man. All good Egyptian men know of our greatest-ever female. Even dogs like me."

Salam's head inclined a little.

Jabari smiled. "Good. Then we will be there soon."

Greatest-ever female? Female Pharaoh? Salam was confused. He was certain their plan was to go now to the Valley of the Kings on the West Bank. Yet, the location they were just discussing was not in the Valley of the Kings at all. No, the tomb they were speaking of was that of Queen Hatshepsut. They were right; she was Egypt's greatest female pharaoh. Interestingly, although very close to the King's Valley as the crow flies, Hatshepsut's temple complex was in fact not in the King's Valley at all. He had to warn Sophie and the others.

An hour later they arrived at a nondescript stretch of dusty road between some low-rising cliffs and narrow gullies. They hauled Salam out of the vehicle and frogmarched him forward, then abruptly yanked him to a stop. A key grated in a lock and the metallic squeal of a door being pulled open made Salam cringe. Strong hands shoved him forward again. Another yanked his blindfold off. Before he could see anything, the door was slammed and locked. He was left in total darkness.

Chapter Sixty-Five

Salam's heart raced.

Adrenalin buzzed in his temples. His eye was still swollen shut. The agony of his fucked-up nose made his stomach churn and breathing difficult. Yet, for whatever reason, Salam was still alive. Though he doubted the reason was good, he at least felt he had a slim chance to make some amends for what he'd done. While he was alive, he was determined to take that chance. Salam waited a few minutes to let Jabari and the others move away. He let his wheezy breaths slow and his rattled mind settle.

Hatshepsut's temple? I must tell Sophie. Salam knew there was no chance of escaping the cell, or whatever it was he'd been locked inside. There was probably an armed guard outside, and how far they'd travelled into the West Bank, he couldn't know. On a whim, he felt in his trouser pockets for his phone. Nothing.

Just then the cell's lock disengaged with a rusty protest and the door squealed open, flooding the space with dazzling desert sunlight. Salam thrust a hand over his eyes and didn't see Jabari walk in. Jabari grabbed Salam roughly by the arm and hauled him to his feet, then shoved him through the open door. Salam stumbled, expecting to be shot dead at any second. Instead, he heard Jabari laughing.

Then a bucket of water was launched into his face... still in the bucket. It crashed into his nose and sent shockwaves of agony coursing through his nervous system. Now he puked and retched until his ribs felt as if they would break. With his head between his knees, Salam waited for the next inevitable attack. Nothing came. Instead, he was hauled to his feet and marched back into the cell, then forced onto a chair. Slowly, he opened his eyes, keeping a hand in front to shield them from the blinding light. Once he was accustomed to the glare, his eyes settled on his tormentor-in-chief, Jabari Hader.

Salam's heart sank. In Jabari's hands was an item Salam recognised from Egyptian antiquity. Realisation dawned.

"Ah, you recognise this object. That's good. It means you know what it is used for."

Salam puked again. When he recovered, Jabari stepped forward and thrust Salam's phone into his hands.

"You are going to text your friends our location. Do it now!"

"I... I can't... I don't have their numbers."

"You think I'm stupid? I have had your phone for half an hour. Sophie? Maria? Your family members? I now have all their numbers saved in my phone. Many addresses, too. So, text them right now and tell them we are at Queen Hatshepsut's temple."

Salam's mind reeled. He had to warn them not to come here. *Maybe if I—*

"Too fucking slow," Jabari spat. "I've changed my mind. Grab him!"

Two of Jabari's thugs grabbed Salam's arms and pinned him against the cell wall. One of them clutched a handful of hair and yanked his head back, exposing the bloodied nostrils of his shattered nose. Jabari stepped forward, waving the tiny artefact back and forth in front of Salam's face.

Salam knew what it was. The small steel rod, a foot in length and reminiscent of a section of a modern wire coat hanger, had a sharp hook on one end. The item had one use. Excerebration… to pull out the brains of a corpse, fragment by fragment, during the mummification ritual of Egyptian antiquity.

The man holding Salam's hair pulled back tighter as his other arm gripped Salam's shoulder. The second man stepped behind and clutched Salam in a reverse bear hug, rendering him completely immobile. He had no strength left to fight anyway, and his efforts to shake off them were futile.

"I am going to pull out your tiny brain, Salam. Even though I am sure my actions will kill you before I really get started, I will complete the task. Then I will send a section to everyone in your contact list. That is, unless you do exactly what I say. Is that clear?"

Salam blinked. He couldn't nod his head.

"I said, is that clear?"

"Yeah… yes… clear," Salam mumbled, tears streaming down his cheeks and saliva dribbling down his chin.

Jabari glanced at his two men and nodded. They let Salam go. He fell back against the cell wall, but somehow stayed upright. He looked down at his trousers. A dark patch had blossomed around his groin. Jabari and his men chuckled.

Jabari snatched Salam's phone back and located the video camera mode. He raised it and aimed it at Salam.

"You are going to remain calm and say that you are at Hatshepsut's tomb and that your friends should come here now. Do it right, I will let you go. Don't do it… well, I think you know the consequences of that decision by now." Jabari wafted the ancient hooked object close to Salam's face again. Salam jerked his head away. He didn't doubt the sincerity of the man's threat. He nodded.

Jabari hit record.

"I… I am at the temple complex of Queen Ha… Queen Hatshepsut. I am so sorry for what I've done. I was a fool. The Rosetta Stone is here. Come now, before it is gone. I am… I'm so sorry." Salam's eyes streamed with more tears as Jabari stopped the recording. They were not tears of fear, however. They were tears of shame and guilt. He had just been forced to lure his former colleagues into the deadly arms of their psychotic enemy.

"Very good, Salam, very good. Now perhaps we can step outside and look around?"

Shell-shocked, Salam took a few deep breaths and followed Jabari out into the blinding sunlight. The harsh light and searing heat caused his head to feel as if it would explode. Pain and anguish coursed through his entire body.

Slowly his eyes focused and he glanced around. Just as slowly, another terrible moment of clarity dawned on him.

My God, what have I done?

Looking about him, Salam knew where they really were. It was not Hatshepsut's tomb at all. He stared at Jabari, who grinned.

They were in the Valley of the Kings.

Chapter Sixty-Six

Luxor International Airport

Omar Abdel-Rahman's sleek jet—one of them—touched down with a whisper onto the private runway at Luxor International Airport. The flight was short, but a nervous tension had gotten into the joints of those on board. Kane couldn't wait to depart the luxury jet and stretch his limbs. No sooner had they stepped onto the scorched tarmac, however, than Sophie's mobile phone pinged, alerting them of an incoming text. She snatched it from her purse and opened the screen. Kane saw her swallow.

"Maria, Hiram," she called out, her face ashen. "It's a video message from Salam."

The others hustled around her and she played the video on her phone.

"I... I am at the temple complex of Queen Ha... Queen Hatshepsut. I am so sorry for what I've done. I was a fool. The Rosetta Stone is here. Come now, before it is gone. I am... I'm so sorry."

Kane inhaled, as the rest of the ARC team flew into action.

Omar immediately barked orders into his mobile phone, and within minutes a fleet of jet-black SUVs thundered towards them from somewhere in the airport. Kane listened in as Omar then instructed someone apparently important to have Queen Hatshepsut's tomb cleared of any visitors currently there. If Kane hadn't already realised it, the man wielded significant power here in Egypt. Just how much power exactly he wasn't sure he wanted to know. Yet, he felt certain that before this was over they were all going to find out.

Within five minutes of touching down in Luxor they were speeding at a hair-raising pace along the narrow, dusty streets of Luxor towards the Nile, where they'd cross to the West Bank on a direct heading to the mortuary complex of one of Egypt's most important queens. They had to dodge malnourished mules dragging wagons loaded with too many bricks. They swerved past kids wobbling around on rusting bicycles. Old women toting baskets of fruit and veg struggled beneath the weight. Camels hobbled around after too many years' service under ten-thousand ferocious suns. Most common of all were the hawkers selling 'genuine' relics from Egyptian antiquity, relics that likely just came off the trundling production line in the hidden backstreet factories.

In their haste, no one saw the unmarked transit van following at a discreet distance.

Less than thirty minutes later—it should have taken sixty—the convoy of SUVs skidded to a halt at the distant entrance to the magnificent tomb of Egypt's greatest female pharaoh—many scholars would argue *greatest*, period— Queen Hatshepsut. It seemed as if Omar's calls ahead had done the trick; there were no tourists anywhere to be seen. *Influence indeed,* Kane thought as he trotted alongside Ridley, Martorana and the others towards what truly was an architectural wonder of the ancient world. Built directly into the towering cliffs behind it, the megalithic, three-tiered mortuary complex, also known as *Djeser-Djeseru*, or the *Holy of Holies*, loomed before them as they traversed the wide, two-hundred-yard flag-stoned approach.

Omar ushered the others ahead, with a couple of his trusted security guys for support. Once they'd arrived at the top of the main entrance steps—Kane, Ridley, Martorana, Sophie, Julian, Jim and the security men—they split into pairs and began making their way cautiously into the shadows of the massive colonnaded tiers. Kane wished he had time to explore and that he were there under differing circumstances. He'd been before, yet it was many years ago and he was being reminded now just how inspiring the structures of the ancient Egyptians truly were. He made a mental note to return with Ridley. He paused as an unbidden sense of foreboding flooded through him, prickling his senses.

If we survive this…

After ten minutes of frantic searching, delving as far as they could physically get into the tomb complex, Kane realised they weren't going to find what they were after. There was no sign of Salam. Nor was there any sign of the Rosetta Stone. The only good news was that they weren't surrounded by gun-toting bad guys. Yet…

"What the hell's going on?" Martorana barked at Sophie once they'd congregated out on the main front terrace to the complex.

Sophie shrugged weakly, her heart thumping. She held out the phone to show Martorana Salam's text.

"Well, it seems as if your boyfriend has played you for a fool, doesn't it?" Martorana said, her voice matronly. It wasn't a question.

Ridley stepped close and put her arm around Sophie's slumped shoulders. "So, what now?" Ridley asked. "Where the hell is it? Where is anyone?"

"We've been set up," Kane declared. "That doesn't mean the stone isn't close. Omar had it confirmed by a friend that the jet with the Rosetta Stone definitely landed here in Luxor within the last couple of hours. It's a big town. But it's here somewhere, here on the West Bank. I know it. I can feel it."

Kane paced the stones, the sun beating down and making his shirt stick to his back. "Where the hell are you?" he muttered.

Kane was suffering. He had done everything he could to make sure nothing like this could happen. They'd spent months organising the security and the logistics, and although it had been a team effort, the buck, he knew, stopped with him. He had to get the stone back. It was a priceless artefact, one of the most important ever found. On top of that, his reputation was on the line. Worse still, so was the reputation of his grandfather, the man who had fought tirelessly for decades to make the return of the Rosetta Stone a reality.

Now it was gone. Kane was going to do everything and anything in his power to—

A series of deafening cracks resounded off the stones and they threw themselves to the ground as an automatic rifle unleashed hell.

Chapter Sixty-Seven

The Mortuary Temple Complex of Queen Hatshepsut

Kane threw himself in front of Ridley. Bullets pounded through the air. Stone obliterated. He pulled her down behind one of the giant columns as rounds from the semi-automatic rifles pummelled the ancient stone above their heads. Fragments shattered and splintered all around them. A hail of granite and marble rained down. Several razor-edged fragments pierced Kane's face and neck. Ridley suffered a few grazes to her exposed arms.

"Jesus!" Kane yelled. "Who the fuck are they?"

"Just stay down," Ridley warned.

A second hail of fire sprayed the colonnade. Kane's eyes darted left in time to witness someone succumb. Their silhouetted form crashed face down onto the stone floor. Kane couldn't make out who it was. He knew it wasn't one of Omar's security men. Which meant…

"No… oh, no, no…"

Omar's men returned fire. The howl of their guns grew even louder. The two gunmen fled for cover.

Kane risked a glance to his right. Martorana crouched low with Julian. They were okay.

Martorana spotted Kane and flashed a stoic glare, as if to say, *It'll take more than a few big guns to scare me.*

Kane looked back the other way. He saw no one else. His heart skipped a beat. *Where's Sophie?*

Omar's security guys stepped out of the shadows of the columns. They advanced on their assailants, their weapons raised out front. They peppered the stone balustrades the men had ducked behind.

Kane seized his moment. He stood up and pressed his back flat against the rear side of his protective column. His eyes flitted about the shadowy colonnade searching for Sophie. He saw nothing. He would have to take his chances to go and search for her. He was about to push off when a blur of movement stopped him in his tracks. Ridley flew from her position and sprinted across the stone expanse between the first row of columns and the next.

"Bollocks." He set off at a sprint after his love. A fresh wave of enemy fire threatened to mow them down like ducks in a range.

Kane and Ridley flattened themselves tight against the gigantic column that towered skyward to support the vast carved ceiling of the megalithic mortuary complex. Bullets pummelled the ancient stones to dust.

"You go left!" Ridley yelled, taking control. "I'll look right. Keep your head down. Ready?"

Kane nodded. "Ready."

"Okay, on three." Kane nodded again.

Ridley offered the merest hint of a grin. "Three," she

hissed and powered off like the supreme athlete she was. She dodged left and right. A trail of bullets tore up the flagstones behind her in a maelstrom of dust and shattered stone.

Kane sprinted in the opposite direction, arms and powerful legs pumping fast enough that the incoming fire couldn't trouble him. In a flash, he'd reached the column behind which Martorana and Julian crouched. He saw immediately who had fallen. After a deep breath, he said, "Have you seen Sophie? Where is she?"

"No. No idea. She must've made it back inside."

Kane nodded. "Sit tight here. Omar's men will keep those gunmen contained. I'll search for Sophie. You keep him safe," he added, nodding at Julian, whose tanned face had paled significantly in the last few minutes.

"Be careful," was all Martorana said as Kane darted off along the colonnade.

Sophie's teeth clenched together so hard she realised she hadn't breathed in far too long. She opened her mouth and sucked in a series of rapid breaths, simultaneously wiping tears from her eyes. She hadn't looked down at her leg yet. Hadn't dared. Her heart pounded and her ears rang. She tried to find the courage to appraise her injuries.

Surprisingly, she couldn't feel any pain. That scared her the most. She supposed she was in shock. It would hurt soon enough.

She glanced around her, letting her gaze drift towards the ceiling. Although she had studied the hieroglyphics of the ancient Egyptians extensively, the ceiling was too high for her to make out any individual carvings. She knew she was in a queen's tomb, one of the most powerful women who had ever lived.

Well, she thought with a heavy dose of irony, *if this is to be where I die, there will have never been a more inappropriate place.* Tears of shame caused a fresh round of streaks down both cheeks. She finally let her gaze drift down to her leg. Then she rolled over and vomited on the marble floor.

Protruding through the skin of her leg was a gnarly stump of lower shin bone, blood and flesh glistening on its end. The upper half dangled by sinewy threads, dripping blood and appearing as though it were about to drop off entirely. She didn't look back at it. She didn't need to. Sophie knew her leg was beyond repair, and if she were to survive, she would lose it.

Only now did she scream.

Chapter Sixty-Eight

Darkness stripped Kane of his sight as he entered the gloomy tomb. He willed his eyes to adjust from the searing bright light outside. He stumbled further forward as gunfire echoed through the cavernous space.

He closed his eyes for long seconds, giving them time to adjust. Another burst of gunfire rattled through the air. Kane tried not to think of the thousands of years of history being torn apart by a group of mindless thieves.

He opened his eyes and dark shapes materialised in his vision. He moved further into the entrance hall of the Queen's tomb complex.

That's when he saw Sophie, slumped behind a column. She'd managed to scamper inside to escape the worst of the incoming fire. So he thought.

"Sophie!" he shouted, closing the distance in seconds.

She didn't respond. He was wrong. Sophie hadn't escaped the gunfire at all.

Sophie's left shin bone was shattered. The lower part of the tibia stuck out and ended at a sharp point.

"Sophie?" he said. "Sophie, can you hear me?" She couldn't. She'd passed out from pain and shock. That was a blessing. Kane fell still and listened. The gunfire had stopped and things outside had fallen silent. He hoped Omar's men had taken the upper hand. It didn't matter. He had to get Sophie out of there and to a hospital. He eased his strong arms beneath Sophie's shoulders and sat her upright.

"Salam," Sophie whispered softly. "Stop it. Leave me alone. I don't—"

Kane ignored her soft whimpers. With one knee planted on the ground he eased his arms beneath her body and lifted her from the blood-soiled floor.

Kane took a deep breath. Memories of previous incidents flashed through his mind. This was exactly the sort of thing he shouldn't be doing anymore. Exactly what he was trying to avoid.

Maybe what his grandfather used to say was right: "It's the adventurous life that chooses us, not the other way around."

Kane winced at the memory, then hauled Sophie higher and headed for the entrance.

He emerged into the bright beyond. Ridley appeared and helped share the burden of carrying Sophie.

"Shit, she's shot..." Martorana stated as she trotted over. "Damn it."

"What's the status out here?" Kane asked.

"Two gunmen, both down. Omar's men took care of them. One of them is down too. But it's over. Jim is..."

"I know," Kane told her. "Poor bastard. Listen, we must get Sophie taken care of, then we have to get moving. We can't risk the stone leaving Luxor."

"No, we can't!" Martorana declared. Fire raged in her

eyes and fierce determination strained her face. Kane felt a new wave of urgency take over.

"Julian," he said, "I'm sorry about Jim. I know you guys were close. Could you do him the honour of helping carry his body back to the vehicles?"

Julian nodded absently. Omar's man stepped forward and took Jim's shoulders. "Grab his feet," he said, taking control. "I'll come back for my man later." Slowly, Julian did as he was instructed. With some difficulty, he managed to lift the feet and legs of his friend and mentor.

Martorana ran ahead to speak with a shell-shocked Omar.

"I'm... I am..." Seldom lost for words, Onar was struggling now. "I'll... I will arrange for her... for her to be taken to Luxor's best private... my hospital. It won't cost you anything. It's the... I'm sorry. It is the least—" Omar's words deserted him.

"Listen, she'll be okay," Kane told him. "Sorry about your man. If we didn't already know it, we're into some very serious shit. The question is, what the hell do we do now?"

Chapter Sixty-Nine

Julian plucked his mobile from his pocket and placed a call. He was struggling to think straight after the shock of having to carry Jim's dead body. Jim had been a respected colleague and a mentor. Most of all, a friend.

Julian looked down at the phone in his hands. His dust-caked face reflected in the glass. *If these callous bastards get away with this, Jim's death will be for nothing.* There was no way Julian would let that happen.

He selected a number and pressed 'Call'. Then he stepped a few yards away from the others, far enough that they couldn't overhear his brief conversation.

He noticed Kane and Martorana glanced at him warily. He understood. There had been enough surprises today that no one knew who to trust. Julian walked across to them and switched his phone to speaker. "Tell them what you told me," he said aloud.

"My guess is Kings' Valley," the man said, his gruff voice enunciating the words with his limited English. "Many secret tunnels. Maybe ISIS, maybe no. Secret base. Many tourists. No problem."

Julian looked around the group and saw shock etched into each of their expressions. Martorana spoke first.

"Is he saying that terrorists have a secret hideout in the Valley of the Kings? One of the most heavily touristed locations in Egypt? Impossible!"

"Yes, that's what he's saying," Julian confirmed.

"Hiding in plain sight," Kane said flatly.

"It's true there are hundreds of as-yet undiscovered and unexplored tunnel networks linking various tomb complexes. Maybe even thousands," Martorana conceded. "How the hell did these guys find them? Moreover, why haven't the bastards been discovered?"

Omar stepped quietly in front of them and studied the group, a solemn expression on his huge, ruddy face. Sweat glistened in the folds of his neck. His jacket was streaked with dust. He inhaled deeply, then addressed them, his voice grave. "I fear he is right, whoever he is?" He glanced at Julian.

"Local contact," Julian offered, unwilling to divulge anything more.

Omar nodded. "Well, I believe he's correct. There have long been rumours that *Daesh* had taken up a kind of residence in some of the lesser-known tunnel systems beneath the Valley of the Kings. Honestly, it wouldn't be that difficult. Since the Arab Spring a few years ago, tourist numbers in the region have declined at an alarming rate. Archaeological teams have also been more reluctant to dig in the Valleys of the Kings and Queens. Government funding has almost entirely dried up. A few sporadic private digs are still active, but more recently away from the valleys, often down at Abu Simbal or at the Saqqara Necropolis south of Cairo.

For several years now the Valley of the Kings has been like, pardon the pun, a kind of tombland." No one laughed. Omar looked at his feet.

"How do terrorists know how to negotiate the subterranean world?" Ridley asked. It was a solid question.

Julian shrugged as Kane seemed to ponder, then answered. "Think about it," Kane said, "no archaeological digs means what? No digging. Maria, you know as well as I do that digging those sites is a specialised skill passed down through generations. Therefore, whole families of diggers have found themselves without work for too long. The people are hungry. No tourists, no digs… it wouldn't take much for a family of hungry diggers and tunnellers to be persuaded to help these guys." He glanced at Omar. The big man nodded.

"It is unproven," Omar said, "but I believe it is likely true." He cleared his throat, then dabbed his lips with his handkerchief and quickly stuffed it out of sight. Julian suspected the man knew more than he was prepared to let on, at least for now. "I have to admit," Omar added, "I myself have considered capitalising on the misfortune of those digging families you mentioned. There was an opportunity there to make some remarkable discoveries while the world's attention was elsewhere, but—"

"But you didn't?" Ridley asked, eyebrows arched.

Omar's gaze settled on Ridley's and held what Julian realised was an accusatory gaze. Omar looked down. "No, I didn't," he said quietly. He then looked up again and said, "No, on my life, I did not. I am sure someone else has. Life is cheap sometimes… if someone, or some group or other, wanted to, they could potentially have claimed the entire Valley of the Kings network from the authorities. No one would have even known."

Chapter Seventy

Valley of the Kings

Alarms rang throughout the network of tunnels and tombs of the Valley of the Kings. Tourists were hustled back out into the bright Egyptian sunlight, complaining to security guards who didn't listen. Although the frustrated visitors didn't know it, it was for their own safety.

Two miles away, Kane and the others watched as Omar ended his call. The call had just resulted in the famous tourist attractions being cleared of all people.

Again, Omar had demonstrated just how well-connected he truly was. Kane began to get a sense that there was more to the huge man than even Omar himself had confessed.

Omar and his remaining security guy, plus Kane, Ridley, Martorana and Julian jumped into the two Range Rovers and sped east and slightly north to the entrance of the Kings' Valley.

As Kane watched the tourist buses rumble away in the

opposite direction he couldn't help but mull over what was wrong. Something just wasn't sitting well and he couldn't shake the feeling something bad was going to happen. Either in spite of Omar, or because of him.

The Range Rovers screeched to a stop in the main car park of the Valley of the Kings. A hundred disgruntled tourists were being herded onto another pair of buses. Tour guides tried placating them with offers of returning tomorrow as the bus doors juddered shut. Then, in a swirling cloud of dust, the buses headed back to the East Bank hotels, leaving the car park deserted.

Kane stepped out of the SUV and watched several stray dogs scavenging around a pile of discarded food cartons.

The remaining members of the ARC team clambered out of the mercifully air-conditioned vehicles and huddled around Omar and his man. Kane assessed the security guard. He was a slight yet angry-looking fellow with a jaw so hard and square it might have been carved out of stone from the Valley of the Kings itself. *Easy to look tough with a semi-automatic weapon slung over a shoulder,* thought Kane, though he got the sense the man would be hard enough without it. The security operative had hardly flinched when his comrade had been gunned down. *Omar must be paying him well,* Kane surmised. He turned to the over-sized art collector.

"So, where do we start?" he asked.

Julian answered first. "Listen, no one can be certain..." He paused, seemingly unsure whether to share what his contact had told him. Kane understood the reporter didn't want any more blood on his hands.

"Go on, Julian, it's important," Kane prompted.

"Get on with it," Martorana demanded.

Julian inhaled. "My guy says that the as-yet undiscovered tomb of Ramses the Eighth is a possible—"

Omar erupted in a snorting laugh that soon developed into a near-choke. He looked as if he were about to have a heart attack. Ridley raced over and placed a hand on his back.

"You okay?" she asked.

Omar plucked a kerchief from his breast pocket and, recovering, dabbed at his lips, then wiped his eyes. "Damn dry climate here," he muttered. "I'm fine, thank you dear. Ramses the Eighth, hey? Not a chance. If that undiscovered tomb has indeed been discovered, I for one would know about it."

Kane noticed the blood splats on the hanky.

Julian shrugged. "That's just what my contact told me."

"Who is this contact again?" Omar looked sceptical, as if he didn't want anyone to believe there was something about Egypt he didn't know.

"Listen, I won't say who it is, but I think you should take his word seriously. He, uh… he knows things."

Omar remained silent. Kane pushed Julian for more.

"He says that a private archaeological team, more or less the same team that was led by Otto Schaden in 2005 and that discovered the tomb of Ramses the Third… well, rumour has it that some of these people have gone rogue. Supposedly, they've discovered the tomb of Ramses the Eighth, the last true Ramesside pharaoh's tomb. Apparently, they're working under new, shall we say, management. Like I said, it's just a rumour."

Omar seemed to consider what Julian had said.

Martorana said, "Omar? Could it be true?"

Omar's head tilted a little, as if the weight of it all was becoming too much. Kane assumed the heat was beginning to wilt them all. Omar raised a meaty hand and grabbed his even-meatier chin, the folds of it spilling over his fingers.

Kane swatted at a fly which didn't get the hint and landed in his ear, watching as Martorana placed her hands on her hips and narrowed her eyes. She glared at Omar with such intensity that if he hadn't been leaning on the SUV, Kane thought he might very well have recoiled.

"Well?" she pressed. "Answer the fucking question."

Omar inhaled, then let it out. The sound was like a car tire deflating. "Yes, I suppose it's possible."

Chapter Seventy-One

"There's nothing else for it," Kane declared. "I'm going in."

Ridley stood next to him, nodding, her face set in grim determination.

"You can't," Julian said. "Hiram, look... I know I've only just met you and I'm sure you're capable. These guys... well, they are not to be messed with. I say we call the authorities and—"

"Total waste of time," Omar chimed in with finality. "The only possible way they could have pulled off what your, um, contact, suggested, is if they had bribed the authorities. Apparently, they offered a bigger bribe than I did. I agree that you shouldn't go in," he added, looking at Kane and Ridley. "On the other hand, there won't be any authorities coming to assist... Take a look around."

They did. They were on their own. The pack of dogs continued scattering rubbish across the car park.

"I'm with Hiram," Martorana told them. "As operations manager, and although this is now strictly unofficial, I have to insist it's just Hiram and myself. Alex, I appreciate your offer. This is too dangerous for a civilian. Julian, you too. You both stay here and—"

"Forget it," Ridley said, her eyes fixed on Martorana's. "I'm here and I'm going to help." Kane watched their eyes meet and was sure both women saw in the other the same unwavering intensity. Kane saw two brave women who would not suffer fools and who would do whatever it took to get back the artefact.

Martorana nodded. Kane suspected her confidence had been dented a little when she'd learned of Salam's betrayal and all that had happened. Yet, her shoulders remained up and as she inhaled and exhaled, eyes narrowing, Kane had no doubt whatsoever she'd still be a formidable ally.

"So be it," she said. "Julian, you stay here with Omar. Omar, do what you can to get some assistance out here. You've talked a good game until now. Show us your true worth."

Julian nodded. He seemed glad to cede to Martorana's commands. Kane didn't blame him. As much as he surely liked a good story, he shouldn't have to die for it.

Omar stepped closer to Kane and Matorana. "I agree I would serve no purpose venturing any further. I'm the wrong side of sixty, with almost four decades of high-living literally under my belt." He patted his significant midriff without smiling. "My days of exploring tombs are over. I can do more good from here, with my phone and my knowledge of the area. I'll start right now." Omar stepped away and started making calls.

"They're probably waiting for you," Julian said to Kane and the others. "With guns. If it's who I think it is, these guys are notorious. We know they're armed, and won't hesitate to kill you if you get in the way of their plans. Be careful."

Kane nodded, then turned to Martorana and Ridley. "Listen, Julian's right. Much as we want to get the Rosetta Stone back, we shouldn't risk our lives to succeed."

Martorana looked in earnest at Kane, as did Ridley. He understand they both knew he'd just lied to them. They would all three of them do exactly that—do everything in their power to see justice served, including putting their lives on the line.

"Sure thing, Hiram," Martorana said, the barest hint of a wry grin curving her full lips. "So, what do you say? You two up for a little tomb raiding?"

Chapter Seventy-Two

Martorana led Kane and Ridley towards the north end of the deserted visitor car park. A gust of hot wind whipped across the concrete, twisting the torn food cartons into a spiral then scattering them around.

Kane watched her trotting ahead. He tried to ignore the fact they were going up against heavily armed men when they had nothing more than torches.

She led them into the shadows of the low cliffs that lined the trail. Kane suspected that whoever had the stone, or whoever they might encounter, were probably already aware of their presence in the King's Valley. So far, they seemed to be one step ahead and would likely have spotters stationed along the route. Yet Kane knew they had no choice. Martorana had employed him to to conduct a successful hand-over of the artefact to the Egyptians. They had executed a flawless mission, too, until things had gone tits up. They couldn't have predicted that. There was no way they could have envisioned a theft on that scale. Despite what their boss, Neil McGregor, had told Matorana, Kane knew they had to do what they could to right the wrongs they'd suffered. Kane knew Martorana felt the same way.

They raced past the now-closed entrance to the tomb of Ramses II on their left, and the tomb of the sons of Ramses II on their right. Next, they passed the tombs of Ramses IV and VII to the left. It meant they were getting close to the alleged site of Ramses VIII. What they'd find when they got there, Kane couldn't know. He was certain it wouldn't be a friendly welcoming committee.

"Wait, it's very likely these guys know we're coming," Kane said, slowing to a walk. "I'm not sure who they are or what their ulterior motive is. My guess is that one group has the stone and wants to sell it. If the other group buying it are terrorists, who knows what they want with it, other than perhaps a statement of power. Maybe they'll want to sell it on again for even more profit to fund their organisation. We can't know. What we do know is that they've allowed us to get this far. They want us to go in to the complex after them, which to me can only mean one thing…"

"What?" Ridley asked. "What the hell do they want?"

Kane exhaled. "They want to kidnap us for ransom."

Martorana nodded. "I think you're right. I don't see any other reason why they'd want us to go after them."

Ridley shook her head. "Our government doesn't negotiate with kidnappers… especially terrorists."

"True," Kane agreed. "I assume they know my family has money. I think it's me they want. I know I'm wasting my time asking this, but I'll ask anyway. Stay behind. Let me go in alone."

Ridley grinned and pinched Kane's cheek. "You're very sweet," she said in the girliest fake voice she could muster. "As usual, you're also right… you're wasting your time."

"I think you and I could be good friends, Alex,"

Martorana said, grinning. "Yep, complete waste of time. Let's go," she added, winking at Kane.

They moved further north up the dusty valley. The tarmac road built for tourists deteriorated into a rough track of rubble and dust. This area was only known to the archaeological team permitted to dig here. If it weren't for the situation, Kane would have felt the thrill of the moment. He was a trained archaeologist. Martorana too. This was what they'd trained to do, yet the stakes were higher now.

Kane stopped dead in his tracks; he spotted several vehicles parked haphazardly at the base of a low cliff, perhaps thirty-feet high. The sun hadn't reached here and the air was mercifully cooler. Kane was drenched in sweat from the hike up the valley.

"Get out of sight," he hissed, beckoning the others against a nearby rock wall. "I can't see anyone."

"I guess this is the entrance," Martorana said, ducking beneath Kane's arm and striding with caution towards a narrow crevice between two natural sandstone formations.

She paused, her eyes wide. She held up a hand to stop Kane and Ridley. "Sshhh… someone's been here," she whispered. "Cigarette smoke. Very recent. We're not alone."

Chapter Seventy-Three

Kane stood still and sniffed. Cigarette smoke lingered in the hot, still air of the valley. Someone had been here just minutes ago.

"Let's go," he whispered. "Carefully."

They stepped quietly between the vehicles, two top of the range SUVs next to three old battered Fiats.

"This is the place," Kane muttered, catching sight of his reflection in one of the 4 x 4's tinted windows.

He led them into the shadowy recess of the entrance. Kane looked around and noticed that it was actually a well-supported structure, reminiscent of many he'd seen before. Professionally done. Apparently well-funded. These guys knew what they were doing.

Martorana snapped on her torch and led them further into the tunnel. A finger of light swept through the gloom. Kane turned on his torch, helping his eyes became accustomed to the darkness. The tunnel was neat and well-organised. Electrical cables ran down one side. Tire tracks worn into the floor. This was a serious operation.

Of Curses and Kings

Kane wondered who these people were. There'd been mention of terrorists. Yet, there'd also been talk of legitimate archaeologists. If so, why had they gone rogue? How had they been corrupted? *Or,* Kane pondered, *were they working under duress?* Had the archaeologists themselves been kidnapped by nefarious forces? That wasn't good either. Nevertheless, he hoped it were the latter. He'd had enough drama with terrorists and other criminals in recent years to last several lifetimes. It's why he'd retired from the exploration game and taken this gig.

He almost laughed at the irony of it all. Almost. Yet, once again Kane found himself in a situation he couldn't ever have imagined. *Join the Artefact Repatriation Committee team,* they said. *It'll be easy and safe,* they said. *For fuck's sake.*

He recalled a line from the Indiana Jones movies, the leitmotif running throughout the series. "Snakes? Why does it always have to be snakes?" Dr Jones said often. *Well,* Kane thought as they crept onwards through the dark tunnel, only their torches lighting the way, *Terrorists? Why does it always have to be terrorists?*

They walked another thirty yards along the narrow passage. To Kane's expert eye, this looked like a new project. As yet none of the archetypal hieroglyphics had been revealed along the surfaces of the excavation. The walls and ceiling of the tunnel, originally constructed over three-thousand years ago, narrowed, seeming to close in on them. Kane knew it was just a figment of the imagination; it was a common phenomenon for people who spent a long time underground. An innate human fear of enclosed spaces and of being buried alive caused it. Though Kane himself wasn't claustrophobic, he'd be glad to get back outside.

"Stop," Maria hissed, her feet slipping on the sandy floor of the tunnel. "Smoke."

Kane smelled it too. He listened, but heard nothing.

They weren't alone. Someone was watching.

Chapter Seventy-Four

Salam sprawled on the floor against the wall of his cell, wishing he were anywhere else but here.

Shame weighed heavily. He'd never felt so useless. He still didn't think he would survive the day. He also didn't really understand why he was still alive. Salam knew only that if he did somehow manage to live through this, he would never forgive himself for what he'd done. Worse than that, nor would Sophie. He loved Sophie, at least in his own way, though he'd never told her. Salam thought she knew it, but she hadn't pushed him to confirm it to her. Further, he hadn't been brave enough to declare it. He was Muslim, and he had been afraid of what his Muslim family and friends would say.

What the fuck was I thinking?

Salam stood on shaky legs and walked to the door of the cell. He knew it was locked, but he had to try it anyway. *If I could just get out of here, maybe I can help.* Perhaps he could make right the things he'd done wrong. How, he couldn't know. He had no idea where Jabari had actually taken the stone. Even if he did, what could Salam do about it anyway? If he interfered, they'd kill him and bury him in the desert. No one would ever know. His death would be as pointless as his brother's had been.

Salam slumped further to the ground. No one would even miss him.

Still… I have to try.

He grabbed the handle of the cell door and pulled. Locked, as he knew it would be. He pulled again.

"Hey, stop that," yelled someone in Arabic outside the door. Though Salam couldn't see anything beyond his four-walled prison, he sensed it was just a boy stationed outside. He yanked hard on the door again to elicit more words.

"Hey, stop it."

Definitely a kid, Salam thought as an idea began to form.

Chapter Seventy-Five

Kane's pulse hammered in his ears and the dry taste of danger clawed at his throat as he hustled along the passage ahead of Ridley and Martorana. When he was a few paces ahead of them, he glanced over his shoulder. There was a good distance between them; enough distance that if anything happened to him, they could get back out of the tunnel before it was too late.

Kane was convinced the bad guys' plan was to capture them for ransom. They were no good to anyone dead, though his mortality was something he could accept. Of course, he might be wrong, yet Kane always took positive action.

He had often found himself in frightening situations in the past. Equally as often, he had asked himself, *What's the worst that could happen?* Well, other than being gunned down, blown up, tortured and buried in a ready-made tomb, the worst that could happen was failing to retrieve the Rosetta Stone and thus failing in his mission. Kane supposed that was pretty bad.

"Stop!" Ridley hissed, and something in her tone made Kane pause his onward march.

"What is it?" Maria whispered.

"You hear that?" Ridley asked.

They fell silent and strained to listen in the gloom. Their torches cast dancing shapes along the dusty walls and ceiling.

Kane knew all three of them had seen their fair share of tombs and tunnels during their various careers. Martorana would've spent thousands of hours in subterranean complexes, both as a student and in her later role working for the British Museum. He knew Ridley had too. Yet, something felt different about this passage. Very different. Glancing at his companions, they felt it too.

Kane recognised the signs of an ancient tunnel. It had been carved into the very bedrock of Egypt thousands of years ago. He wasn't superstitious and didn't choose to believe in such nonsense as ghosts. Yet there was definitely some kind of malignant energy in the air that made the hairs on the back of his neck stand on end.

"Is it... is that a breeze?" Ridley asked, her voice sounding loud and sinister in the enclosed space. The air was still and silent now they'd paused to listen.

Sweat dribbled down Kane's back and sent a chill in the opposite direction. "I don't hear anything," he whispered. His gaze flicked about the floor and walls.

Something moved. A brief flash of motion from the corner of his eye. Kane spun to face whatever it was and dropped instinctively into his fighting stance.

He saw nothing. Was his mind playing tricks on him? He shook his head, then dabbed sweat from his eyes.

Damn it's hot in here, he thought, yet shivered at the same time.

Kane set off again, leading them further into the tunnel complex. At any moment he expected the tunnel to end, but it kept going.

Kane knew that a standard pharaonic tomb didn't usually go this far, this deep into the ground. This was either something no one other than the team who'd discovered it, and now themselves, had seen before, or, it was a recently excavated tunnel and nothing to do with Ramses VIII. Either way, Kane knew they'd already travelled at least a hundred yards beneath the cliffs. Whatever they were going to find—or whoever was going to find them—it would happen soon. Kane's senses heightened at the exact moment the snake bit his neck.

Chapter Seventy-Six

Salam yanked hard on the door once more, then stepped back. He heard muttering outside and a jangling of keys. His plan had to work. His life likely depended on it. He hustled against the front wall of the cell and stood to the left of the door. If his instincts were correct, the youngster would step inside and before he realised what was happening, Salam would seize his moment.

"I said be quiet," the boy said, turning the key in the lock. "I will show you that you should listen to what I say."

The key turned. The door creaked open a little. The barrel of a rifle appeared through the opening, followed by its bearer. To Salam's good fortune, the kid—he was no more than seventeen or eighteen—looked to his right first as human nature decreed. Sam had counted on this random slice of knowledge. It was the opportunity he needed.

He reacted in a flash and pushed the kid hard into the corner. The boy stumbled, dropping his rifle. Salam followed up with a solid kick to the small of the back. The boy fell forward onto his face. Salam grabbed up the rifle, clutched it by the barrel and slammed the stock of it squarely into the boy's chin. Bone crunched beneath the blow. The kid's lights went well and truly out.

"Fuck," Salam hissed, his heart pounding like a pneumatic drill.

Salam closed the door behind the boy and set to work. He slid off the kid's kaftan. Next, he pulled off his own belt and tied the boy's hands behind his back. He ripped a strip of material from the kaftan and stuffed a large wad into the boy's gaping, bleeding mouth. He tied anther strip around the boy's head to secure the gag.

Next Salam pulled off his jeans and shirt and slipped the kaftan over his shoulders. He and the kid weren't dissimilar in appearance. From a distance, Salam hoped it would be difficult to tell them apart. With a final check to make sure the boy wasn't in any danger of dying—he was breathing deeply and slowly, and was in no grave state—Salam sat him upright against the cell wall, snatched up the keys and the rifle, then poked his head out the door.

Inhaling, he locked it behind him and walked away from the cell.

Chapter Seventy-Seven

Kane reeled as the snake clamped hold of his neck.

He didn't feel any pain. He stumbled against the passage wall, trying to clutch hold of the wildly thrashing serpent.

"Hold still," Martorana barked, taking control of the situation and shoving Kane hard against the wall.

"What species?" Kane knew some snakes were deadly in this region of Africa. He hoped this one wasn't.

"Don't know, but it's got horns."

"Fuck!"

"Alex, grab its tail," Martorana commanded.

Ridley ducked around her and, with caution, approached the snake's dangling rear end, perhaps three feet in length. It was already difficult enough. Factor in the darkness and the confines of the tunnel, it was almost impossible.

Kane's left arm suddenly shot back and pinned the reptile's body against the wall, just below its head. The rest of the body thrashed even more. Ridley managed to grab the tail and pull it taught.

Martorana yanked a folding knife from her pocked and flicked open the blade. Kane saw only a flash of light on metal against the writhing, shining skin of the reptile as she sliced downwards with the blade. The sharp edge slashed through the air and dug deep into the creature's flesh. It passed clean through the snake's body, liberating it from its head. The set of venomous snake fangs remained in Kane's neck, the creature's head still attached.

The long body writhed and juddered in Ridley's hands. She threw it to the floor. It dropped with a thud. Kane watched in horror as the body continued to twist and thrash on the stones, kicking up a cloud of dust.

"Kneel down," Martorana told Kane.

She used the thin knife blade to prise the fangs out of Kane's neck.

Kane's deep breathing sounded like a storm in the tunnel. He tried not to think of the sharp blade slicing inches from his throat.

Ridley held the torch close to provide enough light.

"What is it?" Kane muttered when he got his breath back. "Poisonous?"

"It's a snake in an Egyptian tomb... chances are high," Martorana said calmly, no hint of concern in her eyes and the trace of a smile on her lips. "There... hold still... okay, got it." She twisted the final fang from Kane's neck, then pinched the jaw to open the beast's mouth and looked at it curiously. There wasn't a hint of fear in her expression.

Kane slumped against the wall and clutched his neck.

"I'm no expert," she said, "but I believe this little beauty is a horned viper. Don't worry, it's rarely deadly and this one is young and hasn't fully developed its venom yet. Totally fine."

Kane pulled his fingers away from his neck and looked at them. A trickle of blood ran across his skin. "Horned viper? Never heard of it. Guess it could've been worse," he said.

"Any kind of cobra and the Rosetta Stone would be the least of your worries."

"Does it hurt?" Ridley asked, her concern obvious.

"Honestly, no," Kane said. "A little numb I guess. It's funny, I used to love downing pints of snakebite as a kid."

"Ha, me too. Well, anyway now that little drama's over," Martorana said, "and since you'll probably survive, shall we continue on our quest to find more danger?"

Chapter Seventy-Eight

Omar pulled a fresh handkerchief embroidered with his initials from his pocket and dabbed at his brow. In seconds the fine Egyptian cotton, so fine it felt like silk, was soaked in sweat.

"Come and sit in the vehicle, boss," said Tariq, one of his security guards. An AK47 hung casually across his shoulder. "It's air-conditioned. You'll get yourself sick out here."

Omar glanced at the man. Tariq was half right. The hot, thick air felt like fingers around his neck. His gaze swept the car park and settled longingly on the path along which Kane, Ridley and Martorana disappeared some minutes ago.

Omar narrowed his eyes. If only he was younger and fitter he would have been there with them. He took a deep breath, which only resulted in him coughing and spluttering into the handkerchief. When the coughing fit subsided, he pulled the blood-spattered cloth away from his mouth.

"I knew this over-indulged body would let me down

eventually," Omar whispered as he let Tariq lead him over to the vehicle.

"It's alright, boss, they'll get it, I'm sure," the security guard said, helping Omar into the back of the SUV and closing the door.

Omar sunk back into the leather and let the cold from the air conditioning wash over him. He dug through his trouser pocket and slid out a jar of pills. He cracked open the lid and tipped a few into his hand. Then he glanced out of the window, thought for a moment, and tipped out a couple more. He put the pills on his thick, dry tongue, picked up a bottle of water and swallowed them down.

"Tell me Tariq, how long have you worked for me now?" Omar slouched back into the seat and let his eyes half-close.

"Almost ten years."

"Ten years? Ten years of your life you've spent looking after me. Why?"

Tariq adjusted the rear-view mirror to make eye contact with his boss. He shrugged. "You pay me a lot of money. That keeps my wife happy and my children in the best schools."

"Not to mention the diamonds you buy for your girlfriend in Paris," Omar added, smiling.

"How... how did you—" Tariq suddenly looked nervous, his eyes flickering from left to right.

"Don't worry about it," Omar said, holding out his hands. "It's my job to know everything. Your secret is safe with me. I don't care what you do with your money," he added and meant it.

Tariq's thick lips curved into a smile.

"Listen, I have dedicated my life to art and antiquities," Omar said, knitting his fingers together.

"I know, boss. You've got one of the greatest collections in the world."

"Yes. Do you know why?"

"You like art?" Tariq shrugged.

"Well, I do like art, but it's much more than that." Omar sat up straight and looked deep into Tariq's dark eyes. "For too long now art and antiquities have been used as political tools and weapons of power. Governments and the super-rich control them, trade in them, and decide who should see them and who should not. Governments cannot be trusted. These artefacts are national treasures, not just for those who can afford them, but for everyone who feels the passion for them."

Tariq nodded.

"I am not much longer for this world, my friend, and when I go—"

The screeching of tyres over tarmac cut Omar's words short. The big man strained to look behind him. Two military 4 x 4s barrelled across the tarmac and headed up the track towards the excavation. Their chunky tyres threw up giant clouds of dust and sand. On the back of the 4 x 4s, only just visible through the curtain of dust, four men held on tight as the vehicles bounced away across uneven ground. Each was heavily armed.

"Shit!" Omar's hands balled into fists. "Jabari Hader has called for backup." His eyes constricted to pinpricks. "Tariq, we have to do something. Hiram, Alex and Maria will be slaughtered and the Rosetta Stone will—" Omar swallowed and shook his head. "We have to follow them. We must go into the tomb."

Chapter Seventy-Nine

Kane, Ridley and Martorana continued deeper into the network of tunnels. The only sound was the quiet shuffling of their footsteps across craggy bedrock. Believing the terrorists planned only to kidnap him, Kane pushed on ahead.

Given a chance, he wouldn't hesitate to trade his life to ensure Ridley and Martorana would get out of there. He didn't even need to think about it. The dull ache of the twin fang marks on his neck served as a reminder of the danger they were in.

A metallic sound echoed down the passage. Kane held up his hand. Ridley and Martorana stopped immediately. Three torch beams swept silently through the darkness.

"What was that?" Ridley whispered.

"Not sure," Kane said, "but it came from that way."

Standing still, they heard the noise again. Steel, grinding against steel. Like hinges on an old door.

"I don't think it's cursed ancient mummies," Martorana said.

Kane nodded. "It's not ancients mummies I'm worried about, cursed or otherwise."

Kane signalled for them to continue towards the noise. "Keep your eyes open. We're not alone down here."

Then his stomach lurched upwards as the floor gave way.

"Shit! Shit!" Ridley's voice filled the tunnel as she rushed forward. One moment they'd been following Kane down the passageway, the next he'd disappeared in a rumbling cloud of dust.

"Stop, stop, don't move!"

Ridley heard Kane's voice and immediately slid to a stop. She exchanged worried glances with Martorana beside her. The strong beams of their torches did nothing in the thick dust.

"Hiram?" Ridley yelled. The grit clawed at her throat. "I can't see you. Hiram?"

"Look down," came the reply. Ridley did. A giant hole had appeared in the floor of the passageway. Twenty feet below them, Kane was waist deep in sand.

"Lucky this broke my fall." He signalled at the sand around him. He wasn't smiling. Kane struggled to the surface of the sand and retrieved his torch, which lay off to one side.

Ridley examined the scene now the dust had finally settled. The huge hole was maybe twenty feet across and spanned almost the entire width of the passage.

Down below, Kane moved to the far end and tried to scramble out of the pit. The walls were sheer and smooth, and every time he touched the sides, cascades of sand fell into his mouth and eyes.

"I can't climb this," he sputtered, and Ridley watched as he tried and failed to get a firm grip of the rock face. He glanced up towards the torch beams above. "I can hardly see you. Can you climb around?"

A ghostly hint of a head appeared above the rocky parapet as Ridley looked down, then swept her torch around the pit's edge. "I think so," she said. "It looks as though... yes, there's a ledge on that side." The beam of her torch settled on the right-hand side of the tunnel.

Kane peered into the gloom. Ridley was right. It looked as though the floor of the tunnel was supported there by a pillar of bedrock.

"The people using this tunnel must know about this," Kane stated. He fought to lift his feet up and out of the sand again.

Ridley stood with her back flush against the wall of the tunnel and took a step sideways. The ledge was only six inches wide at most. Kane wasn't certain it would hold her weight.

"Be careful," he warned, watching each of Ridley's movements carefully as the dust settled further. Sand and dirt continued trickling down into the pit.

Above, Ridley took another tentative step. She was now directly over the pit. She flattened herself backward against the wall.

Kane stepped towards her, intent on catching her if she fell. Ridley opened her palms and lay them flat against the wall. Kane knew she had faced myriad challenges all over the world in recent years, without a single thought for her own safety.

"I can do this!" Ridley grunted.

You can do it! Kane thought.

"You'll never make it!" Martorana stated.

Dust clung to the sweat on her palms. She took another step. Her knees wobbled for a moment. Without thinking, Ridley looked down. Beneath her, Kane looked up through wide eyes.

Ridley tensed the muscles in her legs and pushed back into the wall. Dust streamed from the ledge beneath her feet and into the pit, swirling around Kane below. She took a deep breath of the tunnel's sour air, then fixed her eyes on the opposite wall and stepped to the side again. Then again.

Half a dozen steps and what felt like several agonising minutes later, Ridley stepped onto solid ground at the far side of the pit.

"You'll have to do the same, Maria," she said. "Just keep your back to the wall and move fast."

Ridley looked from Kane, then to Maria and back to Kane again. Something seemed to have changed.

"Hiram," Ridley said, her arm extended. "What's that?" Her eyes flew wide.

Kane turned to where Ridley was pointing. A well had appeared in the sand on the far side of the pit. Sand swirled and slid insidiously towards it.

Kane looked towards it. "Fuck!" He tried to move away from the growing well. "I can't move my legs," he yelled. He glanced down and realised with burgeoning concern that he'd once again sunk down to his waist in the whooshing sand.

He leaned to his right and pulled out his left leg and felt the right sink lower. He wriggled to his right to try and raise that leg and watched as the sand shifted and his left leg sank lower.

"Bollocks," he yelled, his voice raising in pitch and volume. "I'm really fucking sinking."

"I'll try and find something to pull you out with," Ridley shouted. She turned and aimed her torch down the tunnel's dark throat.

"I'm coming over." Martorana crossed to the causeway at the side of the pit and took her first step out over the increasingly perilous drop.

Kane struggled again. His legs, which were used to climbing mountains, felt like dead weights beneath him. The sand pressed and dragged against his feet and ankles, sucking him in. He succeeded in lifting one knee upward. Sand ran into the gap behind his leg and dragged it down with more force than before.

"Stop moving," Martorana shouted from the narrow ledge above him. "The more you move, the quicker it's pulling you down."

Kane nodded; he knew she was right. He looked up at her, inching her way across the ledge which was now more like thirty-five feet above him. He abstractedly imagined her back in the British Museum again. The image didn't fit. Martorana was born for a place like this.

Halfway across the causeway, Martorana froze. From way below, Kane saw her glance at the tunnel's entrance. The colour drained from her face.

"What is it?" Kane hissed.

"Voices," Martorana replied, her own voice like ice. "People. Coming this way."

Chapter Eighty

Ridley ran down the dark tunnel, her torch whipping this way and that. The passage was narrowing now, just four feet wide and ten high. Her heavy breathing shushed back at her off the bare stone walls. The thick, dust-laden air tasted foul and gritty on her tongue.

Barely a hundred yards from the pit in which Kane was sinking further by the moment, the tunnel widened again. Ridley paused and looked around as an area opened out to her right. She swept her torch into the gloom.

Ridley stood gasping as she spotted several boxes stacked one on top of the other. She hustled over and slid a tarpaulin to the side. A pair of hydraulic jack hammers and an electric lighting system rested beneath. If they needed proof this cave complex had been worked on recently, she'd found it.

Ridley grabbed a coil of hydraulic hose, hauled it over her shoulder and turned back towards the pit. She covered the distance quickly, the heavy duty hose clattering against her ribs as she ran.

"I've got something," she shouted as she neared the edge of the pit and stopped. Martorana was halfway across now and stood frozen against the wall. Kane was now forty-feet below. Neither Martorana nor Kane were moving.

"What's going on?" Ridley hissed.

Martorana turned to look at her. She didn't have time to answer. Raised voices echoed down the tunnel, followed by the sound of pounding footsteps.

"Fuck!" Ridley dropped the hose and flattened herself against the floor of the tunnel. "Maria, move now!" she yelled.

Martorana shook herself into action and started sliding along the causeway towards Ridley. Sand spilled down from beneath her feet. She pressed herself against the wall then leapt to her right.

"Hiram, take this!" Ridley hissed, kneeling up, then looping one end of the hose around her waist and throwing the coil down towards him.

Kane extended his arms high in the air. The sand was up to his chest. The hose landed on the sand a yard away, and Kane reached over. The movement caused him to sink beneath the sand another few inches.

"I can't." Kane strained for the hose lying just inches from his fingers. "I can't reach it. You'll have to throw it again." He struggled back to his standing position. The sand now covered his collarbones. "It's pulling at my lower body, squeezing the blood from my legs and ankles."

Ridley muttered profanities as she coiled in the hose. It was heavy and hard to throw. The voices were louder now. She wondered how far away they were. Her question was answered when the first bullet thronged past her and slammed into the wall of the tunnel somewhere behind her head.

"Maria, move!" she shouted, glancing at the woman still making her final steps across the ledge. Ridley gripped hold of the re-coiled hose, leapt to her feet and swung the thing as far as she could. The hose spun out across the pit. Two bullets scorched the air. Ridley flung herself to the ground again and watched as Martorana jumped across the remainder of the causeway. Dust and sand shot from beneath her feet. Her arms swung out, propelling her onward. She landed and fell forward, colliding heavily with the unforgiving ground. She scurried to join Ridley at the pit edge.

Another round of bullets pounded through the air inches above their heads. Raised voices followed them.

Ridley shone her torch down into the pit. Fifty feet below them, now up to his neck in the maelstrom of sand, Kane clutched hard onto the hose.

A staccato of bullets tore into the edge of the pit, just inches from the women. Ridley glanced upward. She counted half a dozen beams of light moving around in the dust and the gloom.

"Turn your torch off!" Kane shouted up. Ridley did as he said, and the tunnel was plunged into near darkness. She stuffed the torch away and peered down at Kane in the dark below.

"Alex, listen. I'm going to ask you to do something for me," Kane said. "You won't like it, but it's important you do exactly as I tell you."

A moment passed. Then another. Finally, "I'll do anything for you. You know that," she muttered. Her heart beat aggressively in the silence that followed.

Nearby, one of the men issued instructions and another answered.

When they came, Kane's words struck Ridley like a fist to the sternum.

"I need you to walk away," he demanded. "Walk away and get out of here. Now!"

Chapter Eighty-One

In the dark, Kane listened closely as somewhere above Ridley processed what he'd said. He knew exactly what she'd be thinking. He'd thought the same on several occasions during their years together. This time he was certain though, because just before the lights had gone off Kane had seen something. He had seen something that changed everything.

"Listen, I'm going to get out of this," he said. His voice carried easily, echoing off the stone walls. "I know what I have to do now. But you need to get out of here." Kane looked up at the mouth of the pit now more than sixty feet above him. Lights swirled through the dust from the right. Ridley lay in the gloom to the left. "Once the dust clears, those men will be after you," Kane hissed. "You've got seconds to get out of here. I'm going to be fine."

Another volley of gunfire tore through the cave above Kane.

"You promise?" came the reply. The acoustics in the

tunnel made Ridley seem closer than she was. The raspy sound of her voice in the darkness made him grimace.

"I'm going to be better than fine," Kane said. "I've got this."

"Okay," Ridley finally uttered. With a rustle and a swish, she disappeared into the gloom.

Kane remained still for a moment and sucked several deep breaths, ignoring the particles of dust and sand he was inhaling. If this were to work, he needed his lungs clear and prepared. He extended his toes and tried to feel the thing he'd brushed against as he'd stretched for the hose. His toes strained uselessly through the sand. He tried again. The sand grabbed and pulled at his legs. Kane stretched even further, his feet extended. *There it is…*

He froze and moved his foot around something solid beneath his feet. Kane nudged it gently with his toes. It echoed dully and shifted beneath his feet. Kane strained further downwards. The sand was up to his chin now, dangerously close to his mouth. He laid his head backward. Sand ran into his ears and inside his shirt.

There was something beneath the sand. Something that to Kane—maybe in a stupor of delusional optimism—felt like a trapdoor.

Kane stopped moving as he heard shouts echoing down the shaft from the tunnel above. The men were speaking Arabic, a language of which he knew only a few words. It was something close to:

"No one gets out of here alive."

The beams of several torches appeared at the top of the shaft and circled around the pit. It would be mere seconds before one of them spotted him, despite only his face being visible nearly seventy feet below.

"There's nothing down here," another man said.

"There has to be. If you can't find him, I'll send you down there."

The fingers of light searched again. Kane had to move. He glanced at the hydraulic hose which lay like a dead reptile on the sand beside his face. *Always reptiles...* The metallic surface glinted in the swirling lights, inching towards him. Kane imagined the men scrutinising the sand, their fingers curled over the triggers of their automatic weapons.

Kane had mere moments to make this work.

In one swift move he grabbed the hose, stuffed it in his mouth and pulled himself beneath the sand. Silence and darkness, the thickest he'd ever experienced, enclosed upon him like a death shroud.

With her lips set in a snarl, Ridley glanced back to where the mouth of the pit lay smothered in darkness. The beams of several torches now swung every which way through the tunnel, picking up swirls of spiralling dust. The gravelly voices of the men echoed off the tunnel walls.

Ridley didn't want to think of the only man she had ever loved lying at the bottom of the shaft just waiting to be discovered. Waiting to be shot. Her knuckles crunched as her hands balled into fists and adrenalin throbbed through her veins. She should go back there and she should smash the shit out of those men until they cursed the day they'd ever got involved in this. The muscles in her legs tensed in preparation for a mad dash back towards the pit and those fucking men...

"Come on," Martorana whispered, placing a hand on Ridley's elbow. "Hiram said he'd be fine. He's more than capable. We can't worry about him. We've got to find the stone."

Ridley glanced at Martorana beside her. A torch swept their way and glowed in Maria's eyes. Her high cheek bones and the toned outline of her shoulders and arms glistened.

She knew Martorana was right. Kane was more than capable and a skilled fighter. In fact, Ridley knew of only one time he'd ever been bested in hand-to-hand combat. It was against her, the first time they'd met.

Another beam of torch light swept past them. The light paused on the two women. A long shadow extended down the tunnel.

A shout followed.

"Yes," Ridley hissed, grabbing Martorana's hand and pulling them further into the darkness. "Let's find the damn stone and get the fuck out of here."

Chapter Eighty-Two

With the chemical-tasting pipe between his teeth, Kane struggled and twisted lower into the sand. He clamped his eyes closed, pinched his nose, and pulled a breath through the length of hose. A tease of languorous air made it into his lungs. He gasped again and resisted the urge to push upwards. The men, their guns trained on the surface of the sand, would be waiting for him to emerge.

Two breaths later, Kane calmed down. He'd completed several hundred scuba dives before and was used to the system of breathing. He convinced himself this was the same as he struggled deeper beneath the sand. The sand surrounding him was a strange consistency. It wasn't like dry desert sand, as he moved through it rather than over it. Neither was it wet, like he assumed quicksand to be. Kane imagined it was like being trapped inside a giant sand-filled egg timer. Seconds were rushing away and dragging him with them.

Eventually he felt something solid beneath his feet. Despite all his efforts—or because of them—he couldn't have moved more than another few inches deeper into the sand. Kane struggled and forced himself down a tiny bit further until he was crouched on the hard surface. He extended a hand and felt it. Smooth, metallic to the touch. Like the inside of a silo.

Ancient Egyptian my arse.

In complete and stifling darkness, Kane explored the surface beneath him. It angled to the left, in the direction the sand ran away to. It was smooth, allowing the sand to pass over it quickly. Kane continued to feel around the surface. All he felt was the solid, flat metal. No way through.

He took another gulp of air through the tube. Nothing came.

Shit! The end of the hose must have slipped beneath the sand.

His lungs strained to get even the smallest taste of oxygen. Nothing. Kane's lungs seared with pain. He jerked and flicked hard on the hose in an attempt to free it from the sand. He tried another breath. Still nothing. It felt like a ten-ton weight squeezed against his chest. Colours danced and spun behind his closed eyelids.

Kane tried desperately to pull the hose towards him. *If I could... just get the end... maybe... I can shove it through the surface of the sand... without being noticed. Maybe...*

He thought of the men above him, guns trained down, ready to pepper the sand with bullets. Like shooting fish in a barrel. No way out.

His limbs felt weak. The pain in his lungs had reduced to a dull smouldering ache. He couldn't pull the hose towards him anymore. Couldn't push it up. His hands stopped moving. Kane tried to open his eyes, but he couldn't even do that.

It was over.

Chapter Eighty-Three

"In there!" Ridley shouted, leaping into a hollow at the side of the tunnel.

A flurry of bullets roared through the air behind them. The guns howled again. The taste and smell of gunfire clawed at her throat and nostrils. The shooting stopped as a voice carried down the passage. The man was speaking Arabic. Ridley understood most of it.

"You three get down there and get after the women. You other three, if you don't bring me Kane, or at least his body, it will be the last thing you never did."

"We need to go," Martorana whispered from beside Ridley.

"Yes," she said as a plan occurred. "Two more minutes."

"Had a horrible feeling you were going to say that," Martorana muttered back, leaning out and glancing back down the passage. The first of the men was shuffling across the causeway. The apparent leader, a burly man with a wild beard, shouted aggressively for him to hurry up. "We don't have much time."

Ridley pulled the torch from her pocket and, keeping her hand across the lens so as to not give away their location, clicked it on. She pulled the tarpaulin from the digging equipment she'd discovered earlier.

The man's voice echoed towards them again. It wouldn't be long before the first man was across the causeway and heading their way.

"They've got to have a power source," Ridley whispered, searching the pile of machinery.

"There." Martorana pointed at a machine by the wall. "That's a diesel generator. We used to use them on the digs for lighting and that sort of thing. They should *not* be used underground."

"That doesn't matter for us. See, look at the direction of the tunnel. We've been going downward. The smoke will rise towards the surface." Ridley climbed across the jackhammers and other digging tools. She picked up a can of diesel from beside the generator. "Perfect!"

"I'm clear." A shout reverberated down the tunnel behind them.

"Get after them, now!"

Ridley turned and poured two thirds of the diesel in a thick line across the breadth of the tunnel. She and Martorana then retreated, pouring out the rest of the diesel as they walked. When the can had run dry, Ridley pulled out a lighter and snapped it to life. The flame danced wildly in the tunnel's turbulent air. Their shadows flickered and swayed on the rock walls.

Shouting and the sound of storming feet thundered towards them.

Of Curses and Kings

Ridley didn't wait another second. She threw the lighter to the fuel-soaked floor. Flames leapt forward into the tunnel, flaring jerkily away from them.

Her eyes burned in the sudden light. Ridley found she couldn't look away as the flames reached the highest concentration of fuel and a great wall of orange sprang forth. Thick black smoke billowed up the tunnel towards the surface. The men coughed and spluttered from somewhere beyond.

The silhouette of the first man across the causeway ran away from the flames. He was unharmed, but his eyes were wild with fear at the raging fire. Ridley and Martorana moved towards him in unison, both dropping easily into a fighting stance.

The man neared, running blindly from the fire. Ridley swung out her foot and jammed it into the ground. The man hit the deck, face down in the dust. Martorana dropped, seized the man's weapon away and put on the safety in one swift movement.

Ridley looked at her with one eyebrow raised.

"Don't tell me you don't how to use an AK47? Most common toy in the world," Martorana said, smiling wickedly.

Ridley pulled the guy's arms up behind him and pushed down hard. He yowled in pain. "Where is the Rosetta Stone?" she snarled in Arabic.

"I... I... I do not know what you are talking about."

Understanding only the gist of the conversation, Martorana undid the safety and jabbed the weapon into the back of the man's knee.

"Wrong answer," Ridley stated. "Let's try one more time. Last chance, or you'll never walk again."

The young man muttered a prayer then looked up at her.

"That cursed stone has caused nothing but pain. You British should have kept the thing."

Martorana jabbed the gun deeper into the man's leg.

"Okay, okay," he whimpered. "Two hundred yards down there the tunnel splits. Go left. One hundred yards more there is a left passage. Go down the slope and you will see it."

"Okay, good." Ridley nodded. "How many men guarding it?"

"I do not know. Maybe six or eight. They are spread out around the tunnels."

"One more question," Ridley said, her voice softening. She looked deep into the young man's eyes. The fire danced wildly all around them. "How old are you?"

"Seventeen."

"What? Why the hell're you involved in all this?"

"My family always works on these digs. When trouble started, people stopped coming. No more digging. A few months ago, a man came asking for diggers. My father and me came. When we came below ground we knew it was bad. Digging for the wrong reasons. My father said the man was bad and refused to come. My family still needed money. I came." His head fell in shame.

Ridley nodded. "Stand up." The young man rose unsteadily to his feet.

"There is digging equipment up there. Hide under the tarpaulin," Ridley said, "and get out as soon as you can. My name is Alexandria Ridley. When you get out, I want you to contact me. We'll find you a better job. Can you remember that?"

The man lifted his head. A flicker of hope registered in his dusty eyes. "Yes. Alexandria? Like the city?"

Ridley nodded. "Go now."

The man ran off up the tunnel, now unarmed, his slight frame a silhouette against the fire.

Chapter Eighty-Four

The Kane Estate

1983

"What's this for?" Hiram asked, holding up an icepick to show his grandfather, who looked down at his seven-year-old grandson.

Every day, the boy who shared his grandfather's name wanted to be more like his hero. Hiram Snr smiled and knelt beside him.

"This is for all sorts of things," his grandfather said, taking the pick and turning it in his hands. "Firstly, you would use it to climb the mountain." He mimed swinging the long end of the pick into the rocks. "It's also a life-saver if you are falling." His grandfather locked eyes with him. "Most importantly, you could use it to fight off the Sasquatch!"

Hiram's eyes widened. "Sask watch?"

"Yes! Sasquatch. Big foot. It's an ape-like creature who lives high in the Canadian Rockies. That's where I'm going. I want to try and find him."

"Really? But what if he eats you? What if you fall off the mountain and die?"

Hiram's grandfather picked him up and carried him to the window, where together they looked out as the sun arced through the clear sky towards the horizon.

"You know, Hiram, there are worse things than dying."

"Like what? Sask watch?"

"No, the Sasquatch isn't bad," he said, and laughed.

"Like what then?"

"Like never having lived in the first place."

Suddenly Kane was alert again. He felt movement all around him. The sand was rushing faster now. Falling from his body, yet dragging him with it. He felt the warm, welcome sensation of air on his face. He pulled a breath. It slid into his lungs. Revitalising. Delicious.

Life saving.

Then he was moving, too. Sliding on his stomach down the metal surface. Picking up speed. He blinked. His eyes stung with grit. He tried to look around but saw nothing. There was no light here. He tried to grab on to something. Everything was smooth and he was moving too fast.

Kane's mind spun with confusion. *Where am I? What the fuck's happening? Did Alex get out okay?*

His eyes picked up a streak of light. Just a distant flash, coming from behind and below him. He looked down towards it. A square of light just beneath his feet and he was rushing towards it much too quickly.

The light grew and grew, eating the sand all around

him. Then Kane's legs disappeared into the light. Next his hips. He wasn't fighting now, allowing the light to swallow him. He blinked. Colours spiralled. Falling. Falling... faster now.

Then he was still.

Long moments passed. Kane forced open his eyes. His retinas burned with the light's bright intrusion. He pulled in a deep breath and coughed. Sand shot from his nose and mouth. Then his surroundings strained into focus. He heard someone laugh.

"Hiram Kane! You triggered every alarm coming into this place. Lit it up like one of your Western Christmas trees! Aren't you supposed to be good at this stuff?"

Kane screwed his eyes to slits and stared into the bright light. He was sitting on a giant mound of sand. In front of him a metal walkway hung down from the ceiling. Two floodlights blazed in his eyes. Below him, the sand sloped off into the darkness.

"I hope you enjoyed the booby trap. The Swiss and Egyptians built it in the 1890s. We fixed it. What did you think?"

Kane looked up. A large steel cone tapered to a point twenty feet above his head. It was like sitting beneath a giant hopper.

"Throw a rope down for our... visitor." There was movement beyond the floodlights and a rope flew down from the walkway.

Kane caught it in one hand, then appraised his situation. No way out.

"Climb up when you're ready, Mr. Kane. You may not be able to see from there, but I have four men with guns all trained on you... just in case that heroic streak wants to come out again."

Kane sighed, then struggled to his feet and looped the rope around his wrist. With no other option obvious to him, he pulled it tight; using the very last of his spent energy, he shimmied up it. He reached the walkway and two men helped drag him across the railing. Kane stood up shakily and looked down at the sand below. In another situation, Kane would have been impressed by the feat of engineering.

He brushed himself down and looked at the large man before him.

"Let me introduce myself." The man's wide grin glowed beneath the bright lights. "I am Jabari Hader, I now own the Rosetta Stone."

Chapter Eighty-Five

Valley of the Kings

Once they were safely away from the car park and out of sight of the armed men in the 4 x 4s, Tariq and Omar slowed down and cautiously followed the imprints of recent footsteps along the small hidden valley.

Omar paused. He realised his attitude had changed. It was as if he were no longer afraid, and to hell with the bastards. Instead, he felt himself glowing with excitement. *Perhaps that's just sunstroke and heat exhaustion,* he mused and almost grinned.

As they approached the entrance to the alleged tomb of Ramses the Eighth, he paused again. He shook his head, sweat flying off in large beads. "Can it really be what Jim said it was?" he muttered, almost reverentially. "Is it really the undiscovered tomb of Ramses the Eighth?"

"Only one way to find out, boss," Tariq prompted. "We need to move. Come on, I will go first."

Omar nodded, an expression of grim determination

replacing the disbelieving look of wonderment from moments before. Tariq took a couple of tentative steps into what was apparently the entrance to the tomb of Ramses the Eighth, the last surviving son of Ramses the Third, a great pharaoh best known for repelling the advances of more than one foreign invading force. Omar wondered absently if some of that repellent strength still existed in the air around the tomb, somehow preventing them from further passage inside. He followed anyway, panting hard in the cloying confines of the dark tunnel. Yet, he put his natural claustrophobic fears to the back of his mind and surged on, one step after another as they moved deeper underground beneath African bedrock.

Finally, after many decades of witnessing his beloved ancient artefacts in galleries and private collections, usually his own, Omar knew he was about to see perhaps the greatest of all artefacts deep in the belly of Egypt itself. Of course, Omar also knew this wasn't anything like seeing it *in-situ*. The Rosetta Stone had been found in the ruins of an old fort outside of Alexandria. This was special. It still felt like an adventure, and Omar realised he was in his element, finally understanding what drove men like Howard Carter, Hiram Bingham and of course, more recently, Hiram Kane, to do what they did. There was a certain irony about that… here he was, following in the actual footsteps of Hiram Kane. It was because of people like himself, Omar knew, who collected great artefacts and protected them in museums and galleries, which in turn inspired the younger generations to become archaeologists and explorers. Now here he was, following one of those explorers into the subterranean world of an ancient pharaoh carved more than three-thousand years ago.

They surged on, Tariq leading, Omar close behind.

Omar was fascinated by it all. He wished they were there under less troubling circumstances. He could have no complaints. This was all because of him. His mind drifted with notions of regret and shame and—

"Boss, stop. There's something ahead…"

"What is it? Can you see it? Let me through."

Tariq took a few more steps forward and paused. "It's a… it's a snake. Well, the body of a snake. Its head is missing."

Omar hustled past Tariq, almost barging the smaller man out of the way. He stepped closer to the dead serpent and couldn't help but grin. Here he was, beneath ground in a tomb of a great pharaoh in the legendary Valley of the Kings. *There's a decapitated snake on the ground? How exciting!*

"I think we should turn back boss," Tariq said quietly.

"Nonsense," muttered Omar, revelling in the adventure. In his heart of hearts, he wasn't sure what they would find if they continued on. He suspected that despite his wishes, it wouldn't be anything good. At this point, he didn't care if he even survived the day. He was on the cusp of seeing the Rosetta Stone back on Egyptian soil. If he died to get that chance, so be it. It was enough. He had taken some important precautions once this whole scheme had gotten underway many months previous; he knew he didn't have to worry about his legacy. Omar's life had always meant less to him than the artefacts he so desired. Nothing was going to stop him from proceeding down the tunnel now.

"Tariq, you have done enough. I think you should return now to the car park and wait for me there. If I am not back by the time—"

"What's that?" Tariq said, looking over Omar's shoulder at something along the tunnel.

Omar turned, swivelling his huge shoulders at an angle

in order to face back the right way. Thick smoke was wafting towards them, accompanied by some unintelligible noises that might have been human screaming or maybe just wind.

"I am going onward, Tariq. You do what you will."

With that, Tariq watched on as Omar shuffled out of sight into the darkness.

Chapter Eighty-Six

Ridley and Martorana ran on down the tunnel. As the light of the fire died away, Ridley snapped on the torch. After two hundred yards, just as the young man had said, they reached a fork. One tunnel twisted off to the right, while another, the smaller of the two, descended steeply to the left.

Ridley shone her beam down the passage.

"I'll go first," Martorana said, indicating with the gun. Ridley nodded and followed her down.

The roaring of the flames had muted to nothing here. All Ridley could hear was the swishing of their footsteps over the sand. As they walked, Ridley couldn't stop thinking about the young man hiding beneath the tarpaulin in the tunnel above. She'd known gangsters who preyed on vulnerable children before, but hadn't expected it here. This wasn't some distant, war-torn country. This the was the land of her birth.

Twenty-four hours ago, they had all been pumped with their own self-importance, thinking they were doing something so good and honourable. Yet, they were bringing an ancient artifact into a country rife with corruption and poverty. They had planned to stay in a nice hotel, sip champagne, and then disappear on a luxury jet to a hail of kudos and congratulations.

Ridley felt sick from it all. How had she become this detached from the place of her birth? In that moment, she wondered whether they were any better than their colonialist forefathers.

When she and Hiram got out of this, Ridley would ensure they did something about bringing change to this country. For everyone, and not just for the few.

"Tunnel to the left up ahead," Martorana said.

Ridley nodded, looking up at the opening on the tunnel's left wall.

Martorana reached the opening and froze. She held her finger to her lips and beckoned Ridley closer.

As the young man had said, the tunnel dropped steeply downward. A rope hung against the wall to aid the descent. The tunnel was narrow, too, and looked as though it had been cut by hand. Ridley pictured the hundreds, maybe thousands of hours of work put into creating this complex.

Martorana clicked on the AK's safety catch, then tucked it beneath her left arm and stepped slowly into the passage. Gravity caused a drift of sand to cascade from beneath her feet.

Ridley let her get a few paces ahead and then followed. She gripped hold of the rope and leaned into the slope. Her feet slid slowly down the vertiginous passage. The rope cut into her sweaty palms. She wiped her free hand across her forehead; it came away wet. It was hot and humid. Ridley took another step, straining to keep upright.

"Kill the light," Martorana hissed.

Ridley did as she was told and stashed away the torch. A dull orange glow filtered up the passage from an opening on the right.

The noise of movement echoed from somewhere nearby. Footsteps shuffled. A male voice sounded, and another answered.

Martorana reached the mouth of the passage and paused. Ridley inched down towards her. The muscles in her calves ached from the awkward position as she reached Martorana's side. The pair exchanged a glance and then leaned around to look into the next cave.

Ridley did a systematic sweep of the area. When she realised what she'd seen, her eyes flew wide and her jaws parted like the Red Sea.

Chapter Eighty-Seven

Ridley shut her eyes and opened them, expecting the view to change. It didn't. The vision of the cave in front of her stayed resolute, like a recurring nightmare.

The passage they'd had descended entered the cave six feet above floor level. The space was large and well-lit by numerous floodlights attached to the walls. The ceiling was domed and as high as two double-decker buses in the centre. The dark mouths of two other tunnels loomed on the far walls. Those tunnels were larger. Ridley noticed there were tire tracks worn into the floor.

There were also two armed guards in the room. They stood on the far side, talking idly and clearly not expecting company.

Yet, when Ridley noticed what was in the centre, everything else paled into a distorted and silent blur.

Held by the prongs of a large forklift truck, Ridley recognised the packing case which held the item of incalculable value. The item for which they'd travelled around the world with the sole purpose of returning: The Rosetta Stone.

Next to it—in fact, chained to it—was something of far greater value. *Someone* of far greater value.

"Is that... It can't be..." Martorana whispered, blinking hard.

Ridley didn't reply. She couldn't reply.

The world had fallen still and silent. She stared ahead at the shocking scene. Her breath caught in her throat. Her heart skipped far too many beats.

Chained by his neck to the Rosetta Stone, like a villain in the stocks, was Hiram Kane's grandfather.

Hiram Kane Snr blinked as he slid his tongue over his dry, chapped lips. He let his gaze sweep around the cave once more.

He had no idea how long he'd been kept in this position, but his legs and arms ached. He was chained against a wooden crate inside a cave somewhere beneath the earth. The harsh metal of the chains dug into his skin.

Hiram Snr didn't know his exact location. Based on the stifling heat he felt as he'd been dragged in here, the language spoken by his captors and the colour of the native bedrock surrounding him, he would've placed a fairly sizeable wager on them being somewhere in the southern part of Egypt. It was an area he'd visited many times, and if these cowards thought this old man would shy away in fear at being in a foreign land, they were far more stupid than their ancient ancestors. As Hiram Snr knew, the ancient Egyptians had, at one stage been, the most developed society on the planet for 3,000 years.

Hiram Snr glanced at the two men who were supposed

to be guarding him. They stood nonchalant, guns slung over their shoulders and lounging against the cave's far wall.

In the last two days—he thought it was two days though he couldn't be sure—he'd been pushed, prodded, chained, beaten and starved of both food and water. *Like an animal on the way to the slaughterhouse*, he mused. If he ever needed an excuse not to eat meat again, this was it.

Yet, Hiram Snr wasn't vanquished. Far from it. The men guarding him had been lucky the last couple of times he'd tried to escape. The cards were stacked in their favour —definitely not in his; he knew they wouldn't be that lucky every time.

If only he could find a way to level the playing field. He had been kidnapped by these cowards one evening while walking his beloved Champ. A gang had ambushed him from behind, pulled a hood across his eyes and dragged him into a waiting vehicle. A man half his age would have struggled—although he'd put up a bloody good fight.

Hiram Snr suppressed a welling sadness at the thought of his dog. He had been a good ally and companion over the years and that had been no way to say goodbye. When he was through this—when these criminals were either behind bars or bleeding out beneath desert sands—Hiram Snr would mourn that loss. Not now, though. Now he had to stay focused, remain sharp and wait for the bastards to make a mistake.

He glimpsed a flash of light from the corner of his eye. His gaze flicked in that direction, but he but saw nothing.

There it was again. A faint pinprick of light rushing past him.

He strained his eyes in the direction of the source. For a man of his age, his vision was good. Only after the strong words of an optician had he started wearing glasses when he took his classic Aston Martin for a drive. Right now though, Hiram Snr cursed his diminishing eyesight.

There, again! This time he sensed a shape moving beyond the light. *No, not just a moving shape... a face.* His eyes slowly focused. It wasn't just a face. A woman's face. A woman he would recognise anywhere, in this life or the next. Alexandria Ridley.

He shook his head to clear his eyes, sure of whom he'd seen and yet still disbelieving his dust-filled eyes. Yet, there was no doubt. It was Alex Ridley. Hiram Snr nodded to confirm he'd seen her.

Ridley nodded back, then placed her thumb and forefinger together to make a circle. *You okay?* Hiram Snr knew the gesture. He nodded again.

Then, and with a series of points and gestures, Ridley laid out her plan.

Chapter Eighty-Eight

Ridley watched as Hiram Snr nodded again. She hoped he'd fully caught her drift. Although late in his eighth decade, the man was sharp in both mind and body. She had absolute faith that Hiram Snr could do this.

Ridley and Martorana ducked back into the tunnel and waited. A moment later, they heard the famous old explorer cry out in pain. It was so convincing the sound sent shivers down Ridley's neck.

"What the fuck's up with the old bastard now?" barked one of Hiram Snr's minders. Ridley was going to enjoy beating him. She would have to be careful not to snap his fucking head off.

"What do you want, old timer?" the guard spat as he approached their captive.

"My... my... urrggh, it's my stomach!" Hiram Snr mumbled.

Should've been an actor, Ridley thought.

"Unless you want a big fucking hole in it, I suggest you shut your mouth."

"My pills... I need my pills. They are... trouser pocket. Right side. I... never leave the house with... without them. I know they're there. Just give me one of those pills. I'll be... urrgghhh... I will be fine.

"What a fucking mess!" the man said in Arabic to his colleague. Both men laughed.

A spike of rage shot through Ridley. Her muscles tensed and her lips twisted into a snarl.

"Please, I might die if I don't... get those pills. Then... your boss will be really pissed off."

Ridley peered around the wall of the tunnel. The guard was halfway across the cave.

"Just a little closer. One more step, arsehole," she whispered.

"It's... a... stomach ulcer." Hiram Snr grumbled again at a new wave of imaginary pain. Ridley was impressed with his convulsing. She was convinced.

"Just do it to shut him up," the other guard grumbled.

"Okay old man, but listen to this... if you try anything, I will fucking shoot you. Understand?"

"Yes... uugh, yes... yes. Thank you. Thank you!"

The guard took two steps then turned to face him. Ridley's eyes flicked from one guard to the other, waiting for the perfect moment. The guard took another step toward Hiram Senior. Ridley leapt.

She hit the ground two yards behind the guard and closed the distance quickly. The other man shouted a warning. It came too late. Ridley spun anti-clockwise on her left foot and landed a swinging kick deep into the man's ribcage with her right. She felt and heard bones crack beneath her heel. She then pounded a swift jab and reverse elbow into the back of his skull before grabbing the gun and pulling it clean away. The startled guard sunk to the floor in agony. It had happened in less than three seconds.

"Don't you fucking think about it!" yelled Martorana, her voice echoing through the cave. She'd jumped down from the passage and had her gun trained with menace on the remaining guard. "If I see your finger so much as twitch, you won't even have time to blink."

"She's a great shot... put the gun down," Ridley demanded in Arabic, cool and calm.

Fear burned in the guard's eyes. He looked from Ridley to Martorana and back again.

Ridley hoped they wouldn't have to shoot him. Now they could see him clearly, she realised his young age.

"Do not put the gun down," came another voice from the dark mouth of the passage. Two more guards stepped into the cave, their guns levelled at the women.

"Shit!" Ridley muttered. "Maria, don't move. Let's see how this plays out."

The men fanned out, surrounding the two women. Ridley looked at them each in turn, searching for a moment of distraction.

What she got back were three hard, defiant stares. The men were young, maybe teenagers. All three were gaunt. Their dark yellow uniforms hung loose from their underfed bodies. Yet, in their eyes Ridley saw no fear. These young men were used to witnessing pain and death. Maybe even inflicting it themselves.

The men stepped forward again. Ridley and Martorana took a step back. Maria kept her gun levelled at the guy in the centre.

"Put your gun down and come with us," said the young man on the right in good English. "You do not need to die here." The men took another step forward. They were now between Ridley and Hiram Snr.

Ridley glanced around. They were out of options. Backs were against the wall. Ridley pulled a deep breath and started to tell Martorana to lower her weapon.

Then all hell broke loose.

Chapter Eighty-Nine

The guard on the right yelled in agony. His cries echoed around the cave.

Ridley glanced towards him. She didn't hesitate. She surged forward at the guard in the centre. Launching from her right foot, she kicked the barrel of his rifle hard. The cold metal shot upwards and struck the unsuspecting guard on the nose, crushing it in an explosion of blood, gristle and splintered bone. She yanked the weapon from his hands, spun it around and swung the butt like a cricket bat. The unforgiving metal thronged against the guard's temple and Ridley stepped back as he crumpled to the floor.

Martorana also didn't wait. While Ridley was destroying the guard in the centre, she had turned her attention to the man on the left. She stepped to the side in case he fired, then charged forward. She let her gun fall to her side and struck the guard on the side of the face with a vicious elbow, following that up with a hook to the jaw and a jab to the nose. With a swift yank, the stunned guard was relieved of his weapon and sprawled whimpering to the ground.

Ridley and Martorana both turned to the remaining guy on the right. To their surprise, like his colleagues, he lay crumpled in the sand. Behind him, now free from the bonds that had chained him to the Rosetta Stone, stood Hiram Snr. He fingered the abrasions on his neck from the chains.

Until that moment, Ridley hadn't thought it possible to admire and respect the man any more. She should've known better. As with everything any member of the Kane family did, expectations meant nothing; exceeding expectations is what counted. To the Kanes it came naturally.

"What?" Hiram Snr asked, his voice calm as he shook his arms to get the blood flowing. "You can't expect a mere set of cheap manacles to hold me back. I was picking locks before you were born." He glanced from Ridley's startled expression to Martorana's, then back again. A familiar wry grin cracked the old man's face. "Actually, since before your parents were born."

Hiram Snr smiled at Alex and Maria, who continued staring back at him, both shaking their heads.

Last time he and Alex had seen each other, they'd been celebrating his grandson's new job at the British Museum. Martorana was there too. Now their lives were at risk deep beneath ancient desert sands. Hiram Snr felt the distant trill of excitement. This sort of thing used to be his bread and butter.

One of the men groaned from his position, prone on the floor. The sound snapped the old explorer back into the present. "We need to get these bastards out of here, then find that grandson of mine, then get the hell out of here ourselves."

Ridley nodded and looked down at the men splayed

across the floor of the cave. They worked quickly, completely disarming the men and tying their arms behind their backs. They then bound them to a support beam in the furthest gloomy corner of the cave. They wouldn't be seen there unless someone shone a light directly at them.

"Um, what about this?" Ridley pointed at the Rosetta Stone in its packing crate.

"We'll follow the tracks." Hiram Snr motioned at the ground. The indentations of the forklift's thick tyres led into one of the tunnels in the cave's far wall.

"Can you drive one of these things?" Ridley asked. Then an engine stuttered and thrummed to life. She turned to see Martorana behind the wheel of the forklift.

"We use things like this to move exhibits around at the BM all the time," she shouted over the thumping engine. "Normally not below ground."

"Nor under fire from brainwashed maniacs?" Ridley prompted.

"Not normally," Martorana said, winking.

"I don't think they'll shoot at us," added Hiram Snr, tapping the Rosetta Stone's crate. "Damage this and they'd lose everything."

Ridley extended her hand to help Hiram Snr up into the cab beside Martorana, though he was able to jump up and cling on with surprising dexterity.

"What about Hiram?" Ridley asked, concerned.

"That boy has a nose for trouble," confirmed Hiram Snr calmly, as if all the world knew it. "With all this racket" —he pointed down at the engine which whined and stuttered—"you don't need to worry. I'm sure he'll find us soon enough."

Martorana pushed the throttle forward. The engine grumbled in protest for a few seconds, then, with slow and careful motions, she lifted all 1,675 pounds of the Rosetta Stone. When the load was positioned at the right height to protect her, Hiram Snr on one side and Ridley on the other, she released the brake. Glancing down at the truck's control board she found the switch for the front light and flicked them on. Bright white light bathed the tunnel before them.

Hiram Snr heard Ridley gasp. Next he heard the dull repetitive thud of hand clapping reverberating above the beat of the engine.

"Well done!" shouted Jabari, his voice a low growl. "Now switch that off, then step this way with your hands in the air. If you don't, I'll blow this fucker's face off."

Hiram Snr chanced a glance above the Rosetta Stone's casing. A familiar, imposing figure stood in the mouth of the tunnel. Standing just a few feet in front of him, a gun aimed at his back, was his grandson.

Chapter Ninety

"The problem with you people is that you think you're so much better than everyone else." Jabari looked from Kane to Ridley, and then to Martorana. "You want to save the world. You want to make everything true and nice and perfect."

Martorana recognised the head of security, and things fell into place. *Bastard!* She glanced to her left, watching Ridley's eyes narrow as she inhaled slowly, let the gun fall, then reluctantly raise her hands above her head. Next Martorana glanced to the right. Hiram Snr was gone.

She and Ridley clambered down from the forklift and stepped forward, their arms raised.

Jabari continued. "Your second problem is you just aren't honest enough. You are in this to get rich, just like the rest of us." He looked back at Kane. "Is it a coincidence that the Andes mountains you explore in Peru are filled with Inca gold? Of course not." Jabari spat on the floor. "You are no different to the rest of us. You simply dress it up as something else."

Ignoring the man's words, Kane examined the only woman he'd ever loved. The woman who had quite literally gone to the ends of the world with him. The fact she was there now, her face resonating confidence and strength, filled him with pride, and more hope than he warranted. He turned to face his tormentor.

"We are nothing like you," Kane replied evenly, fighting to remain calm. "Everything we've ever done has been to expose criminals, empower marginalised people and promote equality. That has always been my family's passion, started long ago by my great-grandfather and continued by his son, my grandfather. I have merely continued their work."

Jabari smirked.

"Even if you kill us now," Kane continued, his voice rising in volume, "the work we've done will live on."

Jabari considered Kane for several beats. "That is nice," he said, still smirking. "But it does not change the fact that soon you will be forgotten, rotting away in this stinking tunnel. You mention your grandfather," he added, the smirk growing. "Tell me, where is he now?"

Kane tilted his head to the side and stared long and hard at the big man before him. The muscles of his stomach clenched. It felt like fingers closing around his guts. "What do you mean, where is he now? He's at home. In England. This has nothing to do with—"

"Really?" Jabari said, one eyebrow raised. "In England? Safe? Looking down smugly from the security of his ivory tower as the rest of the world falls apart?"

Kane's stomach knotted further as he remembered the two unanswered calls he'd made to his grandfather. *That was unusual...*

"Old man Kane, where are you?" Jabari crowed.

"You're lying," Kane repeated. "He's not here."

"Hiram," Ridley whispered. He turned to face her. Registering the tone in Ridley's voice and the way she lowered her eyes, Kane's stomach turned to lead. "He's telling the truth. Your grandfather is… he's here."

Kane stared at Ridley. Behind him, Jabari's smile grew.

"Checkmate!"

Chapter Ninety-One

"Old man Kane," Jabari spouted again, "the fun and games are over. Time to come out."

Kane's muscles tensed. His pulse thundered in his ears.

"I know a rat like you is used to hiding in the shadows," Jabari yelled. "You've been doing it for decades, putting political pressure on this cause or that cause—like betting on horses. Demanding change from your oak-panelled study, when out here, our people are being starved, beaten and killed. Your time is over. Starting now."

Kane glanced around the cave. The engine of the forklift truck rumbled quietly, its lights not preventing the edges of the gloomy space from remaining in near darkness. Someone could move around the cave's perimeter without being seen.

Jabari's voice hardened now. "I am done messing about. I am going to leave here now and I am going to sell the artefact to the highest bidder... believe me, there are many hungry parties offering ridiculous amounts of money for this old rock. After that, when I am rich... sorry, even richer... I will I enjoy my own ivory tower." Jabari turned thoughtful. "Maybe I will buy the Kane Estate. I am told it has wonderful views. With the great hero missing, I am sure that layabout brother will take whatever I offer for it."

Jabari's words hit the mark. Kane struggled to bite back his anger. Blood drained from his clenched knuckles and his mouth knitted into a snarl.

"I expect he will beg me to take it. I will enjoy living there... I might even keep her alive as a..."—he nodded towards Ridley—"what do you call it in English? A concubine? Anyway, I am done wasting time."

Jabari lowered the assault rifle and fired off two shots. The gun roared in the enclosed space. Two bullets thudded into the sand an inch from Kane's right foot. Kane didn't flinch, though he felt the impact of the shots thump through his body.

As the reverberations died away, Jabari raised the weapon and levelled it directly at Kane's chest.

"Old man Kane, in ten seconds I am going to fire two more shots," he barked. "Each of them will pass directly through your grandson's chest. He will bleed out on the floor of this cave. Ten..."

Kane glanced around in the darkness. To his left, Martorana stood frozen to the spot. To his right, Ridley snarled at Jabari. Kane caught her eye and all noises in the cave faded away. *Got to get us out of here...*

"Five..." Jabari shouted.

Kane broke his gaze from Ridley and turned to face his foe. A thin film of sweat glazed Jabari's brow.

"Four..."

Whatever this man had planned, Kane suspected he still had further use for them. If Jabari wanted them dead, they would be already.

"Three…"

Kane watched as Jabari's eyes scanned the gloom. Kane took a deep breath and held it.

"Two…"

Jabari's finger tightened around trigger. The gun's snout held firm.

"One…"

The word echoed around the cave. Time stood still for a moment; then Kane was enclosed by a cacophony of sound. Someone shouted. Feet pounded towards him. A gun roared.

Then silence ensued.

Chapter Ninety-Two

Crack, Crack!

Omar and Tariq ducked instinctively as the sound of two gunshots reverberated at them from somewhere up ahead.

"What the fuck?" Tariq yelled. "Was that—"

"Gunshots. Let's move."

Tariq hadn't been able to leave his boss when Omar had suggested he go back to the car park. Despite what many people thought of Omar Abdel-Rahman, he was a genuine, kind and decent boss who had done a lot for Tariq and his family. Tariq wasn't about to betray that decency, though at the sound of the gun fire he was suddenly regretting that loyalty. Still, he knew that if he went back the way they had come, he'd likely run into more bad guys. And with that in mind, he followed his boss into who knew whatever hell they'd find.

Omar stumbled forward through the near-darkness of the tunnels, crashing from one side to the other as his wide frame barely fit between the stone walls. From the corners of his eyes he saw ancient carvings blur past and knew they were likely to be *Book of the Dead* texts synonymous with tombs of this period. He wondered absently if his name could soon be added to the hieroglyphic carvings.

They negotiated one sharp bend after another. Omar believed from his extensive research that surely this allegedly undiscovered tomb was in fact that of Ramses the Eighth. Not only that; based on his knowledge, it was probably the most extensive network of tomb tunnels ever found in Egypt.

With each stride deeper into the darkness, Omar felt more certain something bad was about to happen. Then he skidded to a halt as the tunnel abruptly ended and bright lights blinded him. Tariq slammed into him, nudging Omar further into the open space. Catching their collective breath and gathering their senses, both men stood upright and studied the scene before them.

Standing right in front of Omar was the security guy he had employed for the mission. Jabari Hader.

He was holding a really big gun.

Chapter Ninety-Three

Kane hit the sand and rolled.

The cave's stone ceiling spun across his vision. Adrenalin coursed through his veins. He scrambled to his feet. He didn't feel any pain, though Kane knew sometimes the rush of chemicals sometimes caused a delayed reaction.

Losing a finger to a bullet a few months ago during a fight with a Yakuza gangster, Kane hadn't felt any pain until he'd seen the destroyed digit on the floor at his feet.

Kane stood and turned. What he saw hit him like a runaway train. He gasped for air and fought his body for control.

On the sand a few feet away lay his grandfather. Blooms of red blossomed across his shirt.

Kane dropped down beside Hiram Snr and grabbed his hands, enclosing them in his own. He gazed into the wisened face of the man who he adored, admired, and who he had modelled his entire life and ethical moral code upon.

Hiram Snr's chest rose and fell slowly. The pool of blood seeped into the sandy ground.

"Hiram..." His grandfather's voice was weak. Each breath came shallower than the last.

"I'm here for you. We'll get you out of this," Kane said.

Hiram Snr shook his head slowly. "No. This is my time. I'm an old man and... my days of adven... adventure are over. Go now..." His eyes screwed shut, as if a wave of agony was sweeping through him. "Go," he muttered, so quiet Kane had to put his ear right against his grandfather's lips. "Go. Get yourself and that wonderful woman out of here." The old man's eyes flicked towards Ridley.

Leaning back, for the first time Kane truly saw how old his grandfather had become. His papery skin hung grey and slack from his cheek bones. Blood trickled across his thin lips.

"Hiram," the old man whispered, "when you get out of here, there's... something you need to do. You must..." Hiram Snr beckoned his grandson close again. Kane listened intently for a few seconds, then slowly nodded.

"You have always been like a son to me," Hiram Snr managed. "And... and..." His voice faltered now. "I am so... very proud of... of you."

Ridley blinked away tears as Kane cradled his grandfather on the floor of the cave. She knew there was no saving him now. The bullets had torn two holes through his chest and his life was fading away by the second. She looked up at Jabari, the assault rifle still at his shoulder.

"You piece of shit," Ridley hissed, climbing to her feet. "You're a fucking animal. You shot an unarmed old man for no reason."

Jabari watched on grinning, apparently amused and

seemingly curious as to what might happen. He was enjoying himself. Then swung the gun towards Ridley. "And I am not finished yet," he told her, his voice icy cold.

She seethed. "Come on then." She took a step forward and raised her hands. Hiram Snr had been like a grandfather to her, too. She was going to kick the shit out the bastard standing nonchalantly before her, or she would die trying. "Are you going to shoot me too? Fucking coward!"

Jabari raised the gun towards Alex's head and stared down the barrel. "If that is what I have to do, then yes. It won't be a problem."

Ridley took a step forward. Her heart beat hard against the wall of her chest, as if it were trying to escape the ensuing madness. "Yeah?" she said, dropping into her fighting stance and edging forward. "Then that's exactly what you'll have to do."

"No, don't do it!" Martorana yelled, placing a desperate hand on her shoulder. "He's insane and he'll just shoot you."

Ridley shrugged away her new friend's hand.

"Listen to your little… friend," Jabari hissed.

Ridley took another step forward and saw Jabari's finger tighten around the trigger.

If there's one fighting skill Ridley had mastered above all others, it was lightning-fast reactions. Of course, she couldn't outrun a bullet. She could, however, certainly move two inches to get the fuck out of the way. She saw Jabari's finger twitch. She focused her eyes, zoning in on the trigger finger. Blood leached from the knuckle. She saw the knuckle lock and imagined the inner workings of the gun. Took a deep breath…

"Have it your way, bitch. You're going to die anyway."

Ridley ducked and darted left. A shot echoed through the cave. The bullet thudded into rock somewhere behind her.

Two more bullets zipped through the air. Ridley glanced at Jabari's trigger finger. It hadn't moved. Another shot thumped and Jabari roared in pain.

Omar and one of the bodyguards appeared from the mouth of the tunnel behind Jabari.

Ridley glanced wide-eyed at Martorana and nodded. Correctly interpreting the look, Martorana darted back up into the driver's seat of the forklift, snagging her rifle on the way. Ridley looked at Kane. The crack of the shots had shaken him from his trance.

"Get him out of here!" Ridley shouted to him. "We need to move now."

Kane nodded, scooped up his grandfather's inert body and carried him to a safe place on the far side of the cave.

Ridley turned back to a bloody scene which she expected would get a whole lot bloodier.

Jabari struggled to his feet. From what Ridley could see, he'd taken a bullet to the thigh. The fact he was standing indicated the slug hadn't hit bone. The pain must've been excruciating. *Good!*

Jabari didn't hesitate to raise his gun; he fired again. Several shots echoed around the space. Ridley leapt to the side and flattened herself against the cave wall. Shots thunked into Jabari's body. Two pummelled through his shoulders, causing him to drop the gun. Two more exploded in his hip. He cried in pain and collapsed to the floor.

Omar's bodyguard also fell backward, his face a mask of blood and destroyed bone.

Omar glanced at his fallen man, then at Jabari, then at the Rosetta Stone. His eyes widened.

"You've found it!" he shouted, rushing forward.

Ridley stepped over to Jabari and kicked the gun across the floor out of reach, then looked down at the pathetic man.

"Rest in peace, motherfucker," she muttered, then delivered a bone-obliterating kick to his ribs.

Chapter Ninety-Four

"You've found it, you've found it!"

Omar repeated his mantra, staring up at the Rosetta Stone raised high above the floor of the cave on the prongs of the forklift.

Ridley exhaled, then crossed the room and melted into Kane's arms. They held each other for long moments before turning to look at Hiram Snr's body and the body of Omar's fallen security man.

"We need to get them out of here," Ridley said. "We need to take your grandfather home."

"No!" Kane shook his head. His eyes filled with tears as he looked at his grandfather. Despite what must've been a turbulent last few hours of his life, the great man looked at peace. "He's home already," Kane whispered, his face fraught with emotion. "We need to finish our work."

"Come on," Omar shouted. "Let's get this thing moving, we don't know—"

His words were cut short when another shot echoed through the chamber. Kane and Ridley whipped around to see Jabari, somehow propped up on his elbow and somehow holding another revolver.

Omar clutched his expansive side, eyes wide in obvious shock. He turned to face Jabari. Finding a surprising reserve of strength, Omar threw himself at the man.

Jabari's face distorted into a snarl of shock. He squeezed off two more rounds which tore into Omar, before Omar thudded down on top of him. The gun skittered across the stony ground.

Kane and Ridley watched on in their own shock as the two men writhed in an unlikely battle.

Omar wedged a big elbow beneath Jabari, spun, and pulled the man over on top of him. Then, he looped his meaty arm around Jabari's neck and squeezed.

Jabari twisted and fought, grunting in obvious pain, yet he couldn't get free. His left arm, now bent at an unnatural angle, grazed across the ground in search of the gun.

Kane spotted it two inches from Jabari's hand. He rushed across to kick it away. Before he got there Jabari's fingers found their mark. He snagged the gun, lifted it and pushed it hard into Omar's chin.

Omar shook his head, nudging the gun away. He looked Maria Martorana directly in the eye as she sat in the driver's seat of the forklift.

"Do it!" he shouted.

Kane's head spun her way. Martorana's eyes flew wide. Like Kane, she thought she knew what he was implying. She shook her head. *No!*

"Now!" Omar's voice echoed through the space as Jabari flailed to get free.

Martorana glanced at Kane, confusion crackling through the air.

"Maria... now!"

Finally she nodded and edged the forklift truck forward a few feet so the Rosetta Stone was directly above the fighting men, casting them in shadow. Omar gripped tighter round Jabari's throat. Jabari squirmed, somehow raising the gun to Omar's head. His sweaty finger slipped off the trigger.

"Now!" Omar bellowed. This time Martorana didn't hesitate. She grabbed the lever and yanked it towards her.

The others looked on as almost one ton of ancient stone hurtled murderously to the ground.

Chapter Ninety-Five

The Kane Estate

Six Weeks Later

Hiram Kane pulled open the doors of the church and looked outside. Set amid a small wood of oak and poplar trees in the quiet village which bordered the Kane Estate, the pretty churchyard was packed with people.

As Kane scanned the familiar faces in the crowd, his feeling of sorrow and loss dissolved into one of intense gratitude. Gratitude that his grandfather had been such an inspiration to so many people. Further, that they had all turned out for him today, on a bright spring afternoon, to offer their last sad, yet fond farewells. The loss of Hiram Snr had, of course, left an irreplaceable void in the Kane family, but the younger Kane took great comfort in the knowledge that his grandfather had also left the world a kinder, more tolerant and not to mention more enlightened place.

"Thank you so much for a wonderful service." Kane shook hands with the village vicar. Although their opinions of religion differed—like his grandfather, Kane had zero religious affiliations—the vicar was kind, honest, and had reduced most of the mourners to tears with her warm and touching words.

"You're very welcome, my son," the vicar replied. "Don't be a stranger."

"I'm... well, you know I'm not much of a church goer." Kane locked eyes with the woman and felt at ease.

"We all have some kind of faith," the vicar told him. "Yours, I hope, is still in humanity?"

Kane thought about that for a few moments. *Faith in humanity?* That had been tested so much in recent years he wondered how he could ever retain that faith. Then he remembered why he was here today. Because of his grandfather. *What would he think?* He would think that without faith in humanity, what was the point of anything? Kane shrugged. "I'll try, Jan," he said, and meant it." Both smiled, then hugged.

"You're always welcome here, Hiram."

Kane nodded and turned away before tears could prickle his eyes. He took Ridley's hand in his. Together they stepped among the crowd.

"Thank you so much for coming," Kane said as he approached his bosses from the British Museum.

"I'm so sorry for your loss," Neil MacGregor said earnestly, shaking Kane's hand.

Maria Martorana and Alex Ridley hugged. Then Martorana locked eyes with Kane and held them for a long beat. An unspoken message passed between them. They all knew the implication.

"Your grandfather always said how much he enjoyed walking on the estate," Martorana said. "I think that's how he would have chosen to go."

Kane nodded. They had all decided in secret that the details of Hiram Snr's murder in Egypt should remain within the family. Although his body remained entombed in the network of tunnels beneath the desert sands, he would have a grave on the estate. Kane caught Martorana's eye. Both smiled. He would never forget her fierce, undaunted look as she crushed Jabari with the Rosetta Stone. Omar had sacrificed himself and they would forever remember that sacrifice. Kane and Ridley turned and moved towards Julian and Sophie.

"Thank you both for coming," Kane said, shaking each of their hands in turn. "And thanks for everything back in… well, you know. Julian, I'm sorry about Jim. He was a good, brave man." Julian nodded. It was enough.

Kane turned to Sophie. "Any word on Salam?" he asked quietly. She shook her head. That, too, was enough. Kane placed a hand on her shoulder and squeezed. Sophie cuffed away a tear.

Next Kane stepped into the centre of the gathering and asked for a moment of their attention. "My friends, we're having a small reception back at the house. We'd love it if you could join us. Hiram Snr would be delighted to know you were here to enjoy the estate and the gardens he loved so much."

Kane looked out through the kitchen window and watched the sun slide lower in the western sky. Most of the guests had left and now just a dozen or so of their closest friends and family lounged around the house. Kane lifted a bottle of beer to his lips. It wasn't grief or sadness that clouded his mind now; it was the promise he'd made to his grandfather in his dying moments.

"I hope you know how proud he was of you and everything you do, and everything you've done." Ridley's calm voice breezed to him through the kitchen. Butterflies exploded in Kane's stomach and he almost choked on the beer.

He turned to look at the woman he loved. She leant on the doorframe, a beer in her hand. Kane's eyes instinctively slid across her body. She looked absolutely stunning in the long, tight black dress. Kane felt his pulse quicken.

He nodded. "I... I, um... I know," he managed. "Actually, there's something I wanted to talk to you about. Come and sit down?"

Ridley's eyes narrowed as she crossed the kitchen. Kane watched her hips swaying and his mouth felt dry. He took another swig of the beer, then put it on the counter. He put his hands on her hips and looked into her eyes.

"Just before my grandfather died, he told me something and—"

Kane stopped as a knock at the door startled them both. He glanced towards the hallway.

"Don't worry about that," Ridley said, her eyes locking on his with intrigue. "What did he tell you?"

Kane looked back at Ridley. Emotion broiled inside him. "He told me where something was. I suppose it's a bit of a family heirloom."

The knock sounded again. Louder. Footsteps padded through the house and someone answered it.

Ridley nodded at Kane expectantly.

He slid his hand in his pocket. "Well, it's—"

"Bro, it's for you." Danny sauntered into the kitchen. "Some guy. Says it's really important. Called himself Abdullah Sharif, says he's a solicitor acting on behalf of the estate of Omar Abdel-Rahman. Something about an unmissable opportunity…"

Kane and Ridley looked at Hiram's younger brother.

"Um, I'll tell you later?" Kane's eyebrows rose. Ridley shook her head and nodded, grinning. "Good. Don't let me forget… it's important."

To Danny he said, "You'd better show him in."

Epilogue

The MV Montecarlo, Indian Ocean

One Month Later

Captain Hammas stared through the bridge's rain-smeared glass. The wipers whipped back and forth with fury. Though failing, they were attempting to clear a track through the lashing fingers of water.

Several stories below, the 280-metre-long deck of the container ship stretched out before him. A small red light shone from the bow as it rose again on the ocean swell. Piled high with containers, the ship surged heavily through the water. They had deadlines to keep and Captain Hammas did not like to be late.

He glanced at the charts before him, then looked again at the incoming front of bad weather. The veteran mariner grumbled. These waters could be treacherous. They would need to proceed with caution.

"Reduce speed to fifteen knots," Hammas shouted above the rattling storm. "Keep our heading. If anything changes let me know immediately."

The second mate nodded, his grim expression unchanged.

Captain Hammas stepped through the door and onto the outside staircase that connected the bridge to the main deck. The raging wind and rain slapped mercilessly against his face. He gripped tightly onto the railing and took one step at a time. A bulkhead light offered only a dim glow. The steel wall of the ship was laced with thick seams of rust.

Although he could traverse the ship via the inside stairs, the captain liked the feel of the storm on his skin. It reminded him of an important lesson for any mariner—the most important lesson: out here, nature's in charge.

The captain reached the main deck and glanced back up at the bridge, eight storeys above. A dull light radiated through the windows.

He turned and made his way back to his cabin. Once inside, he locked the door, took off his wet coat and kicked off his shoes. He grabbed a glass and pulled the stopper from a bottle of his favoured Irish whiskey. Hammas slumped into his armchair, took a sip of the whiskey and revelled in the luxury—after all, he was the only man aboard with a cabin big enough to contain an armchair. He sighed deeply, let his eyes close and his body relax to the rise and fall of the boat.

His eyes shot open as a knock echoed violently through his cabin. Hammas's eyes flicked around, as though he'd been caught off-guard. He climbed to his feet and opened the door.

"We have an issue captain," the third mate said between deep breaths.

"What?"

"Three men have taken over the bridge. They're armed and have locked and barricaded the doors."

Hammas's knuckles whitened around his glass. "What? Who are they and how the hell did they get on board?"

"We've not been boarded. That would be impossible in this weather. They must have come aboard at—"

"Port Said, Egypt," the captain interrupted.

"Yes sir. They say they're part of the Ealim Jadid group. One of them identified himself as Salam al Halabi."

Abbe Abidi's Apartment, Alexandria

Abbe Abidi was sitting in his usual spot on his balcony at sunset, overlooking Abo Haif Sidi Bisher Beach. Maybe it was just him, but the usually passive waters seemed rougher than he'd ever seen them. Aggressive. Dangerous even.

El-Gaish Road four storeys below was even busier than normal, which was hard to believe. Over the years Abbe had gotten used to the incessant honking of horns and the shouts of irritation from the hundreds of impatient drivers. It was almost like a comfort to him, that collection of sounds, a kind of white noise that reminded him things were as they should be. Despite it all, the world kept turning.

He downed the last of his drink and stood on unsteady legs to go inside for a refill, the latest of many refills this evening and every evening before it. He wasn't sure if he were celebrating or lamenting. Several months had passed since the incident with the Rosetta Stone. The press had stopped reporting on the events and it was almost as if it had never happened. Of course, the artefact was now where it should have always been... back on Egyptian soil. It had been damaged during an incident beneath the Valley of the Kings, during which several people had died. The damage had been minimal and was now repaired.

Part of Abbe was proud to have been a cog in that process of repatriation, albeit a selfish and dishonest cog. Yet, he had gotten away with his role in the drama. The former director—he had taken early retirement, citing stress in the immediate aftermath of the Rosetta Stone incident—now found himself beyond the doubts of even the most sceptical of reporters and authoritative figures in the world of Egyptology, and also within the shadows of the international black market circuit.

Another part of Abbe felt quite the opposite of pride. It was all getting to him. In recent weeks he'd begun experiencing weird dreams. In these dreams he saw himself alone in the desert outside Alexandria, wandering among the dunes, as if lost. Searching for something. Someone? Sometimes he awoke smiling, believing his beloved wife Fatima was there beside him, only to roll over and recall with gut-wrenching clarity that she was gone, a victim of cancer several years previous.

Other times he awoke in a cold sweat, as if he were afraid. Abbe knew he drank too much and knew that drinking excessively was conducive to dark dreams, sometimes nightmares. Every single night he experienced these dreams; often dark, always frightening. Every morning he awoke exhausted, as if he hadn't slept at all. Abbe was exhausted now as he walked slowly through his apartment to the bathroom.

As Abbe relieved himself, he caught sight of his reflection in the mirror and recoiled. Staring back at him was a mummified version of himself; he staggered back, dribbling down his trousers and almost slipping over on the now wet floor tiles. He screwed his eyes shut and dared a look back at the mirror. There he was. Older and thinner than before; yet, it was definitely only him. He shook his head. *I need to lay off the damn scotch.*

Recovering a little, Abbe set about cleaning the bathroom floor, then changed his trousers. Somewhat shaken by the bizarre vision in the bathroom, Abbe made his way towards the bedroom, determined to go to bed and sleep it off. Yet a moment later, he found himself pouring another large scotch, spilling the brown liquid over the sides of the already full glass until it splashed on the floor and the bottle was drained. It was almost as if he'd sleepwalked to the drinks cabinet. He had no recollection of getting there.

Enjoy your drink, my darling.

Abbe spun on his heels at the sound of his wife's voice, heart now hammering in his chest. There was no one there.

"What the hell?"

A couple of weeks ago the *Egypt Daily News* had published an article suggesting that those involved in the greatest theft in archaeological history were bound to be cursed. Somewhat sensationally, the reporter had written that "Nobody in their right mind would dare to mess with thousands of years of royal history and not expect to be cursed. The wrath of ancient pharaohs is as real now as it was at the end of the last dynasty two thousand years ago. Any man would be a fool to risk that. Especially Egyptian professors who should know better."

Cursed? When Abbe had read it he'd scoffed. Nobody believed that crap about curses and kings anymore, especially not a decorated scholar on the subject. It was nonsense of course, and Abbe had actually laughed aloud when he'd read the barely disguised reference to him.

And yet...

The nightmares.

The visions.

The voices he heard...

Abbe found himself out on his balcony again, feeling a little better in the cooler evening air. This time he stood leaning on the balcony rail and looking out across the now dark and turbulent waters of the Mediterranean. He sipped at his drink, smiling ruefully at how he'd almost let himself believe what he'd been seeing and hearing. He let his tired eyes close for just a moment.

Come and join me, darling.

Abbe's eyes shot open, flitting wildly about at hearing the soft, sensuous words of his wife.

Come and join me. I'm here.

Abbe stared straight ahead. There... in the swirling clouds... he saw her. Fatima's pretty face, smiling, beckoning him with lusty brown eyes, willing him to join her. Abbe suddenly felt calm. All the noise from below had ceased. The wind had dropped. The waves had stopped crashing on the beach. The maelstrom in his mind, now still.

It was just them now. Abbe, and Fatima, his beloved wife. Just as it should be.

He placed down his glass on a table to his right. A hint of movement below the table caught his eye. Abbe watched on as first one, then another, then several large black scarab beetles skittered along the tiles and crawled over his feet, then disappeared over the balcony. Scarabs. The protectors. Abbe was safe.

Come and join me, my love.

Abbe heard only his heartbeat in his ears. All other sounds had fallen silent. A sense of calmness and peace enveloped him and he felt at one with himself and with the world as he clambered up onto the small table and stepped calmly into the void.

Next in The Hiram Kane Archaeological Thriller Series

vinci-books.com/shadow-kailash

When his beloved is kidnapped, Hiram Kane embarks on a dangerous mission to save her.

When Hiram Kane's best friend is murdered, he travels to India to pay his respects. However, Kane's world is shattered when the woman he loves is abducted by a ruthless criminal who vanishes into the Himalayas. As Kane delves into the dark world of human trafficking, he uncovers an evil plot threatening the future of Buddhism.

Turn the page for a free preview…

The Shadow of Kailash: Prologue

Mumbai, India

6:19 a.m.

"Move!" barked Azim, the massive overseer, his dark eyes devoid of any compassion. "Move. Now!"

Azim's boss, who Azim knew only as 'The Vulture', watched as his second-in-command raised his hand as if to strike the young woman, who stood at the end of a line of fourteen others just like her. She flinched. It wouldn't be the first time he'd struck her; she wore the welts and bruises to prove it. But not on her face. The men never struck the girls' faces. It was bad form to damage the goods before potential buyers got to see them. Especially, The Vulture knew, in front of him.

They filed out, a procession of withered, frightened and abused young women who not long ago were enjoying drinks with friends in one bar or another, only to have disappeared without warning or trace. The Vulture smiled. He had orchestrated this drill. These were his methods. Thus, he knew not one of these bitches would ever be seen or heard from by their friends or family again.

Of course, the girls hadn't all been acquired together, nor at the same time or place. None of them knew each other, except the two French sisters, and each had gone missing at various stages over the course of the last few weeks. They did, however, share several characteristics in common. They were all young, between eighteen and twenty-five. And they were all pretty. Very, very pretty.

The last place each of the young women had been seen by friends or travel companions was a bar, though not the same one. There was one further common trait they shared; they were all white. After all, The Vulture knew he had to meet his buyers' specific tastes, and only pretty, young, white-skinned girls fitted the profile.

The Vulture looked on, impassive, as Azim shoved them forward, assisted by several of his men. The girls were silent, their distress muted both by fear and the powerful sedatives they'd unknowingly taken with their water. Herding them like cattle up the dank and dingy staircase, Azim threw open the door and led them out. The girls flinched, raising weak arms to shield their eyes, blinded by the sudden burst of dazzling dawn sunlight. It the first natural light most of them had seen or felt in many days, in some cases, several weeks.

In the loading bay an engine stuttered, then grumbled to life, then the shabby truck reversed; its warning klaxon pierced the heavy silence, reminiscent of a woman's desperate scream. The Vulture smiled again, his thin lips curving upward at the ends. The noise mattered little. He owned the dilapidated warehouse, and no one else would be around at five on a Sunday morning in that rundown, forgotten corner of old Mumbai.

One by one the young women shuffled on bound feet into the rear of the truck, too weak and too afraid to resist, some seemingly almost resigned to whatever horrific fate awaited them. Except one woman. She was tall, and her piercing green eyes never left Azim's. The Vulture noticed her, and glancing at Azim, he could tell Azim knew this one was trouble.

Azim followed them in, shoving them forward, himself followed by two leering thugs. The Vulture suspected their filthy imaginations were running wild. But they wouldn't touch the girls. They knew interfering with their boss's inventory would cost them their lives which were forfeit, worthless to him compared to these women, who were priceless to the right client.

Azim glanced now at The Vulture, whose narrowed eyes stared unblinking at his cargo from the shadows. After a moment, and satisfied with his stock, he offered Azim the barest hint of a nod, which the big overseer returned before sliding down the back door of the truck and bolting it shut with a metallic clunk, locking the terrified girls inside with the lecherous henchmen. Azim jumped down from the loading dock, dusted off his suit, and climbed into the driver's seat of a Bentley Arnage 4.4. The rare bronze paintwork on the long, sleek classic car glimmered beneath an already hot sun.

Straightening his tie and smoothing down his bespoke light grey Armani jacket, The Vulture slid down his Gucci shades and descended the steps onto the loading bay and down to his waiting Bentley.

One of his men stepped forward and swung open the back door, and waited as The Vulture climbed in and relaxed into the plush leather interior. The man closed the door gently behind The Vulture as he checked his Rolex.

"Ready, sir?" asked Azim without looking back.

The Vulture caught Azim's eyes in the rearview mirror, then glanced once more at his £15,000, 18-carat Everose gold Pearlmaster 39. The pure gold hands confirmed it was 6:30 am.

He smiled inwardly, though his outward expression oozed cool disinterest. "Yes, Azim. I am ready," he said quietly.

The Vulture closed his eyes and took a deep breath. Then, he leaned forward and patted Azim on his wide shoulder. "It is time to take this meat to market."

The Shadow of Kailash: Chapter One

Agra, India

For once, Alexandria Ridley appeared to be genuinely lost for words. Quick-witted and incredibly sharp, Kane knew Ridley could hold her own in any conversation and in any company; she was always able to crack a joke in an instant, regardless of the situation. Nothing held Ridley's tongue for long.

Yet, after waiting in the pre-dawn cool of an Indian morning for what seemed an eternity, where she'd chattered jovially over hot chai with Kane and dozens of tourists, she finally stepped through the impressive red-brick archway and gazed upon the incredible vista spreading out before her eyes. Kane watched on as it seemed her breath caught in her throat. Few things silenced Ridley. This view had.

Standing beside her, Kane snuck a sideways glance at Ridley, and offered his trademark wry grin. She looked radiant in that faint morning glow, her near-raven hair shimmering in the pale light and her blue eyes seemingly iridescent. Kane was in awe, not only of Ridley's beauty, but of the stunning vista spread out before them. It was the same emotion he had experienced on his first visit to Agra some twenty years before. On that occasion he had stood spellbound, just as he remained spellbound now. Yet, nothing made Kane happier than seeing Ridley enraptured this way, and he'd never seen her looking as peaceful and happy as she seemed in that moment. His heart swelled, and with his two loves nearby — Ridley, of course, and his most beloved example of architecture, and one that remained the very essence of love just a couple of hundred yards away— Kane himself had never been happier.

The sun had not yet risen fully, but enough light penetrated the complex to cause a wonderfully mystical, almost ethereal ambiance about the place. Ridley glanced over at Kane. His tall athletic figure was silhouetted, but she seemed to be admiring him, something he'd never truly understood. He watched as a single, silvery tear escaped one of her wide blue eyes.

Very gently, Kane wiped that tear from her cheek, and in his strong arms, he embraced Ridley in a hug that meant everything to him and, he hoped, to her too. A drawn out, silent minute passed, neither apparently willing to break the spell, until at last, Kane eased his love away from him. Desperate to reveal the truth in his heart—a truth he felt sure she had always known—but reluctant to say too much, he asked her a simple question. "Alexandria Ridley... are you ready to explore the mausoleum of a fallen princess?"

A simple nod and a smile was a more than adequate answer for Kane. He gently grabbed her hand and led her out from beneath the *Drawaza-e-Rauza*—the Gate of the Mausoleum—and Kane let his mind drift as they wandered among the growing crowd along the narrow, beautiful twin reflection pools. He glanced at Ridley from the corner of his eye as she admired the unmatched beauty of the Taj Mahal before them, a veritable siren in the now golden light of an Indian dawn.

Kane and Ridley were old friends from their university years back in England—the memories of which at times seemed to Kane like decades ago, and at others like yesterday. The pair were on a well-earned holiday in India. Officially they were a relatively new couple. Yet, the way they acted around each other meant that anyone who saw them together almost always assumed they were a married couple. Occasionally, upon discovering that, in fact, they weren't, Kane was told they should be. *Tell me something I don't know*, Kane would think, though he'd keep his dreams to himself.

They had shared many adventures together, some fun, others bordering on the suicidal, and remained loyal and trusted friends to this day. Despite Kane's best efforts, however, he'd never quite managed to convince Ridley they were indeed a perfectly compatible marriage-worthy couple. Kane clung to the hope that this trip to India, especially coming so soon after their last, ill-fated adventure in the mountains of Peru, might be the time to sway the tide in his favour. In his heart of hearts, Kane dared to believe Ridley was thinking along the same lines. He also believed that a dawn visit to the Taj Mahal, one of the most romantic destinations on the planet, certainly couldn't do his chances any harm.

Kane knew the story of the Taj well and as they walked, he relayed it to Ridley. "A little over five hundred years ago," he told her, "cruel fate shattered a Mughal emperor's heart.

Shah Jahan's beautiful and beloved princess bride Mumtaz died suddenly in child birth, much too young, and sadly, only a year into their blissful marriage." Kane felt Ridley's grasp on his hand tighten just a little. He continued: "It was written that the distraught Shah of Agra never got over the death of his alluring wife. Instead, and using his unimaginable grief as inspiration, he went on to build what many scholars have agreed... and you know I do too... is perhaps the single most beautiful, artistically perfect manmade structure ever created."

Ridley paused their walk and gazed ahead at the Taj, now bathed in the most wonderful pink glow as the sun slowly showed its face. "It is hard to argue with," she muttered, and Kane sensed the emotion in her words.

"Of course, the Taj Mahal was to become the princess's mausoleum, and ever since... for several centuries... it has been wowing tourists and visiting dignitaries alike, with its symmetrical magnificence and dazzling artistry. Quite simply," Kane said quietly and with genuine feeling, "it surely remains one of humankind's most astonishing creations. Now, it stands as both a testament to the love the Shah bestowed upon his young bride, and, on a more personal level to me, it demonstrates the ingenuity of what humans can create in the name of love and art."

Ridley glanced up at Kane and offered a smile, though in it he sensed as much sadness as joy. He kept his council, though, and he allowed Ridley to lead him quietly alongside the serene reflection pools. The rising sun warmed their faces and the vibrant yellows, pinks and reds of the ladies' shimmering saris were slowly coming alive in the magical morning light.

The builders of the Taj had used the purest white marble and, inlaid with millions of dazzling jewels and adorned with the delicate script of the Koran in a stylised, flowing font, Kane firmly believed it remained an artistic masterpiece.

As the sun rose, inch by inch, so the Taj began to glow further. If a witness to its beauty didn't know of its earthly provenance, Kane mused, it would be easy to imagine its creators being otherworldly, such was its mystical power. He glanced again at Ridley, who couldn't keep her eyes from it. Kane had witnessed the power of the Taj once before during a mid-nineties backpacking trip with his old friend Evan Craft. They too had been bewitched by the Taj Mahal, and India on the whole, and Kane had fond memories of witnessing all the reactions of those others lucky enough to behold the daily spectacle of magic that morning.

And now, as he glanced at Ridley, it was obvious she felt the same. They approached the first steps up onto the building's main platform, but he steered Ridley away from the swelling hordes of tourists. Some were clearly in awe, while others stood snapping selfies they would post once on Instagram, count the 'Likes', and never look at again. Kane had never quite understood that new phenomenon and was dismayed at tourists who had spent all that time and money to travel to such a special place, and yet, once there, they failed to appreciate the moment. To each their own, he mused, and continued leading Ridley away from the burgeoning masses.

Grab your copy...
vinci-books.com/shadow-kailash

About the Author

Englishman Steven Moore grew up by the seaside, thus his first true joy was the great outdoors. His innate love of travel and a degree in anthropology, archaeology, and art history, help inform his fiction writing. Steven also loves painting, photography, and both playing and watching sport.

The travel bug bit the now perpetual nomad early, and to date Steven has lived and worked on five continents, and visited almost seventy countries. Steven combines an age-old writing adage; Write what you know, with his own mantra; Write where you know, and sets most of his novels in places in which he has either lived or spent an extended period of time.

When not on the road, Steven divides his time between Norwich, UK, and San Miguel de Allende, Mexico, which he shares with his rescue cats Ernest Hemingway and F Scott Fitzgerald (Ernie and Fitz), and his rescue puppy, Charles Dickens. Oh yes, and his beautiful travel writer wife, Leslie.

A lifelong love of food, wine, and beer, have demanded a new-found love of yoga and hiking in order to fend off the imminent arrival of middle age.

Acknowledgments

I don't know of any author who can finish a book of any kind without a lot of help and support, and I'm certainly no different. The assistance I've received for this novel and all my books has been both necessary and invaluable.

So, a quick shout out to these lovely folks—I couldn't have done it without you.

Luke Richardson's help in getting this book over the finish line was critical. Thanks, brother.

My gratitude to Anja Peerdeman, Michael Rhew and Tim Birmingham, my crucial BETA readers. Any remaining mistakes are my own. Thanks, guys.

I also want to thank the incredible team at Vinci Books for believing in me and supporting me on my journey. I appreciate you all.

And as always, to the one and only Leslie, my unstintingly supportive wife, I say thank you.

May you always be you!

Thank you! Shukran! شُكرًا! (Arabic)

Steven